City of Halves

City of Halves

Lucy Inglis

Chicken House

SCHOLASTIC INC / NEW YORK

First published in the United Kingdom in 2014 by Chicken House, 2 Palmer Street, Frome, Somerset BA11 1DS.

Library of Congress Cataloging-in-Publication Data

Inglis, Lucy, author.
City of halves / Lucy Inglis—First edition.
pages cm
Summary: Sixteen-year-old Lily is a skilled computer hacker who uses her skills to help her lawyer father win cases when she is attacked by a two-headed dog and rescued by the Eldritche Regan, who plunges her into a London she never knew existed—a world of magic and supernatural creatures that is beginning to invade the human world.
ISBN 978-0-545-82958-8
1. Hackers—Juvenile fiction. 2. Magic—Juvenile fiction. 3. Mothers and daughters—Juvenile fiction. 4. Adventure stories. 5. Paranormal fiction. 6. London (England)—Juvenile fiction. [1. Magic—Fiction. 2. Supernatural—Fiction. 3. Mothers and daughters—Fiction. 4. Adventure and adventurers—Fiction. 5. London (England)—Fiction. 6. Great Britain—Fiction.] I. Title.

PZ7.1.I56Ci 2015
823.92—dc23
[Fic]

2015001493

10 9 8 7 6 5 4 3 2 1   15 16 17 18 19 20/0

Printed in the U.S.A.   23
First edition, November 2015
Book design by Nina Goffi

For Katie Sedler

Chapter 1

"Okay, so what have we got?" Lily's dad paced the kitchen in his shirt and tie, running his fingers through his fading blond hair.

Lily put her chin in her hand and stared at her laptop. "I told you, Dad. Not enough. The guy who sold her the papers is a visa-passport-whatever faker. Facial recognition on the CCTV has had him in the City a few times recently, but he doesn't stay anywhere long enough to get caught. And without him, we're not going to get any further."

Her father rubbed his face, then folded his arms. "What's he doing in the City?"

She shrugged. "Pubs, mainly. Probably meeting clients. Although there are a couple of places he goes that I can't figure out. Most likely dead drops, just leaving the papers for people to come and collect. One derelict alley in Bow Lane in particular."

Her father picked up his briefcase, a long black court gown, and the box containing his barrister's wig. "We've only got a few more days on this one. Till next week at the latest. If we can't find him, they'll deport her."

"I know. But he's left no online trail, and officially he doesn't exist. He accesses his e-mail from random coffee shops. I'll keep trying, but . . ." She shrugged and took a sip of tea from a large white mug.

He rubbed her curly head as he passed. "Good girl. Wish me luck."

She grinned. "You don't need luck. You'll ace it."

"Thanks to my star researcher." He winked.

"For a big corporation with so much to hide, they were sloppy. That firewall wouldn't have kept out the cold, let alone anyone who actually wanted to get into their system." She smiled. "Besides, it was you who taught me how to find fraudulent transactions."

Her father paused suddenly, looking at her.

"What?" she said.

He hesitated before replying. "Nothing." He blinked. "You looked so like your mother then, I . . . it just caught me up short, that's all."

Lily glanced toward the photographs on the table against the sitting-room wall. The most recent had been taken in Temple Gardens on her sixteenth birthday, the vivid autumn leaves behind her picked up by the colors in her hair. She was a smaller, sharper version of the mother she had never met, but they shared the same soft ringlets in a shiny mixture of gold and bronze. They also shared pale skin and large green eyes framed by dark lashes and eyebrows.

Lily's father turned for the door. "There's money on the table if you need anything. Why don't you go and meet your friends?"

"Thanks. I think Sam's busy. Her cousins are over from Canada or something."

"Right. Well, make sure you eat, please." He straightened his tie in the hall mirror.

"*Yes*, Dad. Go, or you'll be late."

He reached for the door handle.

"And good luck!" she called after him. The latch clicked and she turned back to her computer. Through the window the gulls wheeled against a leaden midday sky.

Lily and her father lived quietly, in a routine formed around his work, her school, and shared mealtimes. Their flat was cramped and old, and Lily knew he didn't earn that much, as lawyering went. They lived in Middle Temple on the edge of the City of London, a sort of ancient village full of lawyers, with a dining hall and library, right on the river. Lily's bedroom had white bedding, a desk, and the MacBook her dad had given her for Christmas. She adored it. Next to it was her brick of a laptop, scuffed and scratched from too many accidents. It was full of tag ends of code, script written on long, quiet afternoons.

Coding was something Lily had discovered she was good at by accident, after her school had run a short course in computer programming. But creating programs that compared consumer interest in products through Facebook "likes" had soon morphed into hacking Facebook, then the school system, then the systems of corporations her father was up against in court. It had become like an addiction, one Lily and her father tried to put to good use. What Lily did was illegal, even if it was for the right reasons, but in the last year they had worked on cases as diverse as stopping a major corporation from poisoning its workers and breaking part of a human-trafficking chain.

Recently, though, it seemed to Lily that someone out there seemed to be aware of her—making contact online and then vanishing again, always just as she was about to launch some complicated new piece of code. Lily didn't know who it was, how they knew, or why they never tried to stop her—they always disappeared too quickly for her to find out anything more than a username: apache85. She had not told her father. Not yet. He worried about her too much as it was.

Lily got down from the stool and made herself some toast, which she ate standing at the counter. Her father was always after her to eat, and he'd been even worse than usual this week, as they had pulled two all-nighters trying to track down the passport faker. She yawned and stretched, feeling jaded.

On the fridge, a handwritten note saying *BLOOD* was held beneath a magnet on top of a form from the doctor's office. Frequent blood-giving had been part of Lily's routine all her life, owing to her rare blood type. She had come to hate doctors, and needles, but she didn't complain. Her father was worried, though, that the blood-banking service would cease now that the National Health Service was being dismantled by corrupt politicians, and that made him even more protective. Lily had found him poring over expensive private health care literature recently. Health care they couldn't afford.

She finished her toast and washed up, then sat back down in front of her computer. The dead drops the forger had made didn't seem to make any sense. One in particular, the Bow Lane one, confused her. It had taken too long. She logged into the Corporation of London's CCTV system. They had recently upgraded their security, but it hadn't taken Lily long to find her way back in. She scrolled through the hundreds of camera locations before clicking on the Bow Lane one.

Along with the security upgrade, new cameras had been installed throughout the City. This one was a sophisticated gimbal setup that could revolve within a wheel in any direction. Lily used the trackpad of her computer to spin it, showing her the whole alley. A building that looked like a closed stationery shop came into view, together with a small, dark coffee shop.

She squinted and looked closer. At the end of the alley, where there had appeared to be a dead end, was instead a gate. Lily attempted to zoom the camera. As she did so, the gate opened, and a tall figure in a long, pale coat walked through it. A wide hood was drawn up over his head, concealing his face. The coat hung open, and beneath it he wore a Henley T-shirt, jeans, and boots.

As Lily watched, he reached back and pulled the gate closed behind him. He halted, turning very slightly toward the camera. She tried to zoom in closer, to see his face, and blinked as he disappeared from view. A moment later, the camera screen shuddered and went dark, cracked.

"What the—?" She tried to reestablish the connection, but the camera was out of action. "Okay . . ."

Going to her bedroom, she added a knitted top to her uniform of worn layered T-shirts, skinny jeans, and sneakers. She pulled on her black jacket, grabbed her canvas satchel, the money, and her keys, and left.

Temple was one of the safest, most traditional places in London. There were porters everywhere, and everyone seemed to know everyone else. Barristers in gowns and wigs strode across the frozen paved walks. It was the hardest winter since records began, and the City had been below freezing since before Christmas.

Putting in her earphones, Lily stood out of the way to let one of the clerks rush past before taking the east gate and heading out toward Ludgate Circus and the City beyond. She launched her music app as she walked, thinking about the figure in the alley. She passed the vast bulk of St. Paul's Cathedral with her usual sense of contentment to be in the City of London alone, with its narrow alleys and their strange names. It was easy to spend hours walking around, watching people as they took a break from work. Or the homeless man at the number fifteen bus stop, with his can of super-strength lager and a bag of bread for the birds. And the tall, thin West Indian street sweeper with his waist-length dreadlocks and the mirrored wraparound sunglasses he wore even in the gray light.

But today, Lily headed straight for busy Bow Lane. In the surprisingly empty passage she found the old-fashioned stationery shop. She looked closer. Dust coated the display; the shop had clearly not been open for a very long time. The sky was a narrow pewter lid overhead, dulling the sounds of the city outside. At the end of the passage an iron gate stood half-open, almost obscured by greenery.

That was where he came from.

Lily walked through. The alley was barely wide enough for her to pass, and was lined and roofed with splitting whitewashed planks. At the other end, she emerged into a dead-end courtyard. On one wall a large archway, which had once led out toward the main road of Cheapside, was closed up with massive doors, nailed shut with rough pieces of wood. Above the door, on the grimy old plaster, was painted a sprawling black bird, wingtips like fingers. A crow, or maybe a rook.

She stared up at the building all around her. It was an ancient coaching inn, four stories high and sloping inward, with elaborate balconies running around it on each level. The nailed-up arch would have been for horses and carriages to come and go; Lily had read about them in a book on London's lost buildings. It was dark and quiet and looked empty. *Must be worth a fortune to a developer.*

Then, behind her, she heard a low growl.

She turned. Four yellow eyes blinked at her, glowing blankly at chest height in the wooden alley. Lily swallowed. Low, rumbling snarls reached her ears.

Okay, there is no such thing as a dog with two heads loose in the City of London . . .

The creature paced, weaving back and forth at the inner gateway, never taking its eyes from her. Lily stepped back. It was massive and barrel-chested, and it definitely had two heads. From one of the mouths, a long, pink tongue lolled over the razor-sharp teeth. The other mouth wrinkled as it bared its long fangs, snarling. It was the sound of fury. Madness.

The dog's weaving increased, and slaver ran from its jaws. Lily's knees weakened. She looked around the huge derelict courtyard. It reeked of abandonment. She tugged out her earphones and edged toward the nearest door, which stood slightly open. If she could get inside . . .

The dog saw her move and the snarling escalated. Then, like a greyhound from a trap, it bounded through the gate and burst into the courtyard. Lily scrambled for the doorway, but a second later everything erupted into pain and blood.

The dog pinned her to the ground, her head cracking against the cold paving. Its jaws fastened on her neck, compressing her collarbone, and shook her violently. Claws like broken razors slashed at her jacket, tearing her flesh from ribs to hip bone. She screamed.

There came a pounding on wooden boards. Running. A shadow fell across her eyelids. Boots thudded onto stone. Snarls and yelps echoed around the high walls. She opened her eyes, saw nothing but blurred shapes, and scrambled backward, against the crumbling planks of the building. She curled her legs beneath her just as the body of the enormous animal slammed into the wood by her damaged left side, knocking her to the ground again and showering her with dust. A great head fell into her lap, tongue lolling from the side of its mouth, gums red and slack against yellowing fangs. Lily's heart clattered, her lungs refusing to fill.

A tall, dark-haired boy in worn jeans and a faded red Henley appeared in front of her. She recognized him from the camera. No coat this time. He was eerily beautiful, with crow-black hair and pale skin. He crouched on his heels and pushed up his sleeves, looking at her, head tilted. Lily could feel the blood pumping from her wounds, dripping over her chest, down her ribs, soaking into the waistband of her jeans.

"Please, you need to get help," she managed, her hand

scrabbling for the engraved silver medical alert disk at her neck. It was gone, lost in the fray. "My blood, I need . . ." She couldn't finish.

He took the collar of her jacket between two fingertips, moving it aside. "I think it's too late for that."

Everything went black.

Chapter 2

Lily tried to open her eyes. Her vision whirled. She winced and closed one eye, trying to focus. The boy crouched before her, ripping away the sleeve of her T-shirt up to the shoulder. Her jacket and knitted top had been dumped a few feet away, and her arm was smeared with blood. He caught her elbow in one vicelike hand and with the back of the other slapped her arm hard, muttering about junkie veins. She wriggled in protest, unable to form the words to explain.

"Stay still." On the floor next to him, a large, very old medical textbook lay open. "Give me a vein, make a fist. I can't do it for you."

"Please," she begged, "don't inject me. I can't—"

"I know. Type H, yes?"

"Yes."

"Then it's fine." He cupped her chin in his hand, leaving bloody prints, looking into her eyes. "I promise. And if I don't do this, you are *going to die*."

With the last of her strength, Lily formed a fist, making her blue veins pop beneath white, gore-streaked skin. She didn't even have the strength to wince as the needle slid in. Her head lolled.

"No. Stay awake." His hand caught in her hair, above her ear.

Lily opened her eyes. A needle was stuck inside his bicep, his tight sleeve rucked over it. From it a yellowing piece of rubber tubing ran to a two-chambered silver pump, which linked to the needle inside her elbow.

"No!" she yelped. "Please don't. Please."

"Shut up. Rest."

Her nerves began to sing, as if with electricity. Instantly she felt better and looked around, everything coming into a sharp, crackling focus. A strange sense of calm and warmth flooded her, like a drug. The boy knelt in front of her, eyes alternately on the textbook and the pump. He ran his hand through a tumbled mass of hair cut into an unruly short back and sides, then glanced up. Beneath thick, straight brows, his eyes were gray, with bright gold flecks visible in the flat winter light from the window. Lily's heart seemed to skip a beat, then thumped hard.

"Hello," he said. The pump whirred.

"Hello," she breathed.

He hesitated, then put his hand to her face again. His fingers were warm and dry, palm hard against her cheekbone. Her eyes met his. Lily could hear the traffic on Cheapside. She could feel the blood drying in her clothes. The boy smiled. *Okay, that makes it even harder to think.*

"How do you feel?"

"Weird."

"Weird how?"

"Everything's buzzing."

"That'll wear off."

Lily looked around. She was sitting in a threadbare armchair in what looked like a cross between a flat and a makeshift office. The room was large, with worn floorboards, and against each wall were piles of books, some leaning dangerously. There was no order to them, and some were ancient, with peeling leather and gold covers. A spine gilded with the date 1650 was sandwiched between two recent pulp thrillers. A book on folklore rested on top of *A Brief History of Time*.

There was an empty fireplace, a desk and an oil lamp, the plaster around it blackened in a neat ring. Through a doorway, Lily could see the end of an iron bedstead, the paint badly chipped. She looked down and flinched from the pain in her neck and shoulder, then lifted her good hand to feel the damage. She struggled to sit up.

"Keep still," he said, catching her hand. "It needs more time to work." Reaching out, he picked up one of her earbuds, which still hung at her collar. "These things? Very bad idea. Anything could creep up on you."

"What was it?"

"What?"

"That thing?"

He looked at her bare shoulder. Lily tried to look too, and winced at the pain in her stomach. Her T-shirts sagged, heavy with blood. Soaked and shredded cotton lay over the flesh of her midriff.

"Bandogge." He took a cool, damp cloth from the table and wiped her throat.

"A . . . bandogge? It had two heads."

He nodded. "They usually do. The pain should fade soon."

Lily grabbed his wrist. "There's no such thing as a dog with two heads."

He sat back on his heels, letting her hold on to him. "What was it, then? And you should wait for it to kick in properly. You'll feel stronger soon, Caitlin Hilyard."

She stared at him. "Why did you call me that?"

He pulled the engraved disk of her mother's medical alert necklace from his pocket and held it up. Its chain was broken.

Lily snatched it back. "That's my mother's. I'm Lily."

He watched her for a second. The pump clicked. He looked at it, then cycled the lever a few times. His hands looked strong and capable. A strange black tattoo of what looked like flames sneaked from the cuff at his wrist and down the edge of his right hand.

"Regan Lupescar."

That's so not a real name.

Confused, and suddenly afraid again, Lily tried to stand. Her knees buckled, and he caught her. He was so tall she had to look up, head spinning, to see his face. Over six feet to her five foot one.

"Thanks."

"You're welcome, but like I said, I think you should give it a minute. Let me disconnect us, at least."

Lily looked down quickly, then glanced up under her lashes and saw that beneath the open collar of his well-washed Henley the same tattoo also curled across Regan's right collarbone, licking up his chest toward the hollow at the base of his throat. She realized she was staring and a blush stained her pale cheeks, the flush deepening as she registered him holding her body up against his.

The pump whirred again and she slackened as the pressure in her bicep increased, the rush through her veins making her dizzy. He let her down slowly, and dropped back to his knees in front of her. The silence was awkward, only the noise from the pump breaking the air.

"You live here?"

Regan nodded.

"It's amazing," she said truthfully, as she looked around.

"It's called the Rookery. I inherited it. Along with the family business."

"What do you do?" *No electricity? No computer. Nothing.*

He stilled the pump and slid the needle from Lily's arm, then his own. "Security. I work nights, mainly. What do you do?"

"I'm still at school, you know."

He shook his head and pushed up from the floor, perfectly graceful. "Never went. How do you feel now?" He disappeared into a tiny kitchen, the equipment in his hands.

Lily got up slowly, hearing it clatter into the sink. "Better, thank you," she called after him. "Maybe I should—" She looked down at her injured shoulder. The pain in her neck was gone. She peered, cautiously, beneath her clothes. Her eyes widened as she saw the massive bloodstain over her chest and shoulder, the torn layers of her clothing matted with it. She pushed them aside. Nothing, apart from smears of blood on her skin. Astonished, she touched her arm near the shoulder, which only minutes before had been ripped and bleeding. The blood was already tacky, sticking to her curious fingers. She examined her stomach, covered in clotted blood but unmarked.

Regan reappeared and leaned against the kitchen door frame, crossing his ankles and drying his hands. His boots were dusty and ancient, with stitched leather soles and loose straps around the ankles, jeans tucked haphazardly into the gaping tops.

"You got away lightly, all things considered."

"*Lightly?* How did you do that?"

"Magic," he said.

"There's no such thing."

He raised an eyebrow. "Sure?" Ducking back for a second, he came over to her with a pair of scissors. "Hold." He put them in her hand.

Lily looked up at him. He produced three large old safety pins and began to pin the ripped edges of her T-shirt back together on her shoulder. On the back of his left hand and on two of his fingers was tattooed a soot-black flight of birds on the wing, incredibly clear. Taking the scissors from her, he cut away the flopping sleeves, leaving her with half on one side and nothing on the other.

He gave her a brief grin. "Could be a new trend."

Lily looked down at the deep rips in the material over her stomach. "Maybe for Halloween." She smiled up at him, liking his unexpected playfulness.

He looked away abruptly and went back into the kitchen, shoving the scissors into the sink. Near Lily's feet the medical book lay open. It looked decades old, the print cramped and small.

Coming back to her with a damp tea towel in his hands, Regan cleaned the blood from her face with it as if she were a child. She noticed his top was covered in her blood.

"Sorry." She gestured vaguely to the stains.

He shrugged. "Occupational hazard."

What does that mean?

"There, all done," he said. His gentleness was as alarming as his orders. He stooped slightly to catch her eye, hands pushed into the hip pockets of his jeans.

"I should go." She stepped back.

"Why?" he asked, sounding genuinely interested.

She looked down at her bloody clothes. "Five minutes ago I was bleeding to death. Now I'm fine? And you're . . ."

"I'm what?" he asked quickly, as if he really needed the answer.

"Creepy," she said warily, stepping back.

That didn't seem to faze him. "I'll walk you."

"You don't have to."

"I know. But I'd rather you got out of here in one piece."

"What does *that* mean?" she asked, alarmed.

"Nothing." He shrugged. "Just what I said."

"Great," Lily said, loaded with sarcasm. "Because I've only been walking around on my own for about ten years."

"And you made a *brilliant* job of it today, Lily Hilyard," he returned with equal sarcasm, pulling on the long, dirty-white hooded coat Lily had seen on camera. As he did, he watched her.

"You don't have to use my whole name all the time. Lily's fine. And do you usually stare at people like they're an experiment in a test tube?"

"Is that what I'm doing?" He didn't look away, settling the coat on his shoulders.

"Yes."

"I want to know why you were in my yard. It's not a place people just walk into."

"I'm looking for Harris Stedman."

His face became shuttered.

Lily's eyes narrowed. "He forges papers."

"No forged papers here." He waved at the flat.

She glanced around, as if to study the place. "Yes, I'm sure what goes on here is absolutely legal."

He frowned. "I'm not sure it's *il*legal. Although to be honest I've never really thought about it like that."

"Are you incapable of giving a straight answer?"

He said nothing. Instead, he opened the door for her in a quaint show of manners. "After you."

Outside the door was a long balcony like a gallery, one of four running all the way around the interior walls of the building, flights of ancient wooden stairs connecting them. Doors led off at regular intervals. *Did he carry me all the way up here?* Lily frowned, burying her chin in her coat collar as she followed him down the switchback stairs.

They passed the body of the animal. Lily walked over and studied it: the two massive heads, the powerful jaws. She shivered. Regan was standing behind her, watching. She turned away from the body.

Through the alley they passed the little stationery shop and the coffee place. A man in his twenties with a neat goatee, wearing a tight white T-shirt, a black apron, and a newsboy cap, stood outside smoking.

"Hi, Tom. There's a job for Felix in there, if you see him." Regan gestured to the alleyway with a nod of his head.

Tom's eyes widened. "In there?"

"I know," Regan agreed.

"Okay, I'll tell him," said Tom, and opened the door to the coffee shop, disappearing inside.

Regan pulled up the wide hood of his coat, obscuring his face, and headed out of the alley. The coat looked handmade, antique. He strode out from the hip, totally relaxed. They walked through the busy streets without speaking until they reached Queen Victoria Street. Lily looked at the people passing them, hurrying through the cold with coffees, sneaking a cigarette outside the office fire door. It was a perfectly ordinary weekday, people still slow and grumpy after the Christmas break, facing the new year with heads down, hands in pockets.

"None of them would believe you," he said, as if reading her mind. "Attacked by a two-headed dog? Here in the City? Right."

"Stop trying to freak me out."

"If I wanted to hurt you, surely I'd just have left you to the dog?" He gestured across the street with a nod of his head, just as the pedestrian crossing light turned green and began to bleep. They crossed and walked toward Blackfriars. The station was still under renovation, and scaffolding and workmen were everywhere. A thousand questions crowded Lily's mind as she almost winced at the brightness of their fluorescent orange overalls. She felt strung out. Her clothes were stiffening with blood—*her* blood. Lily glanced down. Inside her dark coat, against her black clothes, no one could see. But she knew it was there.

They passed a pub, men standing outside, smoking. Ahead of them was Blackfriars Road, the road built over the River Fleet. Suddenly Regan jogged forward a few paces. At the bus stop, the homeless man Lily had seen earlier was still sitting, can in one hand, bag of bread crusts clutched in the other. His head was tipped back, his mouth open as he slumped against the back of the shelter. He didn't appear to be breathing.

"Gamble." Regan shook his shoulder. "Gamble!"

Gamble opened one bleary eye. "Whadder you want?" he said grumpily.

"To check you're alive?"

"Don't know why you bother. No one else cares."

"I don't know why I do either," Regan said, annoyed. Then his expression cleared. "I need to ask you something." He pulled Lily forward. "This is Lily. She just met her first bandogge in my courtyard."

The man squinted up at her. "Won't be the last," he said prophetically, pulling a moldy piece of bread from the bag and putting it in his mouth.

"What?" Lily exclaimed, looking over her shoulder at Regan, who was still watching Gamble.

"Have you seen anything in the last couple of days?"

"Nuffing I got any interest in sharing wiv you."

Regan's eyes narrowed. "So that's a yes."

"And if I 'ave?"

Folding his arms across his chest, Regan waited.

Gamble took a long pull from the beer can. "There's a girl missing. Human. I fink the family are traders, in the market. Fruit, veg maybe. Dunno."

"Borough?"

Gamble nodded, throwing the rest of his crust to a pigeon and taking another long draw on the can.

"What has any of that got to do with us?"

"You know that better than me. She was on the bridge, Blackfriars. I seen it. Seen her wiv you, and now she's missing. An' you should check out that building site near Ludgate Circus. The one with the blue boards up. Dunno why, just gotta feelin'."

"Right." Regan turned away. "Like I haven't got enough to do."

" 'Ere! I want a donation for my trouble. Cost of living is only getting 'igher. Lucas an' Elijah ain't never very forthcomin' where the spendies are concerned."

Regan searched through his jeans, pulling money from his back pocket and handing it over. Gamble took it and stowed it in his jacket. He grunted a thank-you.

As they walked away and reached the curb, Regan turned to Lily. "Well, I guess this is good-bye, then." He looked down, lashes hiding his eyes. His face was unreadable. The moment spun out. He put his hands in his pockets and looked out at the busy road.

Lily raised an eyebrow. "Very funny."

He looked unsettled. "I'm not joking. This is the City boundary. You'll be fine from here."

"You and I aren't parting company until you tell me how to find Harris Stedman."

He moved away. "Don't hold your breath," he retorted, walking backward for a couple of steps before turning. Retreating.

"Nor yours." Lily skipped a step to catch up. "So that's Gamble? Who's he?"

He gave her the side eye. "You need to go home."

"Yes, you said," she said blithely, carrying on undeterred. "But there's a girl missing and Gamble saw what happened to her? And that has something to do with me? I want to know."

"I'm not sure if he saw it, or he just thinks he saw it."

"I don't understand."

"Gamble . . ." Regan began, then sighed. "Gamble is a schizophrenic, who goes off his meds constantly, and drinks too much, because he doesn't like what he sees and hears. Sometimes, that and reality get a little mixed up. For instance, I was never on the bridge with a human girl from Borough Market."

"So he does see things?" she asked as they headed toward Blackfriars.

"Things to come, things that might happen."

Lily stopped in her tracks. "Wait . . . he can see the future? You just said he was mentally ill."

He turned to her and shrugged. "The two are not mutually exclusive. He can see lots of futures. It's not always easy for him to know which one will come to pass. Drinking stops the visions, at least for a while. And then he sees things because he's drunk. He often doesn't know the difference. Now, do you want to play sidekick or not?" He jabbed a thumb over his shoulder, toward the river.

They walked in silence to Southwark Bridge.

"Sidekick," Lily muttered, her fingers curling around the phone in her pocket.

"Go ahead, make a call," Regan said, without looking at her. "Think about what you're going to say first, though."

"I wasn't going to call anyone," Lily lied. *I was going to text.*

"Text, then, or whatever it is you people do."

She let go of the phone, indignant. "Who's *you people*?"

"Humans. Everything else is Eldritche."

"Eldritche? And what do you mean, everything else? There *is* no everything else." Lily walked along rapidly beside him as he carved a track through the dozens of people crossing the bridge. They moved naturally out of the way to avoid him, yet most of them barely seemed to see him.

"Shows what *you* know. You thought there was no such thing as a dog with two heads an hour ago."

"Wait." She caught his coat and he turned back. "You're telling me there is something else?"

He looked at her hand gripping his coat.

Lily let go. "Are you saying . . . *you're* not human?"

His perfect face was impossible to read. "What do you think?" He turned away, dropped down the bridge stairs, and began to walk along the Thames path toward the Victorian railway arches of Borough Market. Lily ran after him.

Covered stalls were everywhere, from butchers to fishermen, oyster shuckers and spice merchants, selling every type of food.

One stand had pheasants and ducks hanging up by their necks, limp and dead. Next to it was a juice bar. There was a smell of coffee and baking bread, then the pungent stink of frying onions. The market was heaving with people shopping. Many stood on the corner outside the pub, the Market Porter, nursing pints of beer in plastic cups and chatting loudly. Regan stopped at a wooden stall selling brownies.

"Sorry to bother you," he said, confusing the girl behind the counter immediately. *Hot, dark strangers crawling with tattoos don't usually have manners like Oliver Twist,* Lily thought. "I'm looking for the fruit stall."

The girl looked at him, grinning as if she couldn't help it. "Which one?"

"I don't know. How many are there?"

Lily watched as the girl gazed at him. *Yes, he's totally gaze-worthy. But enough already.*

"Well, there's the Shadbolts'? Family-run, been here for generations."

"That'll be the one. There's a girl there sometimes, I think?"

"You mean Vicky? They're just there, under the arches." The girl pointed.

"Thanks." Regan smiled at her.

Beneath one of the larger arches, exactly where the girl had pointed them to, a big man was filling crates with fruit. Regan walked over to a brick ledge under the next arch and leaned against it. He tugged Lily's sleeve so she leaned against the ledge by his side.

"What are we doing?"

"Checking out Gamble's vision. But the probability is that the person responsible for the girl's disappearance is someone she knows well, probably a member of her family."

"And if it is?"

"If it is, then that's not my job, it's a human problem."

"What, you'll just walk away?" Lily looked sideways at him.

He shrugged. "Yes. Seeing as how most human girls are murdered by family members, not bandogges."

"Today is getting better and better," Lily muttered, folding her arms. "So what's the plan?"

"There isn't one."

"What do you mean?"

He shrugged. "I can't look for the girl because, first, I don't have time, and, second, I wouldn't know where to start. I don't know what motivates you people."

There was a loud cursing from the stall as a bowl of apples tipped over. The big man—Shadbolt, presumably—kicked the crate hard. It broke, and fruit rolled out over the cobbles. He kicked it a few more times before putting his hands to his face, clutching at his hair.

Lily frowned. "Shouldn't we speak to him?"

"Why?"

"He's upset, and maybe he knows something."

"Trust me, if someone's daughter goes missing, they don't want me showing up asking questions about her."

Lily looked him up and down. "Maybe not. But what about me?"

"What about you?"

"I could have known her. We're the same age."

He raised his eyebrows and folded his arms. "Go ahead."

Lily squared her shoulders and walked over to the stall. The heavyset man was tidying up the broken crate, his face grim.

"Mr. Shadbolt?"

"What?" He turned on her.

Lily stepped back. "I'm sorry. I was just looking for . . ."

"Vicky? My Vicky? You know her? You know where she is?"

"No. I thought she might be here."

"Well, she's not. She didn't come home last night. Do you know where she might be? Anyone she might be with? I've called all her friends. I thought she might have a boyfriend—she's been coming and going at odd times—but no one seemed to know when I asked them."

"No. I'm sorry. I haven't known her long."

He shook his head, staring at the broken wooden shards in his hand. "I just don't know where she might be. I know it's not always easy, living with me. I work her too hard. And you know that her and my missus don't get on. Things . . . money, it's been tough lately."

Lily said nothing.

He sighed. "If she gets in touch, will you tell her to come home?"

"Of course I will. I'd better go now." Lily gestured over her shoulder with her thumb.

He nodded, his shoulders sagging.

Lily, seeing Regan gone from the archway, walked back out of the market. He fell into step beside her after fifty yards. He had a large bacon sandwich in a paper wrapper.

"And?"

"Nothing. But at least we know her name. Vicky Shadbolt." Lily got out her phone and launched the Facebook app.

"I told you, they won't believe you," he said. "Here. Eat this."

"I'm not hungry. And I'm checking something."

"What?"

"Vicky's Facebook."

"Facewhat?"

"Everyone knows what Facebook is. Don't pretend." She paused to thumb in a search for Vicky. Regan looked over her shoulder.

"Well, her profile's open. That means anyone can see it. So there won't be anything interesting on it unless she has no concept of privacy at all. She hasn't updated her status since yesterday afternoon, when she said she was babysitting for a neighbor. And there's nothing to say she's seeing anyone. Her newsfeed looks pretty average too."

"Newsfeed?"

"It's like a rolling bulletin of what's happening with your friends. Photos, updates, locations."

He studied the screen with interest, watching how Lily operated it.

"But it'll help me find her other profiles, on messaging apps and stuff like that. The places she *really* hangs out." Lily spoke almost as if to herself.

Regan looked lost.

"You don't have this?" she asked.

"I don't go in for technology much." Reaching over her shoulder, he held his finger over the phone.

Lily held it up slightly. "Why?"

"It's a human thing." He tapped on a photo of Vicky.

"Is that why you haven't got electricity?"

"I've got it in theory, just no one's paid the bills in ten years, so in practice it doesn't work so well."

"Why don't you pay the bill?"

"First, I want to attract as little attention as possible, and, second, my line of work isn't what anyone would call lucrative." Lily could feel his chest against her shoulder. She shifted slightly, putting an inch of space between them. He shook his head in wonder. "So much information. It's like a playground for deviants. I hope you're not on this." He held out the sandwich. "You need to eat. Your body will be using a lot of calories to repair itself, and it's getting cold again."

Lily frowned at him, but she accepted it and took a bite. "Of course I'm on it. Everyone is. Unless you're a conspiracy nutter. You have to be a bit careful with it, but my profile's private. Only my friends can see it." *And anyone with basic hacking skills, but still . . .*

"Got a lot of friends?"

She put her phone away and carried on eating. "Yes. Why? How many have you got?"

"None. Which is exactly the way I like it."

She wrinkled her nose, then chewed and swallowed quickly. "Why would anyone want to have no friends?"

"Easier," he said, turning to leave the market.

"Where are we going now?"

"*We* are not going anywhere. *You* are going home."

"There are about three people on the planet who can tell me what to do. You're not one of them."

He glanced down at her, as she kept pace by his side. He almost smiled. "I bet they're all human, though. And they didn't just save your life."

Lily thought about it, then shrugged. "I suppose you've got a point. So, explain to me, then, about the Eldritche."

He glanced down at her. Then he took a breath. "You know how there's this idea of a balance in the universe?" He lifted his hands and weighed them against each other like scales.

Lily put her fingers in front of her full mouth before she spoke. "Like Buddhists?"

"A little. Well, it's there in our world too. There are different types of Eldritche, three main ones: earth, water, and air. To your lot, they're folklore, fairy stories, but many are just ordinary people leading ordinary lives. However, there are types of Eldritche who embody darkness, entropy. We call them the Chaos. They take different forms, but they're deadly and you can't reason with them. London is a magnet for them."

"Why?"

He blew out a big breath. "That's something of a mystery. None of us really know. Other cities, they get one or two straying in. But London, it draws them. We think there must have been some event, sometime in the past, that knocked out the balance. But what it was, and how to fix it . . . that knowledge has been lost."

"You mean, like chaos theory and the butterfly effect? Where one tiny incident creates some huge change farther down the line?" She held out the sandwich.

He took it, had a bite, and nodded. "Exactly that. And for some reason, there's more of them than ever recently."

"Why? I mean, why are there more of them?"

"I don't know, but I need to find out. And fast. Something is upsetting the balance even more, and whatever it is, it's creating some kind of large-scale negativity. That's what's bringing more Chaos, accelerating it. And more types than ever too. Things I've never seen." He saw her looking at him. "It's my job to keep them out. Or, if they get in, to track them down and deal with them." He handed her the sandwich.

Lily thought back to the dead bandogge in the yard. She shuddered, food forgotten. "Like you did today?"

He lifted a shoulder. "Not sure what other way there is."

She was silent for a minute. "So that's what you meant, about security?"

He nodded.

"And you said it was a family business."

"Yes. My father did it before me. And his father before him." He circled his finger as if winding back through time, and took the last piece of the sandwich she held out.

"There aren't any others to help?"

He shrugged. "Usually I don't need help. The old gates are strong enough to keep most of them out, and I'm just dealing with one or two a night, but—"

"Gates?"

"Yes. The City of London has seven gates. Aldgate—"

"Aldersgate, Cripplegate, Moorgate, Newgate, Bishopsgate, and Ludgate," Lily interrupted, putting the empty wrapper in a litter bin. "The gates in London Wall. I know. And I know that the City of London's had a wall around it since the Romans, and they stopped repairing it a couple of hundred years ago. Then bits of it got bombed in the war, but there's lots of it still around in places. Dad and I walk it sometimes on weekends."

He looked impressed, pausing at the top of the flight of steps that cut through from Carter Lane to Blackfriars Bridge Road.

"But the gates are just symbolic now," Lily said, "aren't they?"

He nodded. "But that's all they need to be. The barrier of the Wall is still, mostly, intact. Although it's weaker in some places than others."

"Like a magic barrier?"

"I thought you didn't believe in it?" he teased.

"Well . . ."

"I think it's more like consecrated ground, for our kind. Except it's wearing off, starting to fail."

"So you go out at night and . . ." Lily looked dubious.

"Search on the streets, and in the subways, and the tunnels and—the bit I really enjoy"—he pulled a face—"the sewers around the Wall—for anything that shouldn't be there, for the things that have managed to get through the gates, or are trying to."

"Security?" She raised an eyebrow. He shrugged, and she burst out laughing. "Security. Now I get it."

"I guard the Wall, and between me and the gates, the things that should stay out usually do. But lately, things have been slipping through. Hiding out in the City, causing trouble."

"Trouble like what?"

"Accidents, deaths, illness. Chaos. But there are ways to predict what they'll do. Sets of behavior particular to each creature."

"Okay." Lily nodded slowly.

"That a bandogge would end up in my yard, well, that's not right. They're night creatures. They stay in the shadows, wait until you're in a dim alleyway after dark and rush you. It shouldn't have just walked in there in daylight."

"It shouldn't?"

"It shouldn't, no. It was particularly powerful, if it was prepared to come into the Rookery."

"Why?"

They walked to the end of the street and turned toward the bridge. "Two reasons. First, the Chaos can sense it when I'm around. And they don't like it. They might be crazy, but they don't actively court suicide. Second, certain places are like sanctuaries. They can be anywhere, but once we find them, we tend to stay there. Usually there's a lot of gates, doors, or thresholds to cross. The Rookery is one: old coaching inn, built around a central space, so all entrances have an outer and inner door. Plus it's my home. Big deterrent. That the dog wanted you enough to cross both thresholds is a very bad sign."

There was the bus stop, with a string of people waiting now, checking their phones, listening to music. Red buses trundled past in both directions.

"Right."

"One characteristic of bandogges is that they're often

attracted to a focus. To things people really want to find." He glanced down at her.

Lily hooked her thumbnail behind her front teeth. "Hmm. So who's looking for you?"

There was a pause, just a beat too long. "Me?"

She looked up at him. "Well, no one's looking for *me*, are they?"

Cabs and white vans sat at the lights, exhausts filling the cold air with fumes. The sky was darkening.

"I think I should take you home," he said at last.

"You aren't *taking* me anywhere."

They stood, staring at each other, stubborn jaws set. Lily spoke first. "Okay, I'll go home. If you'll tell me how to get in touch with Stedman."

He sighed. "Don't start—"

"I need to find him."

"And I'm not telling you where he is. The Eldritche need fake papers too."

"So you do know him!" Lily exclaimed.

He sighed. "Tell me how you tracked him to me."

"The CCTV in your alley. I've seen him visit the Rookery."

He shook his head, his mouth thinning in a hard line. "That camera . . ."

"Well, you broke it, so you don't need to worry about it now. Until they replace it."

"And you were using it to spy on me?" His eyes narrowed.

"No, I was looking for Harris Stedman," she explained, as if to a child.

"And I can't help you."

"You mean you won't."

"Whatever. He's too valuable to my people for me to get him arrested. Like I said, the Eldritche all need papers. We don't get them handed out to us like your mob."

"But Mary Kalhuna will be deported if you don't tell me where he is! She'll be back at the mercy of the people who trafficked her in the first place! We need to prove that she was being coerced to commit crime. They're the criminals, not her. And to prove it we need to have all the evidence that she was trafficked."

"I don't do human problems, I told you."

"I've got news for you. You've got a human problem." Lily pointed to herself.

Regan looked away. "What do humans do when girls won't do as they're told?"

"They compromise."

"That's not in my makeup."

Lily lifted her chin. "Well, you'll have to learn."

His eyebrow quirked up. "I will, will I?"

"Yes. Seeing as we're working together."

He shook his head. "Oh, no. No, no, no. I don't do compromise and I don't do coworkers. Particularly not coworkers who are as breakable as you."

Lily's chin lifted. "I'm stronger than I look. I work out."

He bit the inside of his cheek, trying not to laugh.

She put her hands on her hips. "Don't be patronizing."

"Fine," he said, looking her up and down. "I should check out this construction site."

They fell into step. Lily shifted the strap of her bag on her shoulder. "What are we looking for?"

"Anything that shouldn't be there."

On a plot just off Ludgate Hill they came to a blue-painted wooden fence with a Corporation of London planning permission sign. They walked around it until they found the entrance down a surprisingly empty side street. Despite it being the middle of a working day, the gates to the site were chained shut. Through the metal grille, they could see a building site stretching down many levels into the earth, drooping steel wires and crumbling rubble around the edges. On makeshift pathways and roads beneath them cranes and diggers stood silent and empty. Cameras on metal poles stood inside the fencing, and signs tacked to the boards read DANGER—DEEP EXCAVATION.

"Must cost a lot for all this to do nothing," Lily said.

Regan glanced around, took the chain in both hands, and twisted in opposite directions. It broke with a loud squeal then a crack, the links falling apart. Lily's eyes widened.

"Let's see if it really is nothing," he said as he lifted his boot and aimed a kick at the base of the gate, sending it crashing back on its thick hinges.

He strode down the dirt track toward the center of the site, coat flowing out behind him. A redundant crane loomed overhead and vapor trails from the City Airport jets crisscrossed the frozen sky. Lily ran after him, skipping over the broken ground. He stopped.

"What?"

"Nothing. Yet." His chin lifted and he sniffed the air. The sky was darkening dramatically now. Lily knew the City had its own microclimate and that strange weather was nothing unusual, but she watched the rapidly blackening clouds with unease.

"Get behind me."

"What? Why?"

"This—it's called the gathering dark. It means there's something here. Do it, now."

Lily came to stand behind him. The distant wail of a police car touched her ears. A sudden breeze picked up, whipping dust and stones into tiny funnels that lifted and dropped all around them. A tarpaulin covering a pile of scaffolding began to snap as the wind strengthened. The siren grew louder, approaching fast from the south.

"Whatever happens, stay with me."

"What's going to happen?" Lily said, alarmed.

The whirlwind of dust and stones picked up around them. The wailing grew louder. *Not a police siren. Couldn't be, not that loud.* It was so loud it was hurting her ears, stabbing like knitting needles. Lily looked up toward the street. Then, above the fence, she saw it.

A gathering in the air, almost solidifying, but not quite. It slid through the air, then gathered again on the cab of a backhoe. Lily tried to make out what it was, but it evaporated again just as quickly as it had appeared. The wail had become deafening.

"There, on the cab," she shouted. "There was—"

"I got it," he hollered back over the noise.

Lily's heart ached at the sound. The wind whipped her hair across her face. As she pushed strands of it from her eyes, a woman materialized in front of Regan. She wore a filthy white dress. Her knees and hands were grazed and bleeding, blood-stains spreading across her clothes as Lily watched. She stretched out her hands toward them. The terrible keening that seemed to come from the center of the woman's body made Lily's breast-bone vibrate, and tears sprang to her eyes, spilling on to her cheeks. It felt as if her heart would break.

"Cover your ears," Regan shouted, not taking his eyes from the woman.

Lily put her hands over her ears, but the noise still wrenched at her insides. She began to sob. The woman came closer, her hands cupped as if begging. Suddenly her fingers began to lengthen into claws and her face sharpened. Her mouth distorted, drawing back, and her nose became a wicked beak, her eyes deep pits surrounded by scales. Lily stepped back in horror.

The creature leaped at Regan, clawing wildly at his face. The dust and stones enveloped them, spattering against Lily's clothes, rushing at her tear-wet eyes. She watched as the two of them fought, trading lethal blows. As soon as Regan caught hold of the woman, she evaporated, then rematerialized, striking at his face with her talons. Then she was on the ground, on her knees, her face a woman's again.

Regan stood over her, his fist clamped tightly in her long, straggling hair. The wailing changed pitch, falling to a thin pleading. Her bloodied hands were held out for mercy. Lily watched in horror as Regan drew back his fist, punched straight into her chest, and pulled out the running red lump of her heart.

Lily scrambled for the gate, legs pumping not with blood, but adrenaline. She ran out on to the hill and pelted for home, throwing herself across the traffic at Ludgate Circus and into the back streets. Her feet banged against the pavement, untrustworthy with fear. As she cut into the back alley behind St. Bride's Church, next to the graveyard, something stepped out and hit her so hard it winded her.

Regan caught her as if he'd been waiting in the alley. She collided with his concrete body, momentum slamming her up against him as his arms closed around her. "Stop," he said, not even out of breath. "It's okay, it's just me."

Lily clung to him. The blood rushed in her ears but his heart thudded steadily, as if nothing at all had happened. As if he hadn't just killed that creature.

"Lily?"

"What . . . was that?" She struggled to get the words out.

"Banshee. Must have gotten past me at Ludgate last night. Probably hiding out in there until nightfall." He set her on her feet, pushing her away gently.

Her knees were still unsteady. "But you killed her."

"Not *her*. It. They're just Its."

Lily stared up at him, panting. He looked furious. "What is it?"

"It shouldn't have gotten past me. Things don't."

"Pride in your work?" Lily tried a weak joke, pushing her hair from her face.

He didn't look amused. "We need to go somewhere."

"I thought you couldn't wait to be rid of me?"

He didn't answer. Reaching down, he caught her hand in his, his fingers sticky with gore as they pushed through hers.

Lily struggled to pull her hand away, grossed out. "But where are we going?"

He tightened his hold. "To see some people about this. It's all wrong." He pulled her across the busy road, and up the narrow flight of old stone steps into Carter Lane. For a moment, he hesitated, letting a bike courier fly past. "And the only thing I know is, the day you turn up on my doorstep, everything goes crazy."

Chapter 3

In a side street off Carter Lane they arrived at a bookshop, the windows thick with grime, obscuring the interior. Outside was an old-fashioned iron water pump. Regan worked the handle a couple of times until it spluttered and gushed.

"Here." He held their hands beneath it, rubbing the blood from Lily's fingers before cleaning himself up. Their eyes caught. She stepped back with a mumbled thanks, wiping her hands on her jeans. He said nothing, but pushed the door, and they went inside.

Ancient parquet flooring crackled and shifted beneath Lily's feet. Shelves of books, marked by country, crowded the walls and sat in piles on tables. Asleep on a pile of books in the corner was a tiny thing, rather like a cherub, less than a foot tall. One arm across its eyes, it slept soundly, its dirty naked chest rising and falling, and from its back grew a pair of ragged, dusty wings like a moth's. Lily stared.

A young man with fine, collar-length brown hair was reading a newspaper spread out on the desk, his right hand hovering above an antique globe, as if he would set it spinning any second. Perilously thin, he looked perhaps twenty years old, with a shrewd, pale face, and he wore a three-piece suit and a watch chain. On the front of the desk, in large gold copperplate lettering, a sign said: "ONLY TWO THINGS ARE INFINITE, THE UNIVERSE AND HUMAN STUPIDITY, AND I'M NOT SURE ABOUT THE FORMER."— ALBERT EINSTEIN.

"Who's that?" The young man was still concentrating on the paper.

"This is Lily. She met her first bandogge outside my door."

He looked up, his face sharp, as another young man appeared from behind the shelving, a book in his thin white hands. He too wore an old-fashioned suit, but this time without a jacket. "Bandogge? Where is it now?"

"Felix will take care of it," Regan said. He collapsed into a worn leather chair, indicating the other to Lily. She sat on the edge, clutching her bag across her lap.

The man behind the desk sighed. "He is busier and busier these days." He reached across and held out his hand to Lily. "Lucas."

Lily shook it. His skin was icy, the flesh stiff and unyielding, yet his bones felt fragile and birdlike.

The other man didn't offer his hand, but nodded to her. "Elijah."

"And there's a girl missing. A human girl," Regan said.

Lucas closed the newspaper. "Since when do we interest ourselves in that?"

"We don't. But Gamble thinks he saw her on the Blackfriars Bridge Road. He thinks there's a connection."

"Have you found anything?"

Regan shook his head. "No, that's just it. Nothing. Nothing at all."

"Then it was probably just one of his more outlandish visions. Still, you'd better make sure to tie up the loose ends."

"What, so a girl disappears, and . . . ?" Lily said.

Regan dismissed that with a wave of his hand. "And? Things are becoming even more unsettled," he said to Lucas. "I've just had to deal with a banshee on a construction site off Ludgate Hill." Lucas raised an eyebrow, and Regan held up a hand. "Slack on my part, I know. But that's not the point."

"What's the point?"

"Lily. She's Type H."

Lucas's eyes fixed on her. They were a deep, wise brown, at odds with his deathly pale face and his washed-out hair. He looked back at Regan, then again at Lily. Sitting back, he spun the globe, deep in thought. "You're sure?"

"She was torn up by the dogge, and she was wearing some sort of tag that confirmed it. I used the transfusion kit. And the book."

"And?"

Regan looked over at her. "Lily, would you take your jacket off?

Lily got to her feet, pulling on the zipper. She shrugged out of the jacket, revealing her stained, shredded clothes and filthy arm.

"Incredible," Elijah murmured. "So it's true."

"*What's* true?" Lily was confused.

"That . . ." Lucas glanced at Regan, hesitating.

"That I can heal a human with your blood type," Regan said abruptly.

There was a long silence.

"Is there something you're not telling me?" Lily said.

"No, nothing." Regan shook his head, but didn't look at her.

"Tell me about yourself, if you would be so kind, Lily." Lucas sat back in his chair, spinning the globe as he did so.

Lily frowned. "Like what?"

"Who you are, where you live. That sort of thing," Elijah added.

Lily looked between them. "I, er . . . I'm sixteen. I live with my father in the Temple. I'm a student. That's about it, I think."

There was a silence, then Regan described Gamble's jumbled visions. Lucas steepled his fingers, sitting forward with his elbows on a dusty ledger. "I wish that man could control his alcoholic tendencies. It would make our lives a lot easier."

"Well, he can't."

"I hope you didn't give him money."

"That's not really the point, is it?" Regan said.

They began to argue.

Lily got up. "I'm off." *Because this is seriously insane.*

Lucas got to his feet and nodded. "A pleasure to meet you, Miss Hilyard. And don't worry. Regan will take good care of you. He's the best at what he does."

"I don't need a babysitter!"

Lucas and Elijah were silent at her bad-mannered explosion.

"Thank you," she mumbled.

"He's the Guardian; it's what he does best," Elijah explained stiffly.

Lily bit her tongue.

They reached the door. Regan opened it and held it for Lily.

"Regan?"

He turned back.

Lucas hesitated. "I . . . had hoped we had more time."

Elijah looked away and picked up another book.

Regan nodded, looking down. "Me too."

Outside, Lily looked up at him. "I mean it, I don't need a babysitter."

"Then stop acting like a baby. Lucas is right. Besides, I thought you were the one who wasn't leaving *me* alone."

"Yes, well, that was before I almost got killed again."

He looked genuinely amused. "You're going to let a little thing like that stop you?"

Lily narrowed her eyes at him, then pointed over her shoulder. "You said you had no friends. But they're your friends, aren't they?"

"I wouldn't say friends, no." He glanced over his shoulder as he began to walk away. "More like mentors."

Lily followed. "They're only about your age."

He looked back at her. "Depends on how old you think I am."

She caught up with him, grabbing his arm. "If I have to walk with you, you'll really have to slow down." He came to a halt and they started walking again, more slowly. "Thanks," she said. "So how old *are* you?"

"Nineteen."

"You look older."

He raised an eyebrow. "Thanks. There are days I feel older."

She turned, walking backward. "How old are Lucas and Elijah?"

"Old."

"Stop talking in riddles!"

"They're wraiths."

"Ghosts? I don't believe in ghosts."

He tutted. "Wraiths are physical beings. You felt Lucas's hand? There's a reason people say 'cold as the grave'."

"But—"

"They're dead."

Lily stopped in her tracks. He walked past her.

"I know," he said over his shoulder, "it must be a lot to process. You'll get used to it. They were clerks in an office on that site. They died in a fire their employer started for the insurance money. Back when insurance was a new invention, three hundred years ago or something."

She chased after him. "What?!"

"The bookshop is dual purpose. They're based there because they have to be—all wraiths are limited to the physical location where they died. It's made them obsessed with travel. Places they'll never get to see. So they like books, and the shop acts like a hub for the community. Lucas and Elijah are kind of elders for the London Eldritche."

"And what was that child, with the . . . ?" She gestured to her back.

"Mothwing. They're a sort of bastardized urban fairy. Most of our kind think they're vermin, but the Clerks are fond of them. And they're in decline."

"Why?"

"No idea. They're just disappearing slowly. At this rate it won't take much longer for them to become extinct. Another thing that's bad for the balance. The Chaos, on the other hand, doesn't seem to have any problem with multiplying."

"But how do people not—"

He shrugged. "I told you, humans see what they want to see. Did you ever notice them, before today?"

She breathed out slowly. "No. No, I didn't." They walked on.

"There are things I have to do before the watch begins," he said.

"Can I help?"

He looked at her, amused.

Lily blushed and shrugged one shoulder. "I want to help."

Raising an eyebrow, he said, "You want to work a night watch with me?"

"Yes."

He shook his head, laughing. "You wouldn't last five minutes. Come on, I'll walk you home."

Lily was about to protest when they turned a corner, and almost walked straight into the West Indian street cleaner in his green-and-yellow high-visibility clothing. He was closing the lid on his cart, and slammed it so hard his dreadlocks jumped. The man turned to them and rolled his eyes expressively.

"You!" he said to Regan. "You tink I no got bettah tings to do wit me time? Two hundred poundsa demon dog to push tru da streets until de end of me shift? And den it tek me at least an hour and de half to offer it op tonight as it should be done. To bind it good. Riskin' me ass for gettink arrested lak a crayzee man. Again. Risk losin' me job. Again."

"Sorry, Felix," Regan said with an unapologetic shrug.

"I don't understand," said Lily.

Felix looked at her, his dark eyes piercing. "Accourse you don't unnerstand. Dat is why Felix is de Cleaner and Felix alone. I bind dem, and I sekkle dem tight. Ain't no comin' back when Felix sekkle you." He closed his fist on the air in front of Lily's face.

"I'm sure there isn't," she agreed, although she hadn't a clue what the man was talking about.

Felix tidied his brushes in the rack at the side of the cart irritably. Regan pushed Lily forward. "Felix, just one more thing . . . there's a banshee that needs clearing up in that site with the blue fencing, off Ludgate Hill near the station."

Felix spun around. "Whatchoosay?"

"Clean strike, heart out. Shouldn't take you long to deal with." Regan saluted, walking away.

Felix grabbed the handles of his cart, outraged. "Dat's it! You go. You stroll out wit' your likkle jubee like a *fine* gentleman. Yes. While Felix be here, cleaning up you mess. As *always*."

They made it on to Fleet Street. "He was pretty angry with you," said Lily.

"He usually is these days. I'm making a lot of work for him. It's a love-hate relationship. We just keep the love well hidden."

"Is he . . ."

"Eldritche? No, he's human. Comes from a long line of West Indian obeah men. Born into it."

They reached the Temple in fewer than five minutes. Regan looked around with interest as Lily led him through the alleys and passageways to Falcon Court. "How long have you lived here?"

"All my life. You've never been here before?" she asked.

"No. I don't leave the old City of London much. This is a strong sanctuary," he observed. "You're pretty safe here."

Lily pulled out her keys, running up the stairs to the third-floor flat. Regan loped after her, two at a time. She opened the door, and before she had time to turn around, he was inside, looking around with interest. He paused by the table with the photographs of Lily and her mother.

"Where's your mother?"

"What do you mean?"

"All these pictures are years old. And you told Lucas and Elijah you lived with your father."

"She disappeared, soon after I was born."

He looked at her sharply. "What happened?"

"She's gone. That's it." Lily folded her arms and gnawed her lip, uncomfortable.

"What about the rest of your family?"

"We don't have any. Mum and Dad met in the children's home where they grew up."

He didn't say anything, just looked at the photographs again. "I should go," he said, suddenly sounding distracted.

"I'm not stopping you," Lily said uncertainly, disconcerted by the change in him but not wanting him to leave.

He strode to the door, then turned back, hand on the handle.

He took a breath. "What happened today . . . it must be strange, finding out about us like that."

She thought about it. "You know when people say stranger things have happened? Well, right now, I'm not sure they have."

He laughed. It lit him from within, making him seem younger, and his harsh beauty even more inhuman.

Lily colored up. "Will I . . ." She hesitated. "See you again?"

"You want to?"

She nodded, chipping her toe into the carpet.

He pulled up his hood with his free hand. "You'll see me again." And then he was gone.

Pulling off her jacket and dumping it, Lily opened her computer and turned it on. She began to search the Internet for Regan Lupescar. Absolutely nothing. *Well, it's not as if I didn't expect that. "Will I see you again?" Great work, Lily. Nothing like looking desperate.* Yet the idea of not seeing him again . . .

She sighed and tried to keep her mind on the job in hand. Searches for the Eldritche brought up myriad pages of folklore, but none of it seemed to relate directly to London Wall. Most of it took her to conspiracy theory sites. She scrolled through a few of the more paranoid forums. *The world is full of nutters.* Lily shook her head. Then she frowned, peering closer at the screen as she read a rambling, disjointed post full of accusations against the government. Accusations that the government knew there were non-humans living in society and that they were being monitored. Why? asked the rant. And what was the agenda?

Lily got to the end of it, then, just as she was about to screenshot it, it disappeared.

What?!

For a second she thought the original poster must have deleted it. But then the responses began to disappear, quickly, one after the other. Lily grabbed a screenshot of everything that was left, just in time before the whole thread was eaten from the inside.

Dammit. She refreshed the browser, but the thread was gone. Rubbing her face, she rested her chin on her hand and glanced toward the window. Full dark had descended. Lily turned her attention back to the screenshots, her focus sharp.

She didn't know how long she'd been sitting there when she finally looked away from the screen. It was past seven. She sent the last lot of screenshots to the wireless printer in her father's study and checked her e-mail. It was rare she printed anything out, but if things were to continue disappearing in front of her eyes, it seemed sensible to have a hard copy. Putting the laptop on the coffee table, she got up and went through to the bathroom, stripping out of her bloody things and looking at them. In her rush to find out as much as she could about the Eldritche, she'd almost forgotten the huge rips in her clothes, the blood matting everything together. She stood in front of the bathroom mirror, examining her unbroken white skin, still covered in flaking patches of now-black blood. On the right side of her neck, her hair was even stuck to her throat in places. It crackled as she pulled it away. She eyed the pile of clothes on the floor. *And I walked around all day like that and no one even noticed.*

She breathed a sigh of relief that she would be changed before her father arrived home.

After her shower, her hair hanging in damp rat-tails around her face, Lily picked up her jeans and went to put them in the machine in the kitchen, then bagged and binned the ruined T-shirts. The towel she had wrapped around herself felt unusually harsh against her skin. Her stomach growled and she realized she was starving.

She ran the tap for a glass of water, finding herself somehow fascinated by the sparkling stream, then shook her head. *What's happening to me? Today is getting weirder and weirder.* Quenching her thirst and throwing the rest of the water down the sink, she put the glass on the side and walked back to the bedroom, almost bumping into Regan as he walked into the room from the hall.

She jumped back with a squeak. He stood, frozen, staring at her. Then he spun around so his back was to her, putting his hands on his head like a police suspect.

"When you said I'd see you again, this wasn't what I had in mind," she said.

"I just came to ask you something else about your mother," he said over his shoulder.

Recovered from the surprise, Lily folded her arms. "Ask, then."

"It can wait until you put some clothes on."

She tutted. "I'm wearing a bath towel with more coverage than ninety percent of prom dresses. What do you want to know about my mother?"

He linked his fingers behind his head. "The circumstances."

"Why?"

"Please get dressed."

"Oh, I *am* sorry," Lily said archly. "I didn't realize people who tore hearts out for a living were so sensitive."

He said nothing, his back still to her.

She rolled her eyes. "Well, if it won't offend you too much, I have to get past you."

He sidestepped into the hall. Lily strode past, shaking her head. She glanced over her shoulder at him. His eyes were closed, his hands still on the back of his head.

In her room, she dressed quickly, pulling on more black jeans, a tight, long-sleeved T-shirt, and a looser short-sleeved one with an almost-rubbed-out Yankees logo. She threaded the silver disk of her necklace onto a thin piece of black ribbon that had gift-wrapped her computer at Christmas and looped it over her head. Her hair was already curling as it dried in the warmth of the flat—in fact, she realized, the flat seemed much warmer than usual for some reason. She frowned, then shrugged it off, going back out to the kitchen.

Regan was standing by the table, looking at the pictures of her mother.

Lily folded her arms. "You can look now. I won't offend you, I don't think."

He glanced up, looking almost grateful. *Very flattering.*

"So, what did you want to know about my mother?"

"I don't know. I just thought . . . it was strange."

Lily looked at him for a long time. Her stomach rumbled and fizzed in the silence. She glanced down at it in surprise. "I'm starving. Want to share a pizza?"

"I—"

She was already rummaging around inside the freezer drawers. "They're really good. Dad gets them from a place in Soho. This one's cheese and tomato with ham on it." She held up the box. "It's pretty spicy."

He hesitated. "If you like."

She turned and put the oven on, taking the pizza out of its packaging. "I'm glad you came back, because I have questions too." She looked over her shoulder. "How did you get in, by the way?"

He cleared his throat. "Locked doors aren't really a problem."

Thinking of all the things she'd had to take in that day, Lily just nodded. "Right. As long as you didn't break it. Dad wouldn't like that."

He looked interested. "Your father's a good man?"

Lily trashed the box and cellophane. "The best."

"And you don't remember your mother?"

"Not at all." Lily spoke quickly and without emotion. "My birth was traumatic. Premature. That's why I'm small, apparently. My mum was given a blood transfusion, even though she told them not to. It made her sick instantly. She disappeared from the hospital that night. No one saw anything—she was gone, that was that. Dad's convinced it was some sort of cover-up, to hide the mistake, but he could never prove anything. That was when he left criminal defense for human rights. It was in all the papers. Dad kept a box of the clippings somewhere."

Regan's face was suddenly interested. "He did? Where?"

Lily shrugged. "In his office somewhere."

"Can I see it?"

In her father's immaculate, Spartan office, Lily went to the cabinet where her father had once shown her the box of her mother's paperwork, telling her to look at it any time she wanted. She hadn't looked at it for years, though; it didn't tell her any of the things she wanted to know. Crouching down, she opened the drawer and pulled out the wooden box containing her mother's papers. She frowned.

"What is it?"

She reached inside, opening a folder containing yellowed news clippings. She pulled it out, then looked at the thick, typed manuscript beneath. Tugging it out, she peered at it. "I don't remember this ever being in here. Dad said the university kept Mum's thesis and put it in the library. I didn't know there were other copies. Maybe he wanted one."

Regan came to stand by her shoulder. " 'Inherited genetic mutations and their potential,' " he read out. Then he looked back in the box.

There, uncovered by Lily's moving the thesis, was the paperwork declaring her mother legally dead. Regan read it without touching the papers. Lily eyed it, but she didn't touch them either. "You can do that, after seven years. Dad thought we needed closure."

"Did you get it?"

They looked at the paper, the ink blotted. *Has Dad been crying over this?*

She didn't answer him. Instead, she put the box back into the cupboard and grabbed the folder of clippings and the thesis. They returned to the kitchen.

Regan looked down at the photographs. "You're very alike."

Lily nodded, dumping the papers on the coffee table. "Yep." She walked over to him. "I think it must be hard for Dad sometimes." When she looked up, he was staring at her in that intense way again. "What?"

"Nothing. Just looking."

"Weirdo." Lily went to the fridge and pulled out two cans, handing one to him. "You can take your coat off, you know. If you're staying."

He shrugged out of his long coat. Looking around for somewhere to put it, he looked surprised when Lily took it from him and put it over the back of a chair. "What's this made of?" she asked. "The material feels strange."

"It's fireproof."

She raised an eyebrow. "Fireproof?" Then she shook her head. "Don't tell me. All part of the job." She put the pizza in the oven, then pointed at the sofa. "Sit. Be comfortable."

He sat, looking anything but comfortable. Lily grabbed her laptop and sat down again, across from him. He pulled the papers into his lap, looking at the clippings and the thesis.

"So, your mother . . . she was a student? Like you?"

"*Much* more advanced than me."

"And she was studying genetics?"

Lily nodded. "Like I said, she grew up in a children's home. Never knew her parents. Dad says she was interested in identity."

"And she had your blood type?" He drank from the can.

"Yes. The necklace was my mother's, remember? I have to give my blood all the time, so that it's in storage in case I have an accident or something." She shook her head, laughing. "That's why I was so frightened today. I wish I'd known about you before. Would have saved me years of nurses and needles."

He smiled, looking down. The wing of his eyebrow and the arc of his down-swept lashes were strong and precise. He flicked through the thesis.

"It's made me feel peculiar all day," she told him.

"How?" he asked, without looking at her, eyes still on the paper.

"Almost high. Like I can feel the threads in my clothes."

He flicked over another sheet. "It'll wear off as your body uses it to finish healing. And no one ever heard anything about your mother again?"

"No." She shook her head. "My turn to ask questions."

He waited.

"What's the Agency?"

His eyes narrowed and his fingers made slight dents in the side of the can. "Where did you hear about that?"

"Online. One of the paranoia forums."

"Paranoia forums?" He looked confused.

"You know, tinfoil-hat wearers."

He shook his head. Lily sighed and got to her feet with the computer, sitting down next to him. She arranged it on her lap. "Here, look. I found this earlier."

Regan read through the conversation. Lily was acutely aware of his arm against hers, despite the layers of clothing.

"And anyone can read this? It's just out there?"

"You'd have to be looking for it pretty specifically. And it's not out there anymore. It was deleted as I was looking at it. But we'll get to that. First, tell me what the Agency is."

"It's a government department that monitors the Eldritche."

"So the government knows about you?"

"Yes. Has for a long time. Perhaps always. They watch us pretty closely, as far as we can tell. Not officially—that would involve revealing that we exist—but they're always there, in the background."

"So there's a government agency out there, watching out for people like you," Lily said seriously.

"Monitoring us. Yes. Surprised?"

Lily shook her head. "Not much that governments or corporations do surprises me."

He said nothing.

The oven pipped. Lily jumped up, putting the computer into his lap. He started as if she'd just tipped hot coals onto him. "Keep reading. You can click through them there, like this," she said, showing him.

Sliding the pizza onto a board, she sliced it and grabbed some paper towels. Putting the board down on the coffee table, she clambered back onto the sofa cross-legged and flicked the television on to the news. Images of burning buildings filled the screen, followed by aerial footage of a street rampage as a mob tore apart shops and burned cars. Lily frowned at the screen.

"What?" he said.

"This. Rioting. In Islington."

Regan watched the screen.

Lily shook her head. "I mean, *Islington*."

He hesitated. "And that's weird because . . . ?"

"Wow, you really meant it when you said you don't leave the City. Islington isn't exactly Baghdad."

"It's outside the Wall. Why would I go there?"

She didn't answer, switching over to *The Simpsons*. "Help yourself," she said.

"You first."

"I haven't poisoned it." She folded the squishy end of a slice back on itself and picked it up.

He copied her, looking at the television. "What's this?"

"*The Simpsons*. It's a classic."

"Oh. Right."

Lily paused halfway through chewing her next bite. "You didn't mean that, did you?" He paused too, his gray eyes on hers. "You meant the television."

"I know what a television is," he protested after finishing his mouthful.

Lily watched him for a long moment before taking another bite of her pizza. He had almost finished his. "Have some more if you want it," she said.

"Don't you?"

Lily looked at the pizza thoughtfully. "I *am* hungrier than usual," she admitted.

"And you'll get tired too, after you've eaten. It works like that."

She eyed him. "How many times have you repaired humans?"

He swallowed before speaking. "Never done it before. I'd read about it a lot, though."

Lily's mouth dropped open, the fresh slice of pizza forgotten in her hand. "You didn't know if it would work?"

He shrugged. "I *thought* it would. Like I said. When I knew you were Type H."

"I'm really not getting this thing about you and my blood type. What does it mean?"

"It just means we're . . . that our blood is compatible," he said without looking at her. "It wouldn't work otherwise."

"What, on someone with a more normal blood type?"

"No, it would kill them. Or at least that's what the books say."

"So . . . you could have killed me?" Lily asked meekly.

He picked at the edge of his pizza with a bird-tattooed hand. "I didn't think I would. And you were dying anyway."

They looked at each other. Lily managed a jerky nod of thanks and they ate in silence, then Lily wiped her fingers and pulled the computer back into her lap.

He looked at the third of the pizza remaining. "You really don't want any more?"

She shook her head, preoccupied. "You have it."

He carried on eating. He was neat and orderly but he ate with an edge, as if he were starving but was trying to hide it. For a second Lily wondered if he really didn't have money, if he went hungry. She pushed the thought away. *He looks too good for that. Far too good.* She sighed, shaking her head at herself.

Regan stopped eating, staring down at the pizza in his hand, then back at her. "What?"

"Nothing." She looked at him, wondering how far he could be trusted. *Well, I'll soon find out.* "There's someone watching me, online."

"Explain to me how that works."

"That's the thing. It *shouldn't* work." Lily settled more comfortably, although it meant her knee rested on his thigh. She was getting used to the odd, electric sensation when they touched each other. He shifted slightly, lessening the pressure. She tucked her leg farther beneath herself, severing the contact, keeping her eyes on the screen.

"I go to a lot of trouble to stay hidden online." When he didn't say anything, she glanced at him beneath her lashes. "Dad's work."

He nodded.

"But, recently, there's been someone watching me."

He took another slice of pizza.

"For example, when I was reading about the Agency, someone began to delete the thread. Delete the information."

Regan looked at the screen, as if the answer could be found there. For a long time he said nothing. "So, either someone is monitoring what's put online about the Agency and it was just a coincidence that they deleted it as you were reading it," he said finally. "Or, someone followed you to the . . . thread."

Lily grinned. "I thought you said you didn't do technology."

He raised an eyebrow. "I'm not an idiot." They looked at each other. "What if it's both?"

"I don't understand."

Regan lifted his hands, making vague shapes in the air. "What if someone from the Agency is watching you?"

"Why would they be watching me?"

He settled back into the sofa. "Because of your blood?"

Lily shook her head. "Nah . . ." She hesitated, then looked at him. "You think?"

He folded his arms and trained his gaze on the television. There was no bulk to him at all, but the fit of his wash-worn Henley revealed the curve of his biceps and shoulder, the muscles of his chest, and even his stomach. "Maybe," he said, lapsing into a strange, otherworldly stillness.

Lily half expected him to leave any moment, but he made no move to go. She carried on searching the Internet, occasionally showing him what she found. He would nod, or shake his head. "No, that's not Eldritche. You humans are so strange. Lumping us in with aliens."

"Next you'll be telling me aliens exist."

He snorted with laughter and carried on watching the television. Lily yawned and pushed the computer onto the coffee table.

"Tired?" he asked.

"A little." She rubbed her face. "Well, a lot."

"The comedown from my blood will hit you like a train. From what I've read."

"Oh, good," she said faintly.

"I should go soon. Don't want to miss anything, like last night." He didn't move.

Lily felt her head getting heavy.

"Maybe you should lie down?" He sounded concerned.

She nodded, part in agreement, part shattered, eyelids flickering. "I . . ."

Her forehead fell against his shoulder.

Chapter 4

She woke as her father put his briefcase down at the end of the sofa.

"Hi, sleepy. A whole pizza? Well done. You must have been hungry. You even ate the bones!"

Lily sat up, rubbing her eyes. Her computer was closed up neatly on the coffee table in front of her. Her mother's papers were all gone. The pizza board sat empty. "I was."

"Good girl."

"What time is it?"

"Not that late. Nine thirty. Closer to ten. I'm going to have the same, I think—I'm famished." He went over to the freezer.

Lily got up, stretching. "I'm shattered, Dad. Do you mind if I go to bed?"

"Not at all. Eventful day?"

She smiled. "You could say that."

"Any closer to finding Harris Stedman?"

"I might be. I'll explain if anything comes up."

He looked up from the freezer. "Nothing for me to worry about, though?"

She shook her head. "Nothing. Nothing at all."

Lily woke early the next morning, from the deepest of sleeps, as if a lightbulb had gone on in her head. She opened up her old, frequently wiped netbook, and connected via the most complicated proxy she could find. She began a straight LCG hack of Vicky Shadbolt's Facebook profile. As the program ran, she showered and dressed. Ten minutes later, she was in.

She sat on her bed and checked the messages and the profile. *Yes!* Vicky had posted the IM handle for her phone app. Lily browsed some hack apps and installed one, then ran it after taking a guess at Vicky's make of phone. One more guess and she was in. Vicky's messages were mainly to a Jen Cooper about school, how she hated working on the stall and was bored of babysitting. She didn't mention a boyfriend at all, but there was a series of messages to and from a David Smith. David Smith had no avatar and no other friends. He was older, liked privacy, didn't want to meet her friends.

She looked at the last message. *Oh, no.*

There was a light knock on the door. "I've made some toast. And there's a letter for you from the doctor. I think it might be a reminder about that blood test."

"Thanks," Lily said, distracted. *Blood test?* She clicked through Vicky's Facebook photos, including those in private albums. One added a month ago caught her eye.

"Lily? Are you . . . ? Is everything all right?" her father asked through the door. He started back as Lily opened it.

"Fine," she said brightly. "I have to go out."

"But it's only"—he checked his watch—"ten past seven. Where are you going at this time of day?"

"Following a lead." Lily packed her satchel.

Her father frowned as he let her past and followed her to the kitchen. Lily picked up a triangle of toast and gulped at the tea in her mug. Her father picked up a sheaf of papers from the counter. "Are these yours? They were in the printer."

"Oh, yes." Lily took them hurriedly and stuffed them in her bag. "Thanks. School project."

"Folklore?"

"Um, yeah. Myths, legends, that sort of thing."

He smiled. "I thought you were an all-science, see-it-to-believe-it kind of girl."

Lily nodded. "I was. I mean, I am!" She took another gulp of tea. Giving him a quick kiss on the cheek, she grabbed her keys and left.

"Call me when you know something," he shouted after her.

Lily took the main gate out of the Temple and stuck to Fleet Street all the way into the City, staying visible and away from the edge of the pavement. She walked quickly and kept her eyes open. As she passed the blue fencing on Ludgate Hill she glanced up, seeing the lifeless cranes outlined against the afternoon sky. She hurried on. In ten minutes she was back at the entrance to the alley in Bow Lane. Cautiously she made her way down the narrow passage.

The Rookery courtyard was as desolate as ever, the building looming up around her. She climbed the stairs up to the top floor, then stood in front of the door she remembered, slightly breathless. It opened before she had a chance to knock.

Regan stood there in a pair of distressed old jeans with a torn-out knee and a bright white but ratty undershirt, his feet bare. The extent of his tattoo was remarkable, seeming to cover the upper right-hand side of his chest, his right shoulder, his whole right arm, his wrist, and the edge of his hand—but even more curiously, his left leg, from what she could see through the rip in his jeans, and finally the bridge of his left foot.

"Lily? Did you want something?" he said after a long moment.

"Oh, hi," she managed lamely, realizing she'd been staring.

"Would you like to come in?" He held the door wider.

She walked past him into the freezing flat. "How was last night?"

"Busy. Very busy."

"You were awake all night?"

"Just got in."

"Don't you get tired?"

He shook his head. "Sometimes. Not like you. At least, I don't fall asleep on my visitors like you do."

Lily's face heated. "Sorry."

He scrubbed a hand through his hair from his temple, holding the back of his neck, eyes down. "I didn't mind. It was the highlight of my night with what came afterward, put it that way."

The silence was awkward. Lily took a breath. "Anyway . . ."

He leaned against the desk and folded his arms. "Why did you come?"

She pulled her computer from her bag and went over to the table, where the newspaper clippings were spread out and the thesis lay open. "FYI, taking this stuff without permission was low."

"I know," he said. "But I heard your father on the stairs and I thought you'd come for them anyway. If not, I'd have returned them."

Lily didn't answer that. "Did you find anything in them?"

"No. Your mother's disappearance was never solved."

"Yes, well, anyway," Lily cut across him as the brief flare of hope burned out, "someone was making contact with Vicky through Facebook before she disappeared. Someone called David Smith."

"Human boyfriend?"

"A boyfriend with no other friends?" Lily looked up at him. His expression was blank. "Would that be so strange?"

She looked back at the screen. "Okay, well, try a boyfriend who arranged to meet her on Blackfriars Bridge the night before last? Maybe that's where Gamble's got mixed up. Perhaps he's the same build as you, or something."

Regan crouched down next to her. "Show me," he urged.

Lily pointed to the exchange onscreen. He read it. "We have to find him," he said without taking his eyes from the computer. "How do we do that?"

"It's not quite that simple. I hacked his account too. He's got a blank avatar—meaning no photo of himself—and, from what I can see, is as good at protecting his identity online as I am."

Regan pushed to his feet and started pacing. "Okay. But is this all that unusual?"

"It's not all that *usual*. But it's not just that." Lily sat back in the chair. Regan turned to her, waiting. "Vicky goes to the same doctor's office as I do. Last month she had a blood test."

He shook his head. "Human stuff, I don't get it. Explain it to me."

Lily shrugged. "I'm not one hundred percent sure, but if you think the Agency might be watching me, it seems too much of a coincidence that a girl going to the same office for blood work has an otherwise anonymous, unhackable boyfriend. And there's enough of a connection between this girl and your kind for Gamble to see her with you in a vision."

Regan walked into the kitchen. "Making tea. Like some?"

"Yes, please."

He came out a minute later with a mug and gave it to her. Lily thanked him and sipped. "Where's yours?"

"That's the only mug."

Lily rolled her eyes and handed it over.

He accepted it wordlessly and took a mouthful. "So, what do we do now?"

"Well, I'm due to give blood. I thought we could go to the office and see if there's anything to be found out there."

He sat on the edge of the desk and passed the tea back. "Like what?"

"I don't know. But they hook me up for a while, and I'm usually left on my own. If I can get into their computer system, I can have a look at Vicky's records, and at mine. See if there's anything there."

Regan blew out slowly. "Fine. Where is it?"

"Bride Court."

"Then finish that and let's go."

Chapter 5

The morning was icy as they walked toward the doctor's office. Lily pushed her hands deep into her pockets in a vain attempt to keep them warm. Bride Court was a small turning off Fleet Street, in the shadow of St. Bride's Church.

Inside the office, it was too warm, like all doctors' offices. It was also busy. A woman in the corner was crying, and the counter was two deep. The receptionist, whom Lily recognized, was on the phone, and didn't look up at her immediately. *Like all doctors' receptionists,* thought Lily, *like it's an unwritten rule.*

"I'm afraid there are no appointments for today," the receptionist was saying into the phone, "and for non-urgent cases it'll be at least ten days. We're so stretched." Then she looked up. "Oh, hi, Lily," she said, gazing at Regan in surprise.

"Hi." Lily presented the test form that had arrived in the mail.

The receptionist took it, not taking her eyes from Regan. She smiled. "Have a seat. The nurse will be with you shortly."

Lily looked around. "It's really busy."

"Yes—since the new laws have come in, about the moves toward privatization, everyone's desperate to get themselves fixed now, while it's still free." The receptionist sounded matter-of-fact.

"I can wait, if there's a more urgent case," Lily offered.

"Oh, no, you're a priority around here, you know that," she said, and winked. "Take a seat."

There was nothing in the woman's manner that was any different from usual, Lily decided. Wandering over to the green-covered plastic chairs, she sat down. Regan seated himself next to her. Only a few seconds later, a nurse in a green tunic and black trousers came out.

"Lily Hilyard?" she asked.

Lily got up. The woman smiled at her. "Does your boyfriend want to come too?"

Regan got up, looking away. "I'll wait outside, I think," he said. "It's a little warm in here for me."

Down a corridor and through a swing door, they entered the pathology room. Lily was still bright red from embarrassment at the nurse's mistake as she took her jacket off and sat in the chair the nurse indicated to her. Lily's stomach twisted as she saw her open a new sterile needle packet. *I hate this.*

She took a deep breath and winced as the needle slipped into her vein, then watched, unable to look away from the bag on the metal stand as it filled with dark crimson blood.

"Is that bag bigger than usual?"

The nurse looked at the form. "A little. Not much."

Lily shifted uneasily on the chair. "I'm small and have low blood volume—you know that, don't you? I'm not sure taking more is necessary."

"It's just what's on the form, love." The nurse tapped away at the keyboard of the computer, then got up and walked out. "I'll be back in ten minutes to check on you, okay?" Lily nodded. "Would you like a magazine?"

"No. Thanks, though."

The nurse smiled and left the room.

Dragging the metal stand with her, Lily just made it to the computer before the screen went to sleep. *No lockout.* She breathed a sigh of relief, then pulled a disgusted face. *My God, this system is based on Access. Who even uses that anymore? Still, makes searching easy.*

It took her about three seconds to locate Vicky Shadbolt's records. Lily looked through them—there was nothing unusual, as far as she could see. Vicky seemed fit, healthy, and perfectly normal. Pursing her lips, Lily searched for her own record. *Hilyard* brought up only herself and her father, but she saw that her own record was flagged. She brought it up. There was little on it apart from details of her blood type, a few childhood mishaps, and the usual illnesses. Behind that there was another field, but Lily couldn't access it.

She scowled at the screen, and was about to try something else when she heard a noise outside the room. She killed the database and returned to the original screen, leaping back into her seat.

The door opened and the nurse came in. She fussed over the half-full bag. "How are you feeling?"

Lily nodded. "Fine, thank you."

"Good girl. Won't take long now, then you can be on your way. School today?"

"No. We haven't gone back yet."

"Ah," said the nurse, not really listening. "Right."

"Where does my blood go?" asked Lily.

"The blood bank, dear." The nurse looked at the computer screen, distracted.

They sat in silence until finally the nurse unrigged her and packed the blood bag into a small polystyrene cool-box. As Lily held the cotton ball to the crook of her elbow the nurse lifted the phone handset. "Yes. Hilyard, for collection." She replaced the receiver and taped the cotton into Lily's elbow. "There, all done."

"Thanks," Lily said automatically.

The nurse held out a funny-shaped red lollipop in a clear plastic packet. "Here. Keep your blood sugar up."

Lily took the sweet, mumbling a thank-you. She tugged her long-sleeved top back down to her wrist and pulled on her jacket, feeling slightly faint. On her way out she stopped in the bathroom and splashed cold water on her face before walking out through reception.

Her skin stung in the freezing air outside. She heard the distinctive exhaust of a motorcycle as it roared off from the entrance of the court, blaring out into the traffic of Fleet Street. As she reached the road, Regan was there, his long coat open and his hands in his pockets.

"Bike courier," he said. "Took a small white box."

"About this big?" Lily's hands made the approximate size of the box her blood had been packed into. He nodded. "Did you get the details of the company?"

He shook his head. "No details, just a symbol on the box and 'Urgent Medical Supplies' written above it."

"A symbol? Like a logo?"

He nodded.

"What did the courier look like?"

"He didn't take his helmet off. My height. Dark-haired." He looked down at her. "You look awful."

She shoved her hands into her pockets. "Needles aren't exactly my favorite thing. And thanks."

He shrugged. "Come on, I'll buy you breakfast."

She pulled out the lollipop. "The nurse already gave me it."

He rolled his eyes.

They arrived at the coffee shop in the alley ten minutes later, sliding into a booth, sitting opposite each other. A man with a briefcase was reading the paper and a young woman was working on a laptop, sipping from a thick white mug. A Wi-Fi sticker was plastered crookedly on the beam above the equally crooked counter. Tom stood behind it in a black apron, fighting with a hissing coffee machine.

Regan borrowed Lily's pen, and on a paper napkin drew the emblem he'd seen on the motorbike courier's jacket. Lily looked at the newspapers on the table, all carrying stories of the Islington riots. The streets were calmer this morning, apparently, although one building was still burning and people were being warned to stay inside.

Regan turned the napkin to her. "Like this."

Tom put coffees and oozing ham-and-cheese croissants in front of them. His stubby fingers seemed to be fused into some sort of V-shaped gang sign. Lily waved back, then picked up the greasy pastry gratefully and bit into it, making a noise of appreciation and giving Tom a thumbs-up.

He laughed. "You look more like a cupcake type than a fried-food sort of girl."

"Appearances can be deceiving," Lily said a little gruffly.

"Don't we know it," Tom said to Regan, still laughing. He went back to the counter.

As he turned away, Lily blinked. "Tell me I didn't just see what I thought I saw."

Regan was already eating. "What did you see?"

"He has a *tail*," Lily whispered across the table.

"And very good hearing."

Ignoring him, Lily whispered back, "What is he?"

Regan leaned closer, straight-faced but enjoying the game. "Boggart. Domestic sprite. They're good in the kitchen."

Lily shook her head, narrowing her eyes. "Nice that you're finding all this so funny."

"Funny? It's hilarious."

Lily pointed to the two other people. "And who are they? Do they know?"

Regan glanced over at them. "No, they're human. They don't know. They're those types who like to think they've found this secret place with great coffee that no one else knows about. Tom could clear the table with his tail and they'd still be talking to him about beans or roasts or something." He took back the napkin and wrote down the motorbike's license plate beneath it. "Can you find it from that?"

"There are data-protection issues."

"Meaning?"

"Meaning prison if I get caught."

"Would you get caught?"

Lily took the napkin and looked at the number in his perfect copperplate handwriting. She shrugged. "Probably not. Worth a try, I suppose."

"How are you feeling?"

"Better."

"So what did you find out?"

Lily put her chin in her hand. "I'm not sure. Vicky's records show she's perfectly normal and healthy. There was nothing on there to indicate she was anything other than human."

"And your record?"

"It's flagged. That probably just means something unusual, like my blood type. There was a field too, though—a screen of information—that I couldn't get to."

"So what did we learn?"

"Not much," Lily admitted. She took a deeper breath. "What are you?"

"What do you mean?"

"I mean, you never said. Lucas and Elijah are wraiths, there are . . . banshees and bandogges, apparently. Oh, and boggarts." Lily rolled her eyes. "So what are you?"

"How do you know I'm not just like you?"

Lily shook her head at him, dismissing the dodge. "If I half saw you, getting off a bus or something, maybe. But not when I look right at you. Which is why you've got that trick of not really letting people see you. Whether it's the hood or whatever, they know you're there, but they just move out of your way without really *seeing* you. And let's face it, you're not exactly inconspicuous."

"I'm not?"

"No."

"Oh. Right." He looked surprised. "I'm a halfbreed." He absentmindedly touched the left side of his neck. "My mother wasn't like my father, apparently."

"What do you mean, 'apparently'?"

"I don't really remember her that well. She was killed when I was young."

Lily hesitated. "Killed?"

"Yes. At the Rookery. The Agency abducted my brother. She was collateral damage."

"Collateral damage?"

He looked down and shoved his hands into his pockets. "Are you going to repeat everything I say?"

She shook her head.

He watched her for a moment. "Yeah, well, it's not done, mixing up different kinds of Eldritche. Lucas thinks we were created, because of the imbalance here, centuries ago. Like an experiment—an antidote to the Chaos, if you like. Plenty of the Eldritche think I'm just a necessary evil. Pest control through the generations," he said sarcastically, with a flourish of his hand.

Lily swallowed. "What happened to your father?"

Regan picked at a scratch in the middle of the table. "He stuck around for a few years. But he was always looking for my brother. Or revenge. Or both. Then one night he went out and didn't return. I went to live with Lucas and Elijah for a while, until they got sick of me creeping out and coming home half killed and covered in blood. So I came back here." He gave her a small, unhappy smile. "Took up the reins."

"Do they mean something?" She pointed at the birds on his left hand.

He held it up a little from the table, studying the tattoo as if seeing it for the first time. "Do you know what they sometimes call a gathering of rooks?"

She shook her head.

"It's called a building."

"Oh, like the Rookery."

He nodded and turned his hand to her. "A rook for every year I've survived the Wall."

Lily reached over and took it, holding it in both of her own, thumb pressing over his knuckles. "Five? You've been doing this since you were fourteen?"

He let her hold his hand, his eyes on her. "Yes."

She thought about it for a moment. "You'll run out of space one day."

He shook his head. "I won't have any more. Not now."

"You have got quite a lot," she said shyly. There was a silence. Lily tucked her hands beneath her thighs. "Do you heal? Like you healed me?"

He nodded.

"Anything else?" she asked finally, in a small voice.

"Like what?" He sat back, slouching in the seat, tattooed hand flat on the table.

"Do you get old? I mean . . ."

"I know what you mean. Yes. We age just like you, if we get the chance."

"And special powers?" She winced with embarrassment as soon as the words were out.

"Let me think." He blew his breath out, looking at the ceiling. "I'm strong."

"How strong are you?"

"Hard to quantify."

"What else?"

"I'm fast, immune to your human diseases, and I hear and see better than you. Eldritche don't get sick anyway, so I'm not special in that regard. But I am also good at killing things. Enhanced natural aptitude, which probably isn't as useful as being able to fly, or move things with my mind, but it seems to come in handy in my line of work."

"So, besides being invincible and—"

"I'm not invincible," he interrupted. "I never said that. It'll just take a lot to kill me. But it can be done."

Lily's eyes widened. "What can do it?"

He sat back in the seat, tracing a scratch on the scuffed wooden tabletop. "Outright obliteration. Catastrophic blood loss."

"How many of you are there? Like you."

He shrugged. "Apart from my father and my brother, I don't know if there are any others."

"Why not?"

"Our line of work isn't exactly relationship-friendly." He looked away. "And who would want what I am?"

Lily looked down. "They wouldn't?"

"They shouldn't. Oh, hi. Fancy a date? Oh, sorry, should have said, during daylight hours only, and there's always the chance of death by demon."

She burst out laughing. When she stopped Regan said, smiling, "I think we should go and see the Clerks. Get their take on all this."

They got up and left. Regan raised his hand to Tom as he opened the door to let Lily through. Outside, she looked up at him.

"You don't pay?"

He shook his head. "I own it." He pointed to the closed stationery shop, where dusty paper butterflies made up the window display. "That too. Was my mother's family's business. Printers. And the coffee shop supplies me with hot water in exchange for a very reasonable rent, in cash. It's how I live."

"But no electricity. I mean, that's mad."

"Why?"

"Because."

"Because what? The Clerks keep me in books. Linda at the Barbican launderette washes my clothes, and in this city I can eat whatever I like, whenever I like. What else do I need?"

Lily eyed him dubiously. "I don't know. Is it, like, a thing your family did? Living like that?"

"No, it's just me. After the shaky first couple of years, I thought that with my line of work it's probably best if I leave the smallest dent possible in the world behind me."

They were walking quickly, both with their hands in their pockets. Lily jogged a couple of steps. "Why do you talk like that? As if something terrible is going to happen?"

He halted. "You've seen what I do. One of me to how many thousand of them? You're the smartest person I've ever met, so you calculate those odds."

"Yes, but—"

"But nothing." He turned away. Lily ran to catch up.

They walked to the bookshop, breath streaming over their shoulders, and found Lucas sitting at his desk. This time he was reading the travel supplement from one of the Sunday papers. He glanced up as they came in and reached out, automatically, to set the globe spinning. Elijah was sitting on a ladder wearing a bright white shirt, a tie, and a waistcoat, rearranging a row of books on the top shelf.

"What news?"

"We think Lily might be linked to the missing girl. She's being watched."

"I'd say that was a certainty, wouldn't you?" Lucas fiddled with a goose-feather quill on his desk.

"Please don't talk around me." Lily looked at them, but it was as if she had suddenly become invisible.

"Her mother disappeared from the hospital soon after she was born," Regan went on. "There had been a mix-up and she received the wrong blood." Lucas raised an eyebrow at this. "Lily's been giving her blood regularly. Apparently they store it for her in case she needs it. The girl who was kidnapped had been having tests at the same place. The blood was taken away by a courier on a motorbike." Regan showed Lucas the napkin. "It's a—"

"Caduceus," Lucas finished.

"Yes, but it's not a real one, is it?"

Elijah looked over his colleague's shoulder and shook his head. "No. The wings at the top here are . . . distorted. It's a symbol used by the medical profession."

Lucas spun the globe again. "It's also the symbol of the god Mercury. The symbol of liars and deception. Thievery."

"Wait, you're saying someone's *stealing* my blood?"

The door burst open, sending the bell jangling. A small Indian boy with long black curls stood there, panting.

Lucas got to his feet. "What is it, Master Singh?"

"Mona! Mona is missing!"

Chapter 6

Siddartah Singh sat upon a corner of the table. His short legs swung as he sucked busily on Lily's lollipop. "Mona was sorting the papers this morning, then she was gone." Sid stuck the lollipop back into his mouth.

Lucas sighed, then looked at Regan.

"I'd better get up there." Regan lifted the boy down and opened the door. "Come on, then," he said when Lily hesitated.

Outside, Sid took Lily's hand. "I have to hold hands. It's the law. And he won't do it." He nodded his head toward Regan.

"But you came all the way here on your own," Lily reminded him.

"That was an emergency," he said around the lollipop.

"Master Singh here is a royal pain in the arse," Regan said drily. "Aren't you, Sid?"

"Yes," said Sid cheerfully.

"Why?" asked Lily.

"Persistent nocturnal adventurer. Only been in the country three months, and two weeks ago he got all the way up to Hackney Marshes on the night bus. Like I needed that on top of everything else."

"I wanted to see the hinkypunks and—"

Lily raised an eyebrow. "Hinkypunks?"

"Hinkypunks," Regan said, the corner of his mouth curving up.

"But what *are* they?" she asked, annoyed.

"You know, wisps? Moon fairies? They lead drunks off the paths at night."

"Then what happens to them?"

"They wake up with sore heads and light wallets. If they're lucky."

"And if they're not?"

He shrugged.

"But you don't stop them?"

"No. Why should I? They don't disturb the order of things."

Lily looked down at the little boy. "How old are you?"

"Six," he said, "and a half."

They walked east toward Bishopsgate. Regan found Sid too slow. He walked with his hands in his pockets, long strides frustrated.

"When I'm older I'm going to be his assistant," Sid confided in Lily.

"Who told you that?" Regan asked over his shoulder.

"You said I could. When I was fourteen."

"I did?"

"Yes. You said if I didn't go out after bedtime again, I could start work at the same age you did."

"Ah, right, yes. I remember," Regan agreed. "Let's see where we both are in seven years." He put a large hand on Sid's shoulder. "After all, I'll be so old and worn out by then, I'll need an apprentice."

Sid smiled happily.

It took them what seemed a long time to reach Liverpool Street. When they reached the station, they turned right down

Artillery Lane. Halfway down was an old shop front, its paint neat and smart. It had three stone steps up to the door, and signs in the windows for lottery tickets and prepaid cell phones.

Inside, a stocky man in a turban was standing behind the counter. He had a pockmarked face with a large hooked nose, and bustled out as soon as he saw them, holding up his hands.

"Regan. Praise be." His accent was a singsong lilt that held a cheer he clearly did not feel.

"Gupta. Tell me."

Sid sat down on a pile of newspapers, chewing the plastic butt of the lollipop stick. Gupta Singh frowned. "Sid, how can we expect to turn a profit if you eat the stock?"

Sid pointed at Lily. "She gave it to me!"

Gupta Singh turned back to Regan. "Mona went missing this morning. She came down at four to open up and take in the paper delivery. When I came down at six, the papers were in disarray! All over the floor! And Mona gone!"

A bead curtain at the back of the shop parted and a woman of Lily's height appeared, with a center parting and a rounded figure. She was dressed in a traditional Indian tunic and trousers.

"Mona wasn't, by any chance, having blood tests? At a doctor's?"

Mrs. Singh frowned. "Tests, no. Not Mona. Why would she? We keep her well away from doctors."

"Just a thought. Anything happen in the last couple of weeks?"

"Yes," Gupta Singh said firmly. "Sid, go upstairs."

"But why?" Sid protested.

"Go upstairs."

"You're going to tell Regan what that man called Mona, I know you are."

Gupta Singh looked at his son sternly. "And how do you know what he called her?"

"She told me," Sid said, as if that were obvious.

Mrs. Singh sighed and looked unhappy.

"Mona said she should have cut his thing off and it would have served him right," Sid continued. "Did she mean—"

"Upstairs!" Gupta exclaimed, then began to berate him in a language Lily didn't know, but which she guessed was Hindi. Sid rolled his eyes and got down from the pile of papers, dragging his feet as he went through the curtain.

"And go upstairs and close the door. Let me hear you!" Gupta Singh shouted.

The door slammed. Mrs. Singh tutted and disappeared after her son, muttering as she went. Regan waited patiently, face impassive.

"Mona was knocked down outside Liverpool Street two weeks ago today. Exactly. She was coming home, ten past four. On the crossing."

"What happened?"

"A man called her a bad name and pushed her out into the path of a van. A paramedic on one of the motorbikes opposite the station came to help her. He had seen everything. Mona had to pretend to be in shock. The driver was very distressed."

"So . . ."

Gupta Singh took a deep breath. "One of Mona's contact lenses had fallen out with the impact."

Regan nodded. "With you now."

"*I'm* not with you," Lily said, "at all. Either of you."

"Mona wears contacts because she's got snake eyes," Regan explained. "They're pretty distinctive."

"Oh," said Lily. "Right."

Gupta went on. "Mona is sure the paramedic saw. And while she was pretending to recover, a customer gave him the location of the shop. These humans and trying to be helpful! That is the only leak of Mona's identity since we arrived. The only bloody one!" He shook a thick finger toward the skies.

"What about Sid? No way he could have told anyone at school?"

Gupta Singh shook his head. "Siddartah is a good boy. He knows when to keep his mouth shut."

Regan rubbed his hands through his unruly hair. "Okay. So you think someone has taken Mona because they know—"

"They know she is the only daughter of the Serpent King!" Gupta Singh almost exploded. "She is worth her weight in rubies! They will ransom her and I will be exposed as a fool. A fool who is not to be trusted! Lord Basak Nag will have my bloody balls for this!" Gupta Singh's strong-looking fist smashed down on the counter.

A man came in for some cigarettes and a packet of mints. Regan picked up a magazine from the shelf and pretended to read it. Lily stared at the fluorescent orange and yellow stars stuck to the bottles of wine and vodka behind the counter. The man cleared his throat awkwardly as he paid, then left.

Gupta Singh carried on talking as if there had been no interruption. He shook his fist at the ceiling of the shop. "This is all

I bloody well needed. Mona was the best pupil I ever had, and I go and let her get kidnapped by some gang who will ransom her for a fortune—and my hide. Seven generations! Seven generations, seven, my family has served the Serpent King, training his young, keeping them hidden until their training is finished. And I have to be the one to let him down. I am a dead man, I tell you."

Regan shook his head. "I'm not sure this is what you think it is."

"What's that you say?" Gupta Singh dropped his fist.

"There's another girl missing. A human girl, from south of the river." Regan shifted to Lily's side. "And whatever's going on, Lily here is involved in it too."

The older man looked her up and down. "Who's she?"

"Lawyer's daughter, student, no idea about who we are. Or at least she didn't, until yesterday."

Gupta Singh's face was serious beneath his drooping, bushy mustache. He nodded toward the door. "You'd better lock up and come in the back." He glanced at Lily. "Both of you."

Regan dropped the latch on the door and flipped the sign from OPEN to CLOSED. Lily went ahead of him, following Mr. Singh through the bead curtain into the back of the shop. Behind it was a door to a staircase on the right; on the left were brown cardboard boxes of stock and four-packs of lavatory paper. Ahead was a large metal door. Mr. Singh took the dented chrome handle in his hand and turned. There was a noise of massive bolts shooting back and he swung the door toward him. Beyond, strip lights blinked on with a slight hum.

Lily gawped. The room was large, probably the size of her

flat. On all four peg-board walls hung weapons of every kind, half of which Lily would not have even known how to hold, or be able to lift. There were also spears, swords, and daggers. An ax, throwing stars, and metal cobras. In the center of the room were padded mats, and mannequins dressed in body armor.

"Come, come in," Gupta Singh said somewhat proudly.

Regan looked around with interest. "What's new?"

Gupta pointed at an enormous broadsword on the wall.

"May I?"

Gupta nodded. "Knock yourself out. Then tell me: What the bloody hell is going on?"

Regan took the sword down and swung it easily, experimentally, in a loose figure eight. It whooped through the air, as if enjoying the experience. Then he weighed it in his hands. "Nice. I don't think this is someone in the community, Gupta. I think it might be the Agency."

"Bloody hell," said Gupta Singh finally.

"It's not your fault," Lily said. Then wished she hadn't.

He turned to her. "And what do you know about it? His only daughter! Trusted me to keep her bloody safe, didn't he? Pays for all of this to keep us hidden! The only daughter in five centuries, and I get her abducted by the bloody British government." He turned back to Regan.

"Calm down."

"Calm bloody down?! Mona is like a daughter to me—"

"Yes, I'm sorry," Regan said.

Gupta Singh's purpling face suddenly relaxed a little, and he breathed out slowly. "We love her very much."

"I know." Regan hung the sword back on the wall.

Gupta Singh pulled up a low stool and sat down, his chunky knees apart and his solid belly bulging. "Can you help us?"

"I'm going to try. Try to find them."

"How?"

"No idea. Yet. I'll think of something."

"And then what? One of you against who knows how many of them?"

Regan shrugged. "I'll cross that bridge when I come to it."

There was a shriek from upstairs. All three of them rushed for the door, Regan way ahead. They ran up the stairs into the cramped flat above the shop. Sid lay on the sofa, eyes closed and face pale. Mrs. Singh stood over him.

"He won't wake up," she cried.

Gupta knelt down by his son, shaking him gently, then less gently. "Sid? Siddartah?"

Kneeling, Regan put his ear to Sid's chest, fingers to his throat. He raised his head a little. "He's still breathing and his heart's strong. I think he's been drugged, Gupta."

"Drugged? But who would . . . ?"

Regan held up the chewed lollipop stick he had extracted from Sid's hand.

They left the Singhs looking after their son. Back on Bishopsgate, Lily checked her phone. There was a text from her father asking how the blood work had gone.

Fine x

She pressed "send." "Will he be okay?" she asked, worried.

"Yes. I think so. That candy was meant for you, though, so he got too big a dose. But not by that much."

"I shouldn't have given it to him," she fretted.

Regan waved a hand. "He should just sleep it off. Who's that?" He gestured to the phone.

"Dad. Just checking in."

"Does he check in a lot?"

Lily shrugged. "We keep in touch."

"You're close?"

She nodded. "Yep."

"Right. Let's go and get a tea or something. I need to think."

Outside Liverpool Street was a kiosk. They bought two teas and sat on the wall in the nearby churchyard of St. Botolph's. In the corner was an old man in a Breton cap, with a short handheld scythe. By his boot was a paraffin lantern, burning dully. He was hacking at a crop of nettles, almost the only green in the place apart from the cold-stunted grass. Stopping to look at his work, he straightened up. Lily frowned. Beneath the open neck of his work shirt and his thin scarf, knotted around his neck, his chest was bare bones, like a skeleton. She blinked and looked again. Just a thin old man, working in a churchyard. He looked back at them. Regan lifted his hand. The old man raised his scythe briefly.

Regan pointed to the wall. The old man nodded. Lily sat. Regan swung one leg over the top of the wall, facing Lily as she sat down, and balanced his tea on the stone between his thighs. His knee rested against hers.

"Who's that?"

"Ankou. He's a Breton spirit, a watcher of churchyards. There are a few of them around the City. They keep things neat and safe. And, to be honest, make my life a little easier."

"But . . . why? And why here?"

"Came over with the Norman Conquest, according to the books—that's why they're attached to the oldest of the churches here. They keep souls in, keep souls out." He made a flip-flop gesture with his hand and shrugged. "That's why churchyards are sanctuaries. If in doubt, get into one, or a crypt, and stay there until I find you."

Lily raised an eyebrow. "A crypt? Great." She glanced back at the old man, still hacking at the bunch of nettles. "Don't the people at the church think it's weird that this old guy, with the bones in his chest sticking out, turns up and does the gardening?"

He coughed a laugh. "I told you, people only see what they want. You see it now because you've got my blood in your veins and because you're looking for what's there, rather than what you expect. They probably just think some nice old Frenchman has too much time on his hands."

Lily shook her head and smiled. "So, we're looking for Mona now as well."

Regan nodded, not questioning the use of "we." A day or so's dark stubble shadowed his jaw. The breeze ruffled his hair slightly and his gray-gold eyes were bright and clear in the winter sunshine. "What?" he asked.

She realized she was staring and looked down. "Nothing. About Sid . . ."

"Yes."

"Drugs. Meant for me?"

He nodded.

"But the nurse gave it to me. You're supposed to be able to trust medical people." Lily looked into her cup.

Regan said nothing.

"Why would anyone want to drug me?"

"My guess? So they could take you the way they've taken Mona, and maybe Vicky. They were just making it easier on themselves."

"Who's 'they'?"

"The Agency."

Icy fear gripped Lily's insides. Her hands, despite being warmed by the thin paper cup, were cold again. "But why?"

Regan looked across the street. "Taking people, it's what they do."

He drank the rest of his tea, then threw out the dregs, not speaking. Lily understood. Sometimes it was hard for her to talk about . . . Her brain clicked again, a thought coming into focus so clearly that she took a sharp breath.

"What if they took my mother?"

He looked at her, then looked away across the street, lips pressed together.

She stared at him. "You'd already thought of that, hadn't you? That's why you came around last night. That's what you and the Clerks were talking about."

He said nothing.

"What if . . . but why?"

"I don't know," he said. "But my guess is it's something to do with your blood."

"But Vicky doesn't have the same kind."

"No," he admitted.

"And now they've got Mona." Lily thought fast. "What is she, by the way?"

"Gupta didn't drill it home to you? She's—"

"The daughter of the Serpent King," they said together, then laughed.

"Yes, I got that. But . . . you know . . ."

He nodded. "She's sixteen and looks human enough, but she's got the snake eyes and an odd way of talking. Lispy. She's also a stone-cold killer. Makes me look like a pacifist."

"But she's the same age as me . . ." Lily began.

"You think that makes a difference? It's just the way she was born. She can also regenerate herself."

"Like you?"

"Different. If I lost a limb, I'd heal, but I'd still be a limb short. Mona could regrow it."

"What?"

He nodded. "I know. Amazing talent to have. The Serpent King's children come out of some mountain every ten years. Farmed out to foster families all over India. The world. They're taught to be great warriors by men like Gupta, and how to behave themselves, as far as that's possible. Then they're recalled to fight tribal wars at home. Mona's the first daughter in five centuries. She's deadly, the most talented of all of them. In India she's like some princess deity. When her father finds out she's missing, we're in big trouble. He'll send an army, and they won't care what's in their way." He looked at her. "You seem pretty calm about all this."

"Calm about what?"

"Yesterday, you didn't even know we existed. Now you're asking questions about the daughter of an obscure Hindu god."

Not that calm, no.

He ducked to catch her eye. "What are you thinking?"

That my mother may have been abducted by the government, and the first guy I've ever met who . . . and he's not human.

She shrugged.

"What does"—he shrugged exaggeratedly—"*that* mean?"

Lily glanced away. "I don't know."

He turned his empty cup around by the rim with long fingers, shaking his head. "When we were talking about abilities I'm pretty sure I should have mentioned that psychic wasn't one of them," he said to the air.

She ignored the comment. "So what do we do now?"

He chewed his lip, thinking. "This paramedic sounds like our best lead at the moment. What's the matter? You look worried."

Lily hesitated. "Like nurses. I always just thought paramedics were good guys."

"It doesn't mean they can't be infiltrated. Maybe the Agency has convinced these people they're doing the right thing."

She looked into her cup. He touched her shoulder. "Don't turn around right now, but look over the road from the station. In a minute."

She drank her tea, then eventually turned around as if stretching. A paramedic was sitting on a bright yellow-and-green motorcycle, in a specially designated traffic island opposite the station.

"We don't know that's him, though," she pointed out.

"No," he agreed.

"CCTV, that's the way to find out. It's everywhere around here. You can't move without being on camera."

He said nothing. Lily pulled out her phone and opened the Internet browser. "Shoreditch local information says here that there are two paramedics on motorcycles in this area at any one time."

"So that means at least . . . what? What's a human shift? Six on shifts through the week, maybe?"

Lily shrugged. "I suppose. So any one of at least six to track down. Unless we can get an image of them."

He exhaled. "Okay. So how do we go about it?"

Lily finished her tea and got up. "We check the cameras in this area. Near the crossing. See which ones may have gotten a good view."

He stood. "Lead the way."

On Bishopsgate Lily walked past the crossing, her eyes trained upward, on the cameras bristling from every building and post. "Any of these will be fine, I think." Regan tipped his head toward the posts outside the station.

She nodded. "Two problems, though. First, they're probably official ones for London Transport. The control center will be right inside the station. Too many doors. Too hard for me to get access. I need a private camera on an office block, where the guard sits at the front desk. Not somewhere too small, though, as the small places will have limited storage and probably wipe their drive every week, if not every couple of days. Probably low quality too."

He straightened his shoulders. "Picky, picky."

Lily nodded. "Behind you. First floor. Look, there's the security guard on the desk. That looks perfect."

He came to stand next to her, looking amused. "Have you done anything like this before?"

She shook her head. "No, why?"

"You seem pretty clued up."

Lily shrugged. "Some of us live in the twenty-first century." He gave her a look, and she tried not to smile. "And we need to find them, don't we?"

"Yes," he agreed. "We do. What next?"

Lily wrinkled her nose in concentration. "You create a diversion. One that will get the guard to leave the desk for at least three minutes."

"Right. What will cause the most fuss without getting me arrested?"

"Tell him there's someone with a ladder about to mess with the cameras at the back of the building."

"Wouldn't he be able to see them?"

"Just try, yeah? Security guards are paranoid, it's their job. And tell him there's someone with him, taking pictures of it. And . . . that the guy has long hair and is wearing an Occupy T-shirt."

Regan shrugged and went inside. Lily watched as he leaned over the desk conspiratorially. The guard, a bulky man, picked up a large set of keys and stormed out of the revolving door, Regan walking after him. "Damn hippies!" the guard shouted as Lily headed past them, pushing through the door just as they rounded the corner.

She slipped behind the desk. The system was open, and it only took her a moment to access the main menu. She worked out the date of Mona's accident and clicked on it, selecting Camera 4. The film was divided into fifteen-minute sections. Lily clicked again, and selected the time window. The film began to play. She moved the slider to jump ahead. Mona was clearly visible lying at the edge of the crossing, the paramedic crouched over her. *Too far.* Lily clicked back, and saw a man push Mona straight out in front of the van as she waited at the crossing. An ordinary girl would have been badly injured. Mona lay still. Lily watched as the paramedic ran over, a first aid kit in his hand, and pulled off his helmet.

She paused the screen. The backs of her hands prickled and her heart thudded in her ears as she looked for a printer. There was nothing beneath the desk, but she found it in a cupboard to her left. *On. Perfect.* It took her only a few more seconds to get a print. She exited the screen, returning to the current views, then slid out from behind the desk, stuffing the printout into her bag.

"Who are you?" a man's voice asked behind her.

Lily turned, but kept walking slowly backward toward the revolving door. "I'm doing work experience in IT. Just sorting out a glitch on the cameras. Apparently there are some people at the back of the building—"

He came toward her. "Where's the guard?"

She shrugged. "Sorting *them* out, perhaps? Anyway, it's not a software problem, so perhaps they've broken something."

"Wait there. Where's your pass? What's your name?"

Lily kept walking.

"Stop! I'm calling the police!"

Lily reached the door, shot through, and ran, heading back into the City. Five minutes later she panted to a stop near the Bank of England. Regan jogged to a halt beside her, not even puffing.

"How did you know where I was?" she gasped.

"Saw you leave."

"I was caught by some guy in a suit. But I got it." She pulled the crumpled printout from her bag. Regan took it. "Well?" she asked, when he said nothing.

"Well done."

She grinned. "Look, there's even a number on his medical bag."

Still looking at the page, he put his arm around her and hugged her against his side. Lily hugged him back, just for a second. He let her go and she stepped back, still panting, pushing her hair off her hot neck.

"So? What now?" she asked. But Regan wasn't looking at her, or the page. He was looking up at the roof of the Bank of England.

He swore softly. Lily followed his gaze. For a long moment

she saw nothing—then, at the edge of her vision, there was a metallic flicker. She watched, dumbfounded, as over the roofline of the building slunk a large silver dragon. It moved in short bursts, like speeded-up film footage, then froze, red barbed tongue tasting the air as its gold claws gripped the edge of the roof. It slithered jerkily again, climbing farther up the parapet, staring down at them.

The City carried on its business around Lily's and Regan's still forms. The buses roared as the lights changed.

"What is it?"

Regan didn't take his eyes off it. "One of the City dragons."

"One? How many are there?"

"Seven."

"There are seven of them?" Lily's voice rose in alarm.

He nodded slowly, still looking up. "I'm hoping that only one of them is awake."

"You see dat?" a voice said behind them. "You see what I see?"

Lily turned. Felix stood behind them, brush in his hand. Regan hadn't taken his eyes off the roof. "I see it."

"You kno' what diss mean?"

Regan said nothing.

"You kno' what diss *mean*?" Felix repeated, almost shouting.

"Shut *up*." Regan turned on him.

"You naw tell *me* to shut me mouth," the street cleaner exclaimed. "Diss now *waaaay* bigger dan you and me. Diss now all *Chaos*." He made a huge circular motion with his brush in the air, almost knocking down a man rushing by.

"Watch it, mate!"

Felix saluted him with the broom in a sarcastic flourish, turning back to Regan. "An' last night I too busy wit' some mighty strong hex to sekkle dem garbage from yesterday. Someting disturbing all my usual safe places."

Lily caught the lapel of Regan's coat. "What does he mean?"

"He needs a crossroads, or a junction, to place the bodies on while he binds the spirit."

Felix nodded. "Aye. An' everywhere too busy last night, too open. Wit' some strange feeling. It is comin', I is sure of it now."

"What's coming?!" Lily asked, exasperated with the riddles.

"Explen to de likkle jubee den." Felix sucked his teeth. "Explen how she gon' get snapped like a tweeg."

Regan turned, looking angry. "Don't you say that."

"I say only tru'. De Chaos War, it is here. An—"

"And if you don't shut your mouth now, I will—"

Felix squared up to him. "What you do? What you do to me? I Felix. I de *Cleaner*." With that, he nodded and began to walk away, pushing his cart with one hand and the brush with the other.

Regan set off back the way they had come, with one last glance at the dragon. It crouched, staring down at the city through eyes like gold-mirrored lenses, emotionless. It seemed to see everything, and nothing. Its barbed tongue flickered in and out.

"Hopefully it'll stay around here for now."

Lily waited until they left the main road for a narrow, deserted alley. She turned on him, grabbing his sleeve. "It's a *dragon*! In the City of London. What do you mean, hopefully it'll stay around here?!"

"I *mean*, up there, on the bank roof, and not on the streets," he hissed back.

Lily covered her face with her fingers for a second. "You said the others are asleep."

"I don't know that. But we only saw one."

She dropped her hands. "Will you talk to me? Properly. Please."

He sighed, letting his head drop back. Lily could see the flame tattoo licking over his collarbone at the bottom of his exposed throat. "There are seven City dragons. One for each gate. They're a kind of Eldritche we call the Ancients. Immortal, eternal. They're totally focused on one thing only. You cannot reason with them and they don't understand us. They only understand protecting the City. Usually they sleep, somewhere beneath their gates. I come across them sometimes. In old water mains, crypts, tunnels, anything. They only wake when their area of London Wall, or their gate, is disturbed."

"The banshee?"

He shook his head. "No, not just that. That wouldn't be enough. But there's definitely more Chaos around than I have ever seen, and if they're focusing on one particular gate, that could have disturbed that gate's dragon." He bit his lip, thinking. "They usually stick close to their own gate. My guess is this is the Bishopsgate dragon. But it could be Cripplegate's. Let's hope the Chaos doesn't disturb the others. One dragon I could probably take down, but if the rest wake it'll be carnage." He swore with feeling.

"What do we do?"

"I have absolutely no idea."

"Oh . . . and the Chaos War?"

Looking away, he took a breath. "When the City will be overrun by the Chaos. It's part of a prophecy. Made by a pair of Eldritche sisters when I was a child."

She swallowed. "And it's here?"

"Felix is a drama queen; don't listen to everything he says." He began to walk back toward Liverpool Street. "Let's just keep to the plan for now."

Lily stopped. "But he said I'd get broken like a twig."

He turned to look at her. "Yes."

"Will I?"

"Not if I have anything to do with it. Come on," he said, his eyes sliding away from hers; "let's find this medic."

Chapter 7

Back in St. Botolph's churchyard, they paused for a second by a tiny Victorian tiled building. It looked out of place, a cross between a miniature English church and a Middle Eastern bathhouse, all red brick and elaborate blue and green tiles. The security guard from the office building was sitting on a bench nearby, eating a burger. Two policemen strolled toward them, bursts of voices then static issuing from the radios strapped to their shoulders. Regan grabbed Lily's hand and pulled her back, into the doorway of the tiled building. An elaborately engraved brass plate on the door announced LILITH'S.

He smacked his forehead. "I'm such an idiot."

"You are?"

"Yes." He tugged the metal bellpull by the door. A grille in the wood slid back and the door clicked open, then closed again. Inside stood a tall, muscular man, wearing a Middle Eastern tunic and trousers. He bowed gravely. Regan nodded to him.

Regan pulled Lily down a tiled spiral staircase. They arrived in a huge basement, outfitted as a nightclub. It too was tiled throughout in blue and green. Aggressive dubstep music was playing quietly from somewhere.

The bar was all smoky mirrors, laden with bottles. A tall, pale-skinned woman in her twenties with fire-engine-red matte lipstick, her long hair elaborately braided around her head, was standing over the till writing on a pad. She wore tight leather leggings and a bright white tank top. The smell of jasmine filled the air.

"Regan!" she said, her voice filling the room. "What a wonderful surprise."

"Lilith, I need your help."

"How may I be of service?" Lilith asked, her voice full of amusement.

"Girls are going missing."

"Then you've come with a warning? How kind, my love. But as you know, the club staff can all take care of themselves."

"Yes, I know that. I just wondered if you'd heard anything. Anything at all. Any trouble with the Agency?"

Lilith pulled a bottle of champagne from beneath the bar and poured three glasses. "Please." She gestured for them each to take one, and took the last one herself.

She gestured to a large sofa covered in black cushions in the VIP area. *Being in a club during the day is totally weird*, Lily reflected as she perched on the edge of the sofa, glass held in both hands. Regan collapsed next to her. Lilith watched them, a smile playing on her face.

"Nothing obvious. But there has been an . . . increase in interest, shall we say. From the authorities."

"How so?" Regan asked.

She shrugged and pouted. "Tax inspection, drinks licensing people. They found nothing out of place, of course. Then we were raided twice in one week a month ago. All the usual checks with permits and so on. And since then there have been a couple of . . . unwanted visitors."

"Meaning what? Spies?"

She laughed, a golden flurry. "How very melodramatic, darling. But yes."

"So you kicked them out?"

"Dear Mohammed dealt with them. Permanently." She clicked her fingers. "Then this appeared." A pretty girl in jeans and a T-shirt materialized with a letter and handed it to Regan.

His eyes flicked over the paper. "They want papers for everyone working here."

Lilith sighed heavily.

"Of which, of course, there are none," Regan explained to Lily, handing the letter back.

"They're not . . . human?" Lily ventured.

"Don't be absurd. I wouldn't have humans working for me. Not reliable enough. And one must take such good care of them, like houseplants." Lilith sighed and sipped her champagne. "Anyway, this is all so tedious. Threatening to close me down. Again. This nonsense demand for papers is going to cost me a fortune. Is that passport faker in Hackney still on the go?"

Regan shrugged awkwardly. "I think he's moved. I'll find out."

"What was his name? Stedman?"

Lily looked over at Regan. *Hackney.*

He avoided her gaze. "Like I said, I'll find him."

She smiled warmly. "Thank you, darling."

They got up to leave. Lily put her untouched glass on the table.

"Is my hospitality not to your liking?" Lilith asked, one perfect eyebrow arched.

"Thank you, it's just that . . ." Lily stalled as Regan touched her arm.

"Lilith's teasing, aren't you, Lilith?"

The woman smiled. "Of course. So, I hear this is your little *kismet*." She examined Lily from the tips of her hair to her toes, then back up again. "Absolutely adorable," she said finally. "She would fetch a fortune in one of Abdul's souk auctions among those slobbering camel traders." She looked wistful, then cleared her throat delicately. "Or would have done, back in the day. But now everyone is so . . . enlightened." She sighed.

"Lilith," Regan warned. "Let's go."

"All clear," said Mohammed in his deep, booming voice as he held the door upstairs.

"Thanks, Mohammed."

Outside Lily took a deep breath. Regan shoved his hands in his pockets.

"Why did we have to see her? I thought we were after that medic."

"Lilith has a lot of ears to the ground. And it got us off the street for just long enough for everyone to go back about their business."

"She called me your kismet. What does that mean?"

"Nothing. This community are the worst gossips. Ignore it."

"You and her seem to know each other well."

He cleared his throat. "Well enough."

"What does that mean?"

They came to a halt, staring at each other. "Nothing, only that—"

Lily walked off through the churchyard toward Liverpool Street.

He followed, looking at her curiously. "Are you angry?"

"I just don't like being talked about as if I'm a piece of merchandise." She made a frustrated noise and turned away.

He caught her up, grabbing her arm. "Wait. Are you . . . you can't be *jealous*?"

She shook her head furiously, curls bouncing. "You're so full of it!" She stalked off through the empty churchyard avenue toward Bishopsgate.

She hadn't made it five yards when, from her left, a woman lurched out from behind a large tomb, reaching for her. Lily leaped back, seeing the dirty, crawling clothes.

"Don't let her touch you!" Regan yelled.

Lily stepped back, afraid to take the time even to turn and run. The woman grinned, her teeth loose and blackened where they met her gums. A bright red centipede ran out of her mouth over her chin. Lice scurried openly over her clothes. Lily flinched. The smell of rot was choking.

Regan grabbed her, hauling her backward and throwing her halfway across the churchyard. She hit the ground and a tombstone, bruising her elbow, stones digging into her hand.

The woman stepped forward. The old man in the cap appeared, stepping out from the hawthorn hedge, scythe raised. In a neat motion he severed the woman's head. She collapsed on the grass in a heap, instantly dissolving into a crawling mess. The old man half knelt gracefully, as if about to throw a bocce ball in a distant French square on a sunny afternoon, and tossed his lantern onto the heap. It smashed, setting fire to the heaving insects. There was a terrible hissing, screeching sound. Lily got to her feet and backed away, into Regan, who caught her arms. He nodded to the old man, who nodded seriously in return.

"First dragons, now this. Come on," said Regan, drawing Lily away. She looked back over her shoulder. The Breton spirit was watching the flames. Just an old man having a winter bonfire in a churchyard.

"Things are getting out of hand. Plague demons are serious shit. They can take out whole cities if enough of them get in. I hoped I had more time."

Lily looked down at the ground in alarm, scanning for any rogue insect. "I'm going to get the plague?!"

"Not if she didn't touch you." They were already in sight of the paramedic's traffic island. "Are you hurt?"

Lily rubbed the gravel marks from her palms and touched her elbow. "I'd rather you didn't throw me around quite that hard. But thanks."

He stopped and turned to her. "I meant did I hurt your feelings?"

"You need to get over yourself," she sniffed, brushing her jeans down.

He said nothing.

She put her hands on her hips, looking at her sneakers. "So what do we do now? About Mona."

He bit the inside of his cheek, then checked his watch. "It's almost the same time exactly as when she had her accident. Hopefully the same medic will be on the same shift."

"Fine." *Seems logical.*

"Right, so you need to pretend to be ill, or injured, or something. So you can get a look at him."

"Me?"

"Well, it's no good me doing it, is it?"

Lily frowned. "I suppose. What do you want me to do, then?"

"Pretend to faint, maybe? Can you do that?"

"I suppose I could."

"Fine."

"What if—"

"Don't worry. He won't take you anywhere. No one will."

"But what if they call an ambulance or something?"

"I just told you, I won't let them take you away."

"*Then* what do we do?"

"No idea. But at least we'll know we have the right guy."

She hesitated, then nodded, handing over her bag before turning away and walking toward the station. The motorcycle paramedic was still sitting on the other side of the road, his helmeted gaze focused on the traffic. When she was sure she was in his sight, Lily put her hand to her head and staggered. A young woman moved away, giving her a wide berth. She made it to the wall and slumped to her knees, before collapsing sideways onto the pavement.

For a long moment, no one came. She heard clacking high heels and men's dress shoes moving past her head, ignoring her. Then someone knelt down, placing a hand on her shoulder.

"Hey there, are you all right?" A woman's voice.

Lily stirred, her eyelids flickering.

"Can you sit up?" the woman asked. "She's confused," she said to someone as a pair of heavy boots thudded up nearby. The pavement was freezing and Lily could smell the dust on the stones and the acrid dirt of the city.

There came another hand on her shoulder. "Thanks, I'll take it from here," a man said. *Voice isn't muffled: no helmet.*

"Hello, there. Can you tell me your name?"

Lily pretended to come around a little. *What do I say?* "Caitlin," she mumbled.

"Right, Caitlin. I'm Jack. Can you sit up?"

Lily let him help her sit up against the wall.

"Thanks," she said.

"No problem. Just doing my job. Are you on your own?"

She looked up. He was crouched in front of her in his leathers with the high-visibility jacket over the top. He had short dark hair. *Definitely him.* Lily could not have known from the CCTV printout how kind his smile would be.

She nodded.

"Where do you live? Can you tell me?"

"Chiswick. I came to go to the market."

"Maybe another day." He patted her shoulder and asked her a few questions. Finally he said, "Is there someone at home?"

Lily nodded.

"Can you call them and tell them you're on your way?"

Wait, what if . . . ? "I don't have my phone." *Please, please let this work.*

He knelt down and tugged his phone from his pocket.

"Look, I shouldn't do this, but use mine. I'll go and get you a drink. Something with lots of sugar in it. Have you had enough fluid today?"

She nodded. "I think so."

"Fine. Any preference?"

"No—thank you, though."

He grinned. "No problem. I'll be back in a minute. Don't run off."

"I won't."

As he went to the booth Regan had bought their teas from earlier, Lily opened his phone and quickly searched for a specific app. She set it to install and it did so without an icon, leaving no visible trace of its presence in the phone. Then she sent herself a text to say she was on her way home because she didn't feel well. Her phone buzzed once in response inside her jacket, just as the paramedic walked back, a can of lemonade in his hand. He opened it for her and handed it over.

"There. I shouldn't do this, but I think you're just dehydrated and I suspect you haven't eaten anything. You really need to, you know. You look a bit tired. Are you studying too hard?"

Lily shrugged. The radio on his shoulder crackled into life and a woman's voice rattled out an inquiry. Jack answered, pressing down a button on the handset's side. He listened to the response and let it go.

"Well, Caitlin, I've got to run. Car accident on Shoreditch High Street. Do you think you can get home from here okay?"

"Yes." She smiled. "Thanks. Thanks a lot."

He winked. "No problem. Just doing my job."

Lily watched him go, standing up slowly. She looked at the can in her hand with suspicion. He jumped onto his motorbike, started it, and roared off up toward Shoreditch, blue lights flashing. As he approached the lights they turned red. The bike's siren came on and he shot through the traffic, disappearing under the old railway bridge.

Lily walked back toward Bishopsgate, dumping the can in a litter bin. Regan appeared from the churchyard and fell in step with her.

"Was it him?"

"Yes." Lily dusted her hands off on the backside of her jeans. She explained about putting the app onto the phone. "So"—she pulled out her own phone—"in theory, all I have to do is install it on *my* phone, and we can see exactly where *his* phone is."

Regan watched her download the app and key in a PIN. "How did you learn all this? Do they teach you in school?"

Lily concentrated on the phone. "No. And it's a long story. But it really started when Ellie Watts wanted to know where her boyfriend went when he said he was going to a tutoring session."

"Was he going to a tutoring session?"

"No." Lily turned the phone to him. On the screen was a map with a red flashing dot. "He's exactly where he said he would be. On Shoreditch High Street."

"You sound as if you like him."

She shrugged. "He seemed nice. And we don't know he's done anything wrong. Yet."

He looked at her. "No. Come on. Let's get something to eat."

They ate noodles and hot soup in a Japanese shop near the station that was full of Shoreditch hipsters. Lily glanced around at the cool crowd, with their unusual clothes and extensive tattoos. "You know, you fit right in here."

Regan said nothing, just pretended to stab her through the back of the hand with a chopstick. She grabbed it and they had a halfhearted tug-of-war before Lily laughed and let it go.

"And you know you need to get a phone."

He shook his head and pushed her bowl toward her before picking up his own. "I manage fine without."

"I bet the Agency uses them. And all the technology they can get their hands on. Why give them the advantage? And it would make it a lot easier to keep in touch with Lucas."

"Only if he had one too, which is about as likely to happen as I am to be struck by lightning."

Lily sat back, studying him. He continued eating, ignoring her scrutiny. "Deliberately staying in the nineteenth century won't help you."

"Eighteenth," he said without looking up.

"What?"

"Eighteenth century. It's when Lucas and Elijah were alive. They're pretty much stuck there."

"Doesn't mean you have to be. Is that the real reason you don't have electricity?"

He changed the subject. "This is really good."

"You like Japanese food?"

He shrugged. "I like anything I don't have to cook myself. And hot. In that order."

Lily picked up her bowl, warming her hands on it, washing down the noodles with the savory soup. On the wall was a large peeling poster of Hello Kitty. "I come here with Dad sometimes. He knows all the best places to eat. Particularly the ones that serve you quickly. And lots of it."

Regan finished the last of his food and started on Lily's leftover noodles, which she'd pushed away.

She watched him. "Are you usually this hungry?"

He stopped eating, looking guilty. "You didn't want it, did you?"

Shaking her head, she laughed.

"I just eat whatever's in front of me. Old habit."

She raised an eyebrow.

"Living with Lucas and Elijah. They don't need food."

"So what did you eat?"

"I did fine. The amount of food thrown away around here every day is incredible."

"You ate . . . food that other people had thrown away?" she asked hesitantly.

"I ate what I could get. We aren't all the children of rich lawyers."

"My father isn't rich. *We're* not rich. We don't own our flat, and he does legal aid a lot of the time. We don't even have a car. I told you, my parents grew up in foster care. They came from nothing. The only thing Dad spends money on is me and food, and that's only because he's always trying to get me to eat more.

Everyone in Temple treats us like a charity case, because of what happened to my mum, and because my dad is amazing at what he does, even though it doesn't make money like criminal law. He's never taken a vacation since I was born. The Rookery is worth a fortune. Millions. You're far richer than we are," Lily said in a rush, the guilt she felt over her father's lifestyle making her snap.

He looked at her for a long time, then shrugged. "Irrelevant. It's not for sale. Ever."

Silence.

"You really are close to your father, aren't you, defending him like that?"

"Yes. He's the world's most decent man. He spends his life fighting for people who have no one else to help them. That's why I need to find Harris Stedman. And at least I know he was in Hackney now, no thanks to you."

Regan raised an eyebrow.

A thought struck her. "Is he Eldritche?"

He shook his head. "No. He's a weaselly, dishonest excuse for a human being."

Lily bit her lip, her palms on the Formica-topped table. He sat back, finished.

"You don't like us humans very much, do you?"

He shrugged, not meeting her eyes. "I like you, don't I?"

"Most of the time I really can't tell." Her phone buzzed on the table between them. She looked at it. "He's on the move. Back in this direction. No, slightly east. He's stopped again. Near the fire station. It's probably the depot, or wherever they're based, don't you think?"

Regan looked at his watch. It was old, a vintage thing with a canvas strap. Lily looked closer. It was like a pocket watch with the case pierced out so that the hands were visible beneath. She wondered how she hadn't noticed it before.

He saw her looking. "Elijah collects old watches. He's obsessed with the passing of time. He gave it to me when I left the bookshop. Almost three. Clocking off?"

"Maybe."

They pulled on their coats and headed out of the warmth of the café. Lily shivered in the frozen air. A frost was settling on the City. People headed back in droves toward Liverpool Street, heads down against the cold. Regan, wearing only the thin Henley beneath his coat, seemed unaffected. He tugged up the wide hood, hiding his face.

They soon found the fire station. Jack was letting himself out of a side door, dressed in jeans and a sweater and a thick duffel coat. He turned left and began to walk quickly back into the City.

"That's him," Lily said, pointing. "We'd better hang back a bit. He thinks I've gone home. To Chiswick."

They followed at a careful distance. Jack took the main roads back into the City. Lily and Regan kept well behind him, without ever losing sight of him. After ten minutes, they ended up back at the Bank of England, where Jack headed down into Bank Tube station. Lily and Regan followed.

"Do you have a pass?" Lily asked, pulling her travelcard from her bag.

He tugged one from his back pocket. "Yep. Thanks to Sid and his adventures."

They followed Jack through the barriers.

On the downward escalator, Lily turned around, lifting her chin to look up at Regan. "We'll have to stick closer to him here."

"Why?"

"This place is a nightmare. You have to walk all the way down one platform to get to the next one."

He nodded. "Yes. But depends which line he takes."

"We could lose him. The tracker doesn't work down here."

He tilted his head, not taking his eyes from Jack's back. "We won't lose him."

At the bottom of the escalator, Jack took a left turn onto the Central Line platform but he didn't stop and wait for the train, instead following the arrows toward the Northern Line. The platform was relatively crowded, and he threaded in and out of the knots of commuters.

The billboards on the other side of the tunnel advertised for blood donors, large red letters on white backgrounds. From tomorrow, mobile blood-donation centers would open in the City for a week. Lily's brain registered the date printed on one of the huge posters, and the caduceus in the bottom right-hand corner. *Trickery, theft.* Regan ducked in front of her, striding through the crowds of people in his usual fashion. Lily hurried in his wake, pushing when they closed ranks. Then Regan stopped and turned to her.

"I'll get onto the next car. If he's working for the Agency, he could well recognize me. You stick close to him."

"But he knows who I am too! I should have been on the Central Line to Chiswick an hour ago," Lily protested.

"Tell him you got lost in the station and then saw him. It's plausible enough. Stick close to him. I won't be far away."

He moved into the crowd. The far end of the platform was congested and Jack walked along the yellow line, close to the edge, to avoid the crush of people. Lily pushed and edged her way closer to Jack, until she was just behind his left shoulder. The rails began to rattle far off in the dark.

Lights appeared in the tunnel. The crowds of people on the platform stirred as a hot, metallic wind signaled the arrival of the train. Jack, only a foot in front of Lily, was looking down at the phone in his hand, checking the time. He was standing right at the edge of the platform.

As the train charged from the tunnel, a hand reached over Lily's shoulder, sending Jack falling with a quick shove. Falling out over the tracks, into the path of the oncoming train.

Time seemed to slow down. Jack twisted in the air in a futile attempt to save himself. Lily grabbed for him, their fingers clashing but failing to grip. In that second, a strong hand caught the scruff of her jacket and hauled her backward.

The noise of the impact was deafening. Then the noise from the people crowding the platform, the collective intake of breath. The driver braked instantly, but Jack's body had already been pulled beneath the wheels and onto the live rail. As thousands of volts charged through his mangled corpse, there was an explosion of sparks, then flame as his coat ignited and began to burn fiercely. Wisps of black smoke carried the smell of burning flesh to those on the platform. A woman began to scream.

Lily tried to turn, but the hand on the back of her collar was immensely strong. Mayhem erupted on the platform all around them.

She wriggled. "Let me go."

Abruptly she was released. Turning, she saw the back of a tall man with black hair, wearing a black motorcycle jacket with a caduceus pattern spread across his shoulders, stamped into the leather. He moved through the crush easily, pushing through people like water. As he passed under the WAY OUT sign, he turned slightly and Lily saw his profile. She frowned. Perhaps Gamble wasn't as confused as Regan thought . . .

The man stepped into the exit tunnel and was lost from sight.

Regan appeared at her side. "What the hell happened?"

She jumped. "We have to get out of here," Lily said. "The . . . I can't explain here. Someone pushed him. It's the Agency, I know it is."

Regan almost towed her through the crowd, pushing people out of the way if they didn't move quickly enough. It became almost impossible to take a step as the exodus began. As she passed the first exit tunnel, she glanced into it, but she couldn't see anything but the coat and shoulder pack of the man in front of her. Announcements came over the loudspeaker, but the noise of the crowd was too much to make out what it was saying. The scorched smell was overpowering.

At last they made it to the exit, the bottleneck suddenly clearing as people ran for the escalators. There was no sign of the man in black. They made it out of the barriers and went back the way they had come in. By the exit Lily noticed a large dragon mural built into the tiles by the designers of the station.

They ran up the final few stairs into the fresh, cold air.

Regan threw his hands up and cursed. "Did you see his face?"

Lily tried to catch her breath. "I—"

Regan's jaw tightened. "I can't believe I lost him," he burst out angrily.

Past his shoulder, by the Mansion House, Lily caught sight of a black van creeping forward. "They haven't lost us. Behind you," she said, "that van. It's them. They've seen us."

He didn't look, but took her arm. "Come on, then. Let's give them a run for their money."

They began to walk swiftly down the fortified western wall of the Bank of England.

"Where are we going?"

"The dragon's lair."

"What?"

"We'll be fine."

At the end of the street they arrived at a busy junction, with roads coming from all directions and a broken traffic cone acting as a makeshift roundabout. The van was in a short queue of traffic behind them, and as they crossed the road the light turned green and it followed them. Regan pulled up his hood and walked into a narrow alley to the north of the massive blank-walled Bank of England, off the ancient street called Lothbury, Lily on his heels. The van immediately turned in after them, lighting them up in the headlamps and making it hard for Lily to see ahead of her in the glare. Regan seemed unfazed, and led her and the van deeper into a maze of small streets. Most of them had only a few doorways, and the windows were high, well above Lily's head.

"Where are we going?"

"Nowhere. Look up."

Lily glanced up at the dark sky. She saw nothing, then a flash of silver streaked between the buildings high above them, a lashing tail just visible for a second as the dragon landed, cat-like, on the edge of an old office building.

"It knows we're here," she said, staring.

"Yep. It will also know they're here. And my bet is, it won't be happy about that. Plus, it'll be getting hungry as it wakes."

"Hungry? For what?!" Lily asked in alarm.

They turned left, into an alley almost too narrow for the van to follow, but it turned in a few seconds behind them, stalking them, engine rumbling softly. Lily's chest tightened. The alley was lit with a solitary orange sodium lamp, high up on a bracket above them, a relic of the 1960s. It cast an ugly light over the street, which was so narrow the pavements were reduced to pointless strips on either side. Lily and Regan walked down the center of the road, the van creeping behind.

"Slowly," Regan warned.

"They're going to run us down!" Lily exclaimed in an urgent whisper.

"No, they want you. And they probably know running me down won't work."

From high above them came a rumbling, purring noise. It was hard to hear over the growl of the van's engine, but it was lower, deeper, stranger. Regan turned again, straight into a dead end. The van turned in immediately behind them, blocking them in. They stopped and faced it. Lily put her hand up to shield her eyes against the glare of the headlights.

The rumbling grew louder, escalating to a roar as the dragon landed on the roof of the van. Rearing up on its hind legs, punching down, its thick talons shrieked through the metal as it ripped open the top of the vehicle like a tin of sardines, peeling the sheet metal back as if it were foil. The driver's door opened but slammed against the brick of the alley wall, not wide enough for anyone to get out. The dragon's head disappeared inside.

Lily had never heard men scream before. A hand pressed briefly against the inside of the windshield, the palm white. It was replaced a second later with a red splatter. The dragon grabbed something and shook it like a dog shaking a rat, resurfacing moments later, jaws crunching, blood running from its mouth, a strip of black clothing dangling. It gulped thickly, like a lizard with an awkward mouthful, before reaching one huge gold-clawed foot into the cab and grasping the passenger, plucking him out. As Lily and Regan watched, the dragon launched itself toward the rooftops, spreading its undersized wings against the black sky, emitting a piercing cry before it disappeared into the darkness away to the west.

Silence fell in the alley, followed by running footsteps and the roar of an approaching engine. Then Regan swore.

"What?" Lily exclaimed.

"No, you don't!" He ran, stepping up onto the van's bumper, its hood, and then its shredded roof.

The engine screamed to a halt, echoing around the alley. Lily ran toward Regan, trying to see through the gap between the van and the wall. She saw an agent getting onto a large black motorbike, ridden by the man in black leather. The man on the bike held something in his ungloved hands. His helmet obscured his face, but it seemed to her that he was looking, not at Regan hurtling over the top of the van toward him, but at the doorway where she stood. She watched as he pulled the pin from a grenade and threw it, with the accuracy of a baseball pitcher, into the back of the van.

Time slowed down. Regan shifted his course instantly, dropped down, and grasped Lily's arm as the bike roared from the alley. Pushing her hard into the brick doorway, he hemmed her in, his arms around her, as the grenade detonated. A wave of hot gas hit them, blowing Lily's hair back and spattering the exposed side of her forehead with hot grit. He curved his shoulder around her even more, keeping tight hold until the only sound was a popping and burning. The air stank. He straightened up, brushing black speckles of stone and carbon from her face.

"Are you hurt?"

She shook her head, looking up at him.

Her phone rang loudly. She pulled it from her pocket, hand shaking.

Chapter 8

"Hello?"

"Miss Hilyard?"

"Lucas?"

"Yes, indeed. How remarkable. This thing actually works. Where are you?"

Lily looked around. "Somewhere near the Bank of England."

"Is Regan with you?"

Lily held out the phone. Regan took it. In his abrupt way he described what had happened that day. The conversation was brief. Lily's legs weakened. She leaned against the alley wall, hands on her knees, concentrating on breathing in and out, staring at the burning shell of the vehicle a few yards away.

"Lucas, we should get out of here. He told Lily his name was Jack. Fine. Oh, and Lucas, when did you get a phone? I thought they weren't for people like us." He listened to the answer, grunted, then passed the phone back to Lily.

They made their way back to Bow Lane. Tom's was closed, but Regan pushed open the door anyway. Tom was shutting off the coffee machine. He said nothing as Lily sat down and pulled out her computer. She searched for the news of a death on the Underground. There was only an announcement that Bank station was closed due to a fatal accident. *Accident*, thought Lily sourly.

Regan sat down next to her.

"What will happen when they find the van?" she asked.

"No idea. My bet is we won't hear a thing."

"So people can get torn apart by dragons in the middle of London and no one will ever hear about it?"

"You may not have noticed, but they weren't exactly the good guys. And don't exaggerate; it was only one dragon. By the way it headed west, it's the Cripplegate one. I'll check it out tonight. Hopefully its belly will still be full by then."

"Why did it attack them?"

"I had a hunch that the dragon wouldn't be too keen on the Agency."

"Wait, a hunch. You led me in there . . . on a hunch?"

He shrugged. "It worked, didn't it?"

She held up a finger. "May I remind you that some of us aren't virtually indestructible? And how many more of these Ancients are still asleep beneath the pavements?"

"Well, there's the Thames River God in the Rock Lock beneath London Bridge. He mainly ignores us land dwellers. And the giant brothers, Gog and Magog, who're buried beneath Guildhall in a kind of stasis. But as far as I know they've never woken up. They're the last stand. If they wake, the City as we know it is finished anyway."

"You're joking now."

"No. They'll level it. Everything. And start again. You really do look pale."

"That's probably because I've just seen a man die under a Tube train, another one get eaten by a dragon, and almost been blown up," Lily said. She bit the edge of her lip, feeling the adrenaline still buzzing through her veins.

"Destroying any evidence, classic Agency tactic."

Tom came over and pushed two teas across the table with his strange, stubby hands. "Thanks," Lily said gratefully, grasping the handle of the mug.

He nodded. "No problem."

Lily picked up the mug, but her hands were shaking so badly the tea slopped over the sides, scalding her fingers. She put it down again hurriedly, laying her hands down flat on the table to stop them trembling.

Regan turned her face toward him, tucking her hair behind her ears. "Hey, hey, come on."

She turned her cheek into his touch, catlike. Then she remembered the man on the platform, on the bike, throwing the grenade with such deadly accuracy. Remembered his height, the distinctive black hair, so dark it had a petrol-like sheen. She pulled away, ducking her head. Regan let his hands drop instantly.

"I'm sorry," she said awkwardly. "Your brother, is he like you?"

"A halfbreed? Yes."

"That wasn't . . . I—"

"What?"

She shook her head. *It can't have been. If his brother was abducted by the Agency, he wouldn't be roaming the Underground killing people.* "Wait, I've got an idea." She turned to her phone and opened the Web browser, searching Twitter for anything to do with Bank station. She pointed at the screen. "Here, look."

"What?"

"There."

"I don't see . . . 'fatality at Bank station' 'man on Northern Line at Bank' . . . so what?"

"No, here." She tapped the screen with a thin, nervous finger where @Louise501 had tweeted OMG, *just heard it was @bikermedic who was killed at Bank. Can't believe it. Crying!*

Lily clicked on @bikermedic's profile. Jack Lewis hadn't tweeted for a few days, but his last few tweets had all been images. Lily opened them up. "These are all Ruskin Park. I recognize the bandstand. And he refers to it in the captions as his back garden, so he must live close by."

"So he lives near the park? How does that help us?"

She shrugged. "I don't know. Wait, let me look further back. He might tag his location."

Regan shook his head. "You people are insane. Why would you tell anyone your location?"

Lily poked her tongue out at him. "Look."

@bikermedic Finally! Keys to new flat! Great to have my own space!!! :)

He looked at the screen, then wrote down the address quickly. "Okay, let's go."

Lily took a hurried gulp of the tea. It was strong and sweet. She mumbled an excuse and slid out of the booth to the bathroom, where she washed her hands and face. The shadows beneath her eyes, which had been vague thumbprints that morning, were now purple smudges. The sensible part of her brain was telling her that she should go home, right now, and forget all of this. It was screaming: *Go home and forget him.*

She stared at her reflection.

I couldn't forget him if I tried.

Lily took a deep breath. She went back and drank as much of the hot tea as she could manage.

"Ready?"

She nodded and looked over to where Tom was standing near the coffee machine. On the counter was a small pile of left-over pastries. He glanced up at the ceiling and made an odd, chattering noise. As if from nowhere between the beams, two small mothwings appeared, shinning down the wooden supports onto the counter, grabbing up the pastries in their grubby hands. Even as they were cramming them into their mouths, Tom lifted them down one at a time and chided them softly. They scrambled into the corner and sat there, a jumble of pale limbs, rags, and dusty wings.

"I found them near the entrance to the courtyard. They were terrified. No idea what they'd seen. They keep babbling about traps and snares." Tom watched them eat. "But you know what they're like, they don't make much sense at the best of times, even less when they're frightened."

Regan watched them. "Someone's picking them off," he said, thinking. "But who? And why?"

They walked down to the St. Paul's taxi stand. Regan looked up and down it before walking to a cab halfway down the line. It was the oldest of the lot, an ancient Fairway, belching black diesel fumes from the back. The driver was enormous, crammed into his seat. He wore a shirt, a narrow tie, and a broken old brown jacket, the sleeves pushed up over his massive tattooed forearms, which rested on the wheel. The tattoos were bleary, but Lily could vaguely make out they were matching West Ham football team insignias. The man was hideous, with a fat nose and thick, wet lips, and a tweed flat cap rammed onto his gigantic, patchily shaved head. Regan bent to the half-open window.

"Evening, Stanley."

The driver looked at him sourly. "What do you want?"

Regan handed over the address. The man took it in his sausage-like fingers. "Get in, then."

Regan held the door for Lily and they climbed inside. Regan folded himself into the corner. Lily sat down abruptly as the cab moved off. *Great moves, Lily. Very cool.*

"Camberwell. Figures, with the Northern Line and everything."

Regan said nothing, staring out at the lights of the City. His wrists rested on his thighs, his hands hanging. His legs were too long for the space, making his knees higher than his hips, but he still sat with a strange grace. Lily looked away.

"You'll never guess," said Stanley, his gargantuan form hunched over the wheel, cap crammed against an oily patch on the cab's roof.

Regan dug a thumb and forefinger into either side of the bridge of his nose and suppressed a sigh. "Never guess what?"

"Who I 'ad in the back of this cab."

"Tell me."

"Guess."

"Stanley, just tell me."

"No, guess."

"For the love of—"

"All right, all right, keep yer 'air on! Cor blimey, ain't you touchy today?"

Regan put a hand to his forehead in mock grief. Lily hid a smile.

"Colonel Amanvir. Flew in half an hour ago, wanting to see Gupta."

A soft whistle escaped Regan. "They've obviously got watchers here, then."

"Who?" asked Lily.

"The Serpent King's bodyguard. Amanvir is its leader. He's the oldest of the living children. Sort of like a statesman. And an assassin."

" 'Zackly," Stanley said emphatically from the front seat.

"Poor Gupta," Lily said.

Regan nodded. "Yep. Poor Gupta."

"They won't really cut his balls off, will they?" Lily whispered to him.

He shrugged. "If that's all they did, he'd probably think he got off lightly. A visit from Amanvir only usually has one outcome."

"Can't you stop them?"

"Well, I probably could, but that's not part of the contract Gupta made. It's an honor thing; he'll accept what's coming to him. But it won't be pretty. The bodyguard are the sort that like to play with their food, if you get what I mean."

They were silent. Lily stared out of the window, worried.

"Anyway, as I was sayin', did you see them football scores?"

"No."

"Two nil against Millwall at 'ome." Stanley shook a huge clenched fist at his absent opponents.

Regan said nothing.

Stanley's sharp eyes were framed in the rearview mirror. "I can tip you out 'ere, y'know."

Lily swallowed a giggle. Regan glanced at her, then looked away, laughing. "Camberwell will be just fine."

Stanley smirked, gesturing at Lily. "What's this one anyway? Ain't nivver seen it before."

"This is Lily."

Stanley sniggered. "Awright, Lils?"

"Yes, thanks," Lily called from the back.

"Proper little flower, ain't it?" His eyes flicked back to Regan. "I seen bigger scraps on a butcher's apron."

Lily sat farther into the corner, folding her arms and looking down.

"Looks 'ooman to me."

"Yes," Regan said.

Stanley shook his head in an exaggerated fashion as he ran yet another red light. " 'Ooman women ain't nivver nuffink but trouble, mark my words. Even the pretty ones. Nivver touched an 'ooman woman. Wouldn't know where to start!"

Lily looked out of the window at the darkened city flashing by. She pulled out her phone and opened the notes app.

What is he?

She passed the phone to Regan. He stared at it for a moment, then his long fingers picked out the letters for a reply, the screen lighting up his face.

Troll

Lily giggled, then clapped her hand across her mouth and scrunched her eyes shut to hold it in. They were all silent for a moment. When she opened her eyes again, she saw Stanley staring at her in the rearview mirror. She ducked her head.

They hadn't spoken another word when they arrived outside a Victorian house in Camberwell five minutes later. Regan jumped out.

"Can you wait?"

Stanley narrowed his already hooded eyes, then pulled up the cab on the side of the road and turned off the lights.

Lily stood on the pavement in front of the house. There were two bins outside, marked 49A and 49B.

"Which one did he live in?"

He looked at the name tags on the door. "B."

"Which one is that? The door just says both."

He pulled a small leather wallet from the inside of his coat and extracted two metal tools from it. "Keep watch," he said, and began to pick the lock.

Lily glanced around but the street was empty. Lights were on in various houses, but the curtains were closed. A man approached with his dog. The dog paused to sniff at the base of a tree. It bought them just enough time for Regan to deal with the lock. They slipped inside. To their left was a door marked FLAT A. The noise of a television blared through the wall. Regan pointed to the stairs. They climbed to the first floor and he started work on the second lock.

A moment later, they were inside a neat, if shabby, flat. The streetlight outside gave them just enough light to see by.

"You check the computer, I'll check the flat."

As Regan walked into the bedroom, Lily flicked on the desktop. *No password. Excellent.*

Jack's computer had few icons on the home screen. One folder was marked *bills*, another *work*. Lily clicked on the work one. Inside the folder was a series of spreadsheets that covered various dates. Lily opened the latest. It was a detailed report of the patients Jack treated during working hours. Their names and a description. What was wrong with them, where they were, the outcome . . . and a column for whether they showed any signs of being Eldritche. At the end were the dates and times when he had filed a report, if they did show signs.

Lily turned on the printer beneath the desk. The only sound was it churning away.

"Lily?" Regan said quietly.

"Yes?"

"We've got company."

Lily joined him at the window. A van had pulled up in the street, CRYSTAL CLEANING written in huge letters down the side. It was the same make and model as the van that had been torn to pieces in the alley near Lothbury only a few hours earlier, just painted differently. Two men got out, wearing white paper suits and white dust masks. They went to open the side doors. Lily ran back to the computer, opened a browser window, signed into her e-mail account, attached the whole folder, and sent it to her secondary e-mail.

"What are you *doing*?"

"E-mailing documents to myself via the Internet. We've got hard copies, but it's harder for anyone to see we've been here this way. Not much harder, but it might just slip through." The computer churned away, sending the e-mail. Lily swore, tapping the desk, watching.

"Right," Regan said, looking mystified. "E-mail. I've read about it. You'll have to show me how that works sometime." He disappeared, looking for a way out.

The mail sent. Lily purged the printer history, cleared the cookies and the browser, and then found a particularly dubious file-sharing site. It took another five seconds to find and download a very nasty piece of malware she'd read about, one that wiped hard drives. Almost instantly, pop-up windows began to cascade and the computer became unresponsive. Lily turned off the monitor just as the front door clicked downstairs: The men had gained access. Lily found Regan in the bedroom, unlocking a window that let out onto the flat roof of the kitchen extension downstairs.

"Go, go," he whispered urgently.

Lily ducked through, landing as quietly as she could on the gravelly surface of the roof. Regan slid through after her and let the window drop. The lights came on inside the flat and he ducked, looking down from the roof onto a narrow path between the houses. Then he jumped, landing silently some fifteen feet below. He turned and looked up at her. "Come on!" he hissed.

"I can't jump that," she hissed back. "I'll break my legs."

There was a pause. "I'll catch you. Just jump."

Lily hesitated. She saw a figure move past the bedroom door. She jumped.

He caught her easily, an arm around her back and the other beneath her knees.

"Thanks," she said, breathless, realizing she was holding on tightly to his neck. *Lily Hilyard, get a life and get him to put you down.*

"No problem." He set her on her feet.

They went out into the street. As soon as they did, Stanley's cab crept forward, bulbous old headlamps flicking on. They jumped in and he eased out of the long, tree-lined South London street at a gentle pace.

As soon as they were back on the brightly lit roads, he grumbled, "Dint like the look of that lot."

"No," Regan agreed.

"You get what you wanted?"

Regan looked at Lily.

"I think so," she said, leaning forward slightly toward the glass hatch.

"Good," Stanley grunted.

Lily turned to Regan in the back of the cab. "He was reporting to someone every time he saw or discovered someone Eldritche. He reported Mona."

"Was there anything else on the computer?"

She shrugged. "Whatever there was, it'll be wiped by the virus I just downloaded. It'll take them a while to get anything from it."

As they hit the road to Blackfriars Bridge, there was a light Stanley could not avoid stopping at. As they waited, three large mobile blood units pulled up next to them, heading into the City. Lily touched Regan's arm and tapped the glass.

"Remember, from the Tube station? Starts tomorrow."

He leaned across and looked at the units.

Lily chewed her lip. "What if . . ."

"What?"

"What if it's not a blood-donation drive? What if it's testing? On a large scale."

"Testing?"

She nodded. "Blood—that seems to be the connection. The connection between you and me, and what the Agency wants from me."

"Testing for what?"

"I don't know. Being Eldritche?"

He shook his head, vaguely scornful. "You know if you're Eldritche, Lily. You're born with it."

"Then not that, but something else?"

"Where to?" asked Stanley, before Regan could reply.

"East gate into Temple, please," Regan said.

Stanley dropped them outside. The cab rattled off into the night.

"I'll see you in the morning, then, I guess?" Lily said, suddenly shy.

He smiled. "I guess you will."

She clutched the sheaf of papers. "I'll look at these. If I find anything . . . well, bye, then." She raised her hand.

"Bye," he said, tipping his head toward the gate.

Lily headed through the covered passage to the church square. It was already dark and the place was deserted. She didn't see the man in black slide open the side door of a van parked at the entrance. The man who had escaped from the back of the van in Lothbury. He jumped straight out into her path, momentum carrying them both to the floor, grazing Lily's chin. Pulling her to her feet, arms clamping tight around her, he dragged her toward the van. She kicked and fought as he lifted her from the ground, his arms like a band around her waist, trapping her hands.

"Should have taken the sedative, it would have been much easier on you," he hissed in her ear.

The van began to creep forward. She struggled harder. He grunted, but held on to her, his grip tightening.

Lily squirmed, hands locking over his. The man laughed in her ear. "A little fighter, are we?" Then he swore as Lily elbowed him hard in the side and kicked her heel back into his knee. The man dropped her. The van sped forward and he hauled her toward the open side door, hand around her arm just above the wrist, banging her knee on the footboard as he made it inside and dragged her after him. He held her down with one hand and slid the door closed with a thud. The van reversed sharply, then crashed to a halt.

The door opened as Regan's fist punched straight through the metal paneling and was removed in one piece from its hinges. He sent the door crashing onto the cobbles, then reached in and hauled Lily out. The agent grabbed for her and she kicked out at him, hard, leaving him behind. The van shot into first gear, screaming for the gate, its rear doors dented, a huge gap in its side. The agent hung from the open doorway.

"Next time," he shouted as the van roared through the gate, smashing the automatic barrier as it went.

Regan dragged Lily behind him across the square, almost too fast for her to keep up, pulling her through the door into her building. He threw the lock and pushed her up the stairs in front of him. Her hands shook as she tried to get the key in the door. He took over and did it for her, pushing her inside and following.

In the flat he shut the door and threw the latch, going to the window and looking down.

"Are they still there?" Lily panted.

He shook his head, coming back to her. "I don't think so. They won't hang around, not after that." He tipped up her chin, looking at the graze. "Does this hurt?"

Lily blinked. Tears welled up in her eyes. She shook her head, pulling her chin from his fingers. Almost without meaning to, she slid her arms around his waist and pressed against him, hiding her face in his chest. He was still and awkward, then put his arms around her, holding her cautiously.

"Lily—"

She stood as tall as she could on her toes and caught the edge of his coat, tugging him down. "Thank you," she breathed.

"Lily," he said again, almost a whisper, "we're not—"

The door to her father's study opened.

"Oh, excuse me," he said, surprised.

Lily untangled herself as if she'd been burned and stepped

away. "Dad, this is Regan." She pushed her hair back self-consciously.

Her father came forward, mug in one hand, the other held out. "Ed's fine," he said cheerfully, shaking hands, his eyes taking in Regan's tattooed hands and neck.

Lily cringed inside.

"I'm about to make a cup of tea, if anyone would like one?" Her father went to the kitchen counter and pushed the kettle on. "Did you hear that terrible crashing? Sounded like an accident down on the Embankment. I hope no one's hurt."

Regan shook his head. "No, we didn't see anything, did we? And thanks, but I think I'd better get to work. See you, Lily." He started toward the door. "Don't worry, I can see myself out."

The door clicked shut behind him. Silence fell.

Okaaay, so this isn't going to be awkward at all.

Her father busied himself making tea. "Remarkable tattoos," he said without looking at her.

"Er . . . yes."

"Very distinctive," her father said with a brave but totally fake smile. "Must have cost quite a bit."

Lily shrugged.

"And very good-looking, in as much as I understand that sort of thing. If it weren't for the tattoos he could be one of those male models . . . but what do I know? They all have tattoos in the magazines these days! Looks about twenty, maybe?"

"Nineteen."

"Known him long?"

"Not that long, no." Lily ran her thumbnail along the edge of the counter. *So, this is excruciating. . . .*

"Where does he work?"

Lily hesitated. "In the City."

"Doesn't look like an investment banker."

"No. He's in security."

"Ah. Right. Where did you meet?"

She grabbed her bag. "Enough with the questions, okay, Dad?"

He held up his hands. Lily went to her room.

"Do you want something to eat?" he shouted from the kitchen a moment later.

Lily rolled her eyes. "No, I'm fine, thanks."

"Have you eaten?"

"I did eat, at lunch," she shouted, then hesitated. "*We* had lunch," she amended, coming back to the kitchen. "At the Japanese place near Liverpool Street."

Her father took a breath and nodded. "Great. That's good to hear. I have some work to finish. But I thought after that we might go out for dinner."

"That would be great," Lily said truthfully. "I'd really like to. Somewhere close, though. I've got some work to do too, before then."

He smiled. "A couple of hours? Can't be much longer." He frowned. "What did you do to your chin?"

Lily tutted in what she hoped was a convincing fashion. "I tripped and crashed into the wall in the courtyard just now."

He winced. "Not like you to be clumsy."

"I know. I played it off."

"Put some antiseptic on it."

"It's not that bad." Lily lay on the sofa and pulled her computer toward her, then let it drop onto the cushions with a sigh. Her arm and knee felt badly bruised and she was still buzzing with adrenalin. She leaned her head on the arm of the sofa, her mind turning over all the events of the day, then groaned and pulled a cushion over her face.

"Are you all right?" He put a mug down next to her.

She grabbed the cushion and sat up. "Yes, thanks." *Which may not be entirely true.*

"Look, I'm pretty much finished with the work—"

"But you said a couple of hours."

"Oh, I know, but I'm hungry too. Let's drink this and go."

In the square by Temple Church, Lily paused, looking cautiously through the passage and out into the yard beyond. There were only a couple of cars there now, no van.

"Can we go to Hall?" she asked suddenly.

Her father looked surprised. "But you hate Hall. Why don't we go to the Italian place up near Holborn?"

Lily shrugged. "I don't know, I just fancy it tonight. Staying close to home." *The home I almost just got abducted from.*

He grinned and offered her his arm. "Fine by me. I think they're serving treacle pudding."

As usual, Lily wasn't dressed properly, but as usual the porter and the waiting staff chose to ignore that. Most of them had known her so long she was like one of their own children or grandchildren. The vast dining hall of Middle Temple, known to everyone as Hall, was a paneled room filled with long wooden tables and benches. Portraits of judges, centuries dead, gazed down from the walls around them, which were studded with coats of arms and lists of names. The atmosphere was at once tranquil but filled with busy conversations, conducted in hushed tones. Silverware and glasses clinked. Candles burned in silver candelabra.

Everyone sat together, which was part of the reason Lily didn't like it. As her father was one of the most prominent lawyers in the place, they always ended up with men sitting down next to them, interrupting their conversation and droning on. Still, the droning was good for one thing—they never knew what piece of information they were giving away to Lily and her father, what tiny gem might provide a breakthrough on something they were working on. The food was what Lily imagined a boarding school would serve. Her father said that was half the appeal for most of the people who ate there.

They ordered their food from the waiter, who gave them a choice of two things, chicken or beef. "And you should have something green," her father said.

The waiter arrived with a bottle of white wine. He poured them both a glass. She looked at her father, surprised.

"What?" he asked.

She shook her head. "Nothing."

A man in a blue suit came over and shook her father's hand. "Magnificent win today."

"Thanks."

The man sat down uninvited on the bench close to her father. "Did you hear about Michaels?"

"No. I hear they're going to appoint him judge any moment, though."

"Not after what happened today." The man lowered his voice. "Locked his entire staff in the conference room and was disarmed by police later in the outer office."

"Disarmed?"

"Said he'd seen something. Something terrible. Was just trying to keep them safe. Complete psychotic break, apparently. He's in the loony bin as we speak."

"What had he seen?" Lily interrupted.

The man stared at her.

"You remember Lily?" her father asked.

"The very image of Caitlin, what?"

Her father rearranged his knife and fork. "Isn't she?"

The man in the blue suit got to his feet, and cleared his throat, embarrassed by his mistake. "Sorry, Ed. Bloody clumsy of me, that."

The terrible silence that descended whenever people blundered over her mother settled over the three of them.

"But what did he see?" Lily pressed.

"Like the Hound of the Baskervilles or something. He was jabbering on, that's all. Anyway, think about it, Ed. You know where we are." He walked off, barking a greeting to another man at a nearby table.

"Did he mean Charlie Michaels? The man with the chambers

next to yours?" Lily asked. *A bandogge? Here in Temple? Regan said it was a sanctuary.*

"Yes. I missed all this. I was in court all day." He looked worried. "Poor Charlie. I'll call his wife when we get in. I knew he was under pressure, but this is awful." Shaking his head, he paused before speaking again.

Lily was only half listening. How could she contact Regan? She cursed his antiquated views on mobile phones.

"Lily, I think we should talk."

She jumped guiltily. "About what?"

He held out his hands flat. "I know we've never spoken about . . . boys, but—"

"Dad, really, there's no need." Lily took care not to sigh with relief.

"No need, as in you know everything, or no need, as in there haven't been any others?"

"Both. None." Lily fiddled with her fork, determinedly not looking at him. "Smart mouths and flat chests aren't a winning combination."

"Don't you ever look in the mirror? You're beautiful, Lily."

She rolled her eyes. "All dads have to say that, but thanks."

"I mean it. And I think I'd rather thought you'd start out in the, er, relationship business with . . . someone from school, perhaps." He cleared his throat. "Matt's a nice boy, and he's obviously quite keen on you from what I've seen."

Lily pulled a face. "Matt? You *are* joking."

Her father took a breath. "It's just that, well, Regan seems, er, quite, grown-up and—"

"Please tell me you are not trying to have the Sex Talk here," Lily hissed across the table, looking around at who might overhear.

"I'd rather not either, but I'm trying to be a responsible parent," he said with dignity.

She shook her hair back. "Well, don't worry. They teach it at school until they put you off the idea. You signed all the papers for the classes years ago."

"I did? Oh. Right. So," he said hopefully, "we don't need to talk about it?"

"No, we really don't."

Her father cheered up considerably. "I meant it when I said we all should go out for something to eat."

Lily looked around, unable to imagine Regan sitting among the Temple lawyers. "I think he's shy."

He cleared his throat disbelievingly.

"Maybe *shy* is the wrong word. I don't know."

"You mean he's reserved?" he suggested.

She nodded. "Yes, I think that's more what it is. His family, he lost them when he was young. His parents and a brother."

"Were they in an accident?"

"They . . . disappeared. Here in the City. He doesn't really know what happened to them."

He looked surprised. "Extraordinary for you to have that in common."

"Yes. That's what we think too."

They were silent for a few moments. "Go on, then, tell me more."

"After that he was fostered and brought up by two very old men," Lily went on, thinking about Lucas and Elijah. "They're strange, and old-fashioned."

"Really?" He steepled his fingers, looking interested. "In what way?"

"Hm, well, they're really formal and polite and there's no television or computers, or anything. Just rows and rows of books."

Her father raised an eyebrow. "They sound even more old-fashioned than me. But books are good."

"And there's books everywhere in his flat. Just everywhere."

"Oh, his flat?" her father said politely.

Lily stalled, realizing she had given away more than she intended.

"Where's that then?"

"Um, near Cheapside."

"So, you've been to his flat. And he's been to ours. And you've met the only family he's got."

Their food arrived and there was a pause as they fiddled with their cutlery.

"Good," he said firmly, as if to himself. "That's good. Now, eat before it gets cold."

They chatted in short, stilted bursts over their food.

"What happened to your mother's necklace?"

Lily touched it on the end of the black ribbon. "The chain broke."

"Shame. We'll get you another. We should really get you a new one altogether. With your own name on it."

"I like this one. It's the only thing I have of hers. And it has my emergency code on it instead of hers, so it's fine."

He watched her for a while. "You know, like you, she never knew her mother. She was only a few days old when she was found outside the police headquarters. Up near the Barbican."

"Wood Street? She was born in the City? I didn't know that."

He shrugged. "She might not have been, but that was where she was found. I always thought that was why she was so driven. It was a tough start in life."

Lily nodded, always eager for any tiny scrap of information her father allowed to slip out from the tight grip he held on everything to do with her mother.

"I often wonder what she might have achieved," he said, lost in thought. "She had so much potential."

Lily sat forward. "The thing she was working on, the doctorate—"

"Inherited mutations. She was obsessed with genetics. I think she linked it to her own identity. Like finding things out about herself that she'd never been told, and could somehow read from her DNA. She already had job offers from two or three companies, and the government."

"The government?" Lily's ears pricked up.

"Yes, but she said she wouldn't work for them as they didn't have a clear ethical stance. She didn't like the people who interviewed her. Although she did say that they had plans to create an incredible new facility. They showed her the plans, even down to her office."

"Where?"

"I don't know . . . not Westminster. Somewhere else. No, can't remember. So, what's brought all this on?"

"I don't know," Lily said slowly, shrugging one shoulder.

"Regan isn't encouraging you to dig through all this, is he? I don't want it to become some sort of obsession between the two of you. Lost family members."

Lily shook her head. "No, it's not like that. I just wondered if you had a theory, about why she disappeared. That was all."

He watched her. "Not as such. For a while I convinced myself she had just wandered out of the hospital, confused. But she would have been found. And she was too sick for that, or so the doctors told me."

Lily bit the inside of her lip.

"Things weren't easy at the time. I was working hard, wanting to establish myself. Your mother had put herself under intense pressure to finish her thesis, and then you were born, so early."

Looking down at the table, Lily fidgeted. "I'm sorry."

He looked surprised. "What for? It's not as if you could help it. Here we are, sixteen years later, trying to find ways to blame ourselves. But the reality is, Lily, your mother is dead." He looked toward the window, the candlelight showing up the lines on his handsome face.

They finished their meal. As always in Hall, her father signed a small piece of paper instead of paying. A bill appeared each month, like clockwork. They started the short walk back to the flat. In the shadow of a buttress on Temple Church she saw a figure hunched against the wall. It was Gamble. Next to him on the ground was a can of lager. As they passed him, he called out.

"Got something for Gamble, have yer?"

Lily stopped in her tracks.

"Come on, Lily. He shouldn't be there. I'll call the porter when we get in." Her father's voice was sharper than usual.

Lily hesitated.

He squinted up at her, one eye tightly shut, the other bleary and bulbous. Then he nodded firmly, almost tipping forward. "I seen it. And 't'ain't shiftin' from my mind. Terrible bad."

"It is?"

"It ain't good. No it ain't," he told himself. "'T'ain't good for you, nor him. But you got to remember . . ."

"Remember what?"

"Lily," her father called from somewhere in the hall.

"What you have to do! Remember Candle . . . no, that's not it," he faltered, then brightened. "London stain." Then belched.

Acrid fumes of alcohol and tramp-stench reached Lily. She grimaced. "Stain? What stain, Gamble?"

She pulled some spare change from her pocket. His hand lifted out of habit, though his head was down, almost between his knees. Lily tried to drop the money into it without touching his blackened fingers, the nails rimed with filth. It rattled and clinked down on to the stones.

Gamble's head came up. "Throwin' yer bloody charity at me. Gerrout of it. Just bloody gerrout!"

Lily backed away. Her father took her arm. As they entered their courtyard, through the yellow pool of light from the lamppost, he squeezed her shoulders.

"Don't worry," he said. "Gambling is a terrible addiction. One of the worst. And you have to accept there are some people you just can't help."

Back in the flat, Lily turned on the television and slumped onto the sofa, taking five minutes before she looked at Jack's e-mails. Her father grabbed a pile of thick white paper and sat down near her, beginning to read. It seemed like only a minute later when he put his hand on her head.

"Lily? Up to you, but probably time for bed."

"Oh." She unfolded her arms, rubbing her face. "What time is it?"

"Almost eleven. You've been asleep for a while. Sorry, I lost track of time."

Lily stumbled to the bathroom. She turned on the shower and threw her clothes on the floor, standing under the hot water. Yawning, she toweled her hair and ran a comb through it before pulling her nightshirt from the back of the door. After brushing her teeth she buried her clothes in the laundry basket and wandered through to her room.

"Night, Dad," she called again, hand on the doorknob.

"Night." He looked up from his papers, the light of the TV on the side of his face.

In her room Lily clambered into bed and sighed, snuggling down.

Her eyes flew open as a hand covered her mouth. Before her loomed a filthy figure with wild hair in a black cycling mask. She wriggled, kicking out.

Regan pinned her down, reaching behind his head and ripping the neoprene mask off forward, shaking his head in disgust at her struggling. "It's *me*."

Lily put her hands around his wrist and pulled. He sat on the edge of her bed, breathing hard, and dumped the mask on the floor. Cold air from the open window flooded over them. His clothes were torn and bloody and he wasn't wearing his coat. Across his face, above the clean outline where the mask had been, were black finger marks, and he smelled of grease, dirt, and rust.

"What are you wearing *that* for? It's enough to give someone a heart attack."

"You'd wear one if you had to work in the same stinking conditions I do!" he shot back.

"Are you okay?" She pushed up onto her elbows, looking at his torn shirt.

"I'm fine."

Her fingers touched a large rip in his shirt. Beneath it his skin was filthy but unbroken, his stomach hatched with sharp, flat muscles and the roiling flames of his tattoo. "What happened?" she breathed.

"Busy night," he said. "I need you to do something for me."

"What?"

He passed her the old laptop from the desk. "Help me. Look for anything unusual happening in the City."

Lily pushed up against the pillows, opening the computer, regretting leaving her new one on the sofa. "This is ancient, and slow. And I thought you didn't do technology."

"I'm taking your advice, and I need a heads-up."

"Like what?"

"Anything." He wiped his bloody, dirty face on his shoulder. "Dead people is usually a giveaway. But failing that, accidents, anything out of the ordinary."

Her eyes flicked up. "A man here in Temple today locked all his staff in the conference room and had a meltdown. Said he'd seen something terrible. Was just trying to protect them."

"What did he see?"

"I couldn't find out more without giving myself away, but I think it was a bandogge. But his chambers are right next to Dad's."

"A bandogge? Here?"

"You said it was a sanctuary, a strong one," she reminded him. "You said it was safe."

He nodded, then shrugged. "But I suppose if they're going to come into the Rookery, they'll go anywhere."

"Was it looking for me? Or Dad?"

He thought about that. "I don't know. You, most likely, and was drawn in by your connection with your father."

Lily frowned. "So he's not safe either? What's out there tonight?"

He tilted his head to one side to stretch his neck slightly. "So far? Two dragons . . . demons . . . some very bad things. There's too much going on. I need to know where my priorities are."

The laptop illuminated the room finally. Lily crossed her legs beneath the covers. "I'll tell you, if you tell me where to find Stedman."

He stared at her. "That's blackmail."

She shook her head. "It's bartering. Information for information."

They looked at each other for a long time.

"You first," he said.

"Nope. You first."

His jaw clenched, but he gave her the address.

She frowned. "But that's Stoke Newington."

"You think I'm lying?"

"No. Okay. My turn." She typed quickly. "Nothing. Nothing I can see. Everything's fine. Wait. On the Tube?"

He groaned under his breath. "Not the Metropolitan Line?"

"How did you know?"

"It runs along the old northern border of the City, straight under three of the gates. Terminates at Aldgate. It's like a sinkhole for the stuff I need to keep out, particularly tonight."

"Tonight?"

"Felix. We've taken a calculated risk and he's going to use the Museum of London to try and settle the dog and the banshee. We're running out of time; they'll rise if he doesn't get them bound good and tight tonight."

"Great," Lily muttered.

"The museum is built on the roundabout on London Wall. And it's deserted at night."

"So why don't you use it all the time?" Lily frowned.

He pushed his hair back. "There's a slight problem with it . . . in that stored beneath the roundabout are about eighty-five thousand sets of human remains."

Lily stared at him.

"The human archaeology department of the museum. Plague pits, graveyards, murder victims, every set of human bones dug up in the City for a century. It's not really the kind of place that takes the sending of spirits into eternal darkness that well." He pulled a face.

An alert came up on Lily's screen. "There's signal failures at Barbican, Moorgate, and Aldgate."

He swore almost silently.

"What?" Lily whispered.

"Barbican is Aldersgate, or maybe Cripplegate. I'll have to go there, deal with it, then be on hand to back Felix up." He ran a hand over his face. "Okay. Anything else?"

"I don't know where to look!" Lily murmured, eyes on the screen. "And even if I find something, how am I going to be able to tell you about it? I can't call you."

There were footsteps in the hall. They fell silent. "Lily?" her father said from outside the door. "Don't stay up on the Internet. Try to get some rest."

"Okay, Dad. Got it."

They waited.

"I've got to go," Regan said almost without sound. "Thanks."

She nodded. They watched each other. He leaned over and bumped his nose against hers gently, their mouths an inch apart. It was clumsy, almost human. The floorboard outside her door creaked. He got up from the bed, suddenly too quick and elegant to be real, taking her face between his warm, dirty hands and pressing a kiss to the side of her forehead.

The floorboard outside her door creaked again. "Do I have to come in there and turn it off myself?"

"No, Dad!" Lily squeaked. "I'm turning it off now!"

"Good girl. Sleep well."

She turned to where Regan had been. But there was only the open window, a faint thud, and retreating footsteps as he landed thirty feet below on the cobbles and disappeared into the night.

She stared after him. "Sleep? Are you *insane*?"

Chapter 9

Lily wriggled into her jeans under the covers, tugging on two pairs of socks and three different T-shirts. She pulled on a black beanie for good measure and lay still, waiting for her father to go to bed. It didn't take long. Ten minutes after his bedroom door closed, Lily slid from the bed and pulled on her boots. She wrote her father a note in the light of the gas streetlamp below her window, telling him she'd gone out early on a lead. Dropping her bag across her body, she picked up her keys extra slowly to avoid them scraping on her desk, and crept into the hall. It took her what felt like an age to reach the door and make it out onto the landing. As it clicked shut behind her, she waited for a second, then ran as quietly as she could down the brightly lit stairwell.

Outside the cold hit her like a hammer and her newly washed face stung. She put her head down and made for the river gate. How to get out without any of the porters seeing her would be a challenge. Luckily a party was just ending in Middle Temple Hall, and Lily slid down the side of the gate just as a row of taxis ferrying guests home distracted the porters. She made it out onto the Embankment and headed east. It took her almost fifteen minutes to get to the Museum of London. St. Paul's Tube station was closing up as she passed, the station guards pulling the flexible metal gate into place. They were talking and laughing in the cold.

Lily skipped over the road, avoiding the last old-fashioned number eight bus lumbering onto Cheapside down to Bow. Because the Museum of London was entered via the London Wall roundabout, the way to get to it was a strange, hidden escalator on the approach road. The escalator had been switched off for hours. Lily clanged up it and onto the walkway leading into the center of the roundabout. As she passed into the huge black-brick wheel, like a wall of death, and into the Museum's garden, she realized she'd made a terrible mistake.

Lily looked down from the balcony, into the dark of the garden, which was lit by dozens of candles stuck inside jam jars. As the icy breeze slid over the jars, the flames guttered and flickered. At one end of the garden was a huge Green Man art installation, shadows playing on his contorted face. Inside a strange circle made of white glittering salt crystals stood Felix. He was still wearing his sunglasses, but instead of his high-visibility gear he was dressed entirely in black. On the ground before him were the corpses of the bandogge and banshee, more crystals piled on top of them. He raised his arms and began to chant. It sounded like something between an order and a spell. Instantly the wind picked up and the candles guttered. Lily stood, bolted to the ground, as the crystals on the bodies began to shift. Lily cast a glance at the Museum entrance. It was dark and empty, the foyer lit with dull floodlights, deserted. She looked back at Felix. His chant had sped up and his arms were raised above his head.

She shouldn't have come.

What am I doing? Creeping out in the middle of the—

St. Paul's began to strike midnight. The wind rose again and Felix's lamps guttered wildly. Lily looked up. The night sky was now a roiling mass of clouds. Felix's voice rose over the sound of the bells, louder and louder. Outside, below them in the cold London night, a motorcycle screamed west, and a siren broke out. The white crystals were spinning in tiny cyclones, rising up from the bodies. Lily stared, gripping the cold metal handrail as white shapes began to rise with them—the spirit of bandogge and banshee, spiraling out of their bodies, spinning, forming, and reforming.

Then Lily saw with horror that more thin white apparitions were appearing from the air vents leading into the subchambers of the Museum.

"Felix, no," she muttered under her breath, shaking her head. She looked down into the garden, twenty feet below, then spied a ladder and a pulley system, which Felix must have used to let the bodies down. She ran to it, scrambling, legs banging on the rails as her boots clawed for the treads. Hand over hand, she was in the garden moments later. As she turned from the ladder Lily's stomach lurched. She was surrounded by a crowd of dead Londoners.

Gripping her bag strap, she stepped back against the wall. Felix was lost in his chant, head thrown back, arms still raised. The white figures before him danced and spun, writhing to escape his spell.

Lily gulped as the figures around her solidified and crowded closer. Men, women, and children of all ages were closing in.

Children covered in rags and grotesque sores. A highwayman, his neck at a peculiar angle. A woman in a huge hooped dress. A man naked to the waist, one leg crushed as if from a terrible accident. Lily felt something tugging on her jacket. She looked down and started back again, knocking over the ladder. There was a vine crawling over her jacket and jeans, up her legs. She watched in horror as more vines began to spurt from the Green Man's mouth.

Felix was bellowing above the whipping crystals, and the spinning figures of the Chaos creatures began to intertwine, screaming and howling over Felix's chant. Lily put her hands over her ears. A clap of thunder broke directly over the round-about and she hunched down, away from the sound.

Suddenly, over the handrail, there was a flash of pale material and the thud of boots on the soil. Lily turned her head. *Regan!*

He was fighting a creature that looked like a cross between a vast golden house cat and a lion without a mane. They smacked into the turf, the huge cat-thing buckling back on its haunches. Regan reared up over it, inked fingers digging into the creature's throat.

"Get out of here. This is not your fight," he threatened, pushing the creature away from him. It slumped, bones heavy, onto the grass before slinking away, growling resentfully. In two bounds it hit the wall of the garden then landed on the handrail above them. With one last look over its shoulder and a purring growl, it disappeared into the darkness at the entrance of the Museum.

Salt lashed Lily's face. A cataclysmic clap of thunder broke over the roundabout, and Felix fell to the ground. In an instant, the specters pulled their hands from Lily and retreated, sucked back into the ground and the air vents, back to where their bones lay. She shook off the vines as they unfurled from her limbs, crawling back into the stone mouth of the Green Man. Regan skidded to a halt in front of her, knees on either side of hers in the gravel path edging the lawn.

"What the . . . what are you doing here?" He sounded angry and exhausted.

"You're hurt."

"I'm good. Fine." His hair was everywhere and blood ran down one side of his face from the hairline to his jaw. He wiped his eye with the back of his hand.

"You're not!" Her voice was shrill.

"I will be . . . just give me a minute. Long night, that's all. Put something under the last Moorgate train. Didn't go quite as smoothly as I was hoping. We need to help Felix." He nodded to where the street cleaner was already on his feet, swaying like a drunk.

"Whatchoo' doin' takin' on a chindit?" he berated Regan in a slurred voice.

Regan let his head drop back and looked up at the night sky, weary. "That cat's been acting up lately. Needs a proper hiding."

He got up and put his arm around Felix's waist, supporting his weight by looping the Cleaner's arm around his neck. He propped him up against the vent and ducked out from underneath his arm. He turned to Lily, who had struggled to her feet.

"Look, I need to go. There's stuff still out there, and only me to take care of it. I need you to do something."

She nodded, looking up at his filthy, bloody face.

He gestured around the garden. "Clear all this mess up? Try not to leave a trace. Then get Felix out of here, to his car. He should have recovered enough by then. He's usually just tired and a little woozy afterward."

Lily hugged herself and nodded. "Be careful."

His fingertip grazed her cheek so lightly, from her eyebrow to her jaw, she wasn't sure it had happened. "Always." Then he was gone.

It took Lily a long time to clear up, even with Felix's directions. The salt that couldn't be collected had to be swept into the grass. Outside the black walls, the occasional car went by. Once or twice, there was a siren. The jars needed emptying of their candles, which were packed back into boxes and into black holdalls. The jars were wrapped and stowed away in a duffel bag.

By the time Lily had clipped the bags one by one to a pulley that Felix had already rigged up, and gotten them out of the garden, he was looking a little better. All that was left on the grass was a scorch mark where he had been standing. Lily checked her watch, surprised to see it was past four o'clock. *Four hours?! How long was I being touched by dead people?* It took even more time to unrig the pulley, retrieve the ladder, and get all the stuff into Felix's old car.

"Jubee, diss was good work," he said in thanks, turning to her.

She smiled. "No problem. Happy to help." She looked around. "Is he still out there?"

Felix looked at his watch. "I say he likely headed home now. Dies off this time."

"Are you okay to drive?"

"I fine." He waved a weary hand. "Home, shower, on the job at nine. See you aroun', jubee."

As the car rattled off into the night, exhaust blowing noisily, Lily stood uncertainly on the freezing pavement, watching it go. Then she walked slowly back to the Rookery.

Before long, she was pushing open the door to the office. It wasn't locked. Inside, the paraffin lamp on the wall cast a pale yellow glow around the room.

"Hello?" she called, uncertainly.

"Hang on!" Regan's disembodied voice called from somewhere. A long second later he appeared from the bedroom, bare-chested, in just a pair of clean jeans, scrubbing his damp hair with a towel. "Are you okay?" He eyed her warily.

She stood uncertainly in the office, hands on the strap of her bag, trying not to look at his washboard stomach. "Yes. Felix has gone home. I think we got everything."

"Right." He nodded, towel in his hands.

"I, er . . . Dad thinks I . . . I don't think I can go home without getting caught and—"

"Oh. Well, make yourself at home," he said, gesturing to the flat.

Lily watched him go through to the bedroom and fish a holey gray T-shirt from a drawer, pulling it over his tousled head in one sweep. On the end of the bed was a blanket of brightly knitted woolen squares. Its cheery look was out of place in the room, decorated only with more piles of books arranged around the walls.

"I just meant I don't think I can risk getting back into the flat without Dad catching me," she clarified in a rush.

He shrugged. "Then stay, like I said. Get some sleep. I'm going to. Tonight was enough to tire even me out." He lay back on the bed and crossed his ankles.

Lily hesitated in the doorway. "Um. Where should I . . . ?"

He propped himself up on his elbows. "Where do you think?"

She put down her bag carefully, pushed off her boots and coat, and lay down next to him on her back. He blew out the candle and settled back. They were silent.

"Well, I'm glad this isn't awkward," she said into the darkness after a minute.

He turned onto his stomach and looped a long arm across her waist. She stiffened. His shoulder covered hers. "Lily?" He sounded drowsy and close.

"Yes?"

"Please stop talking." His voice faded and she realized to her surprise that he was already asleep, exhausted. And heavy.

She woke with a start, alone. Sitting up, she pushed her hair out of her eyes and looked around. The flat was still freezing and there was no sound from the outer room. Checking her watch, she saw it was just before eight and outside the window the sky was lightening. As she stretched, she felt something on her right wrist. It was a bracelet made of knotted red thread, which closed with a glass bead the size of a marble. Like a marble, it had a swirl running through it, but the shimmering dust within swirled and spun around the red thread, constantly in motion. Lily stared at it, curious, as she got up. She found the bathroom, which was as Spartan as the rest of the flat but copious hot water sputtered from the taps, steaming in the cold room. Then she went to the kitchen and made herself a cup of tea. The milk carton sat on the counter, without need for refrigeration. She sat in the office to drink it, and took out her phone. There was a text from her father asking her to check in. She called him.

"Hey, Dad."

"Morning. Where are you?"

"On my way to check on a lead on that guy we were discussing." Lily and her father were always deliberately vague on the telephone, in case their calls were monitored by any of the opposition.

"Oh, right. You went early."

"I know. It was on my mind and I wanted to get on, as we're so up against it." Lily breathed a sigh of relief that her plan seemed to have worked out.

"Good girl. Well, let me know how you get on. And be careful."

"I will."

They finished the call and Lily drank her tea. There was no sign of Regan. She washed the mug and headed out.

Chapter 10

Walking down to Bank, Lily waited at the number seventy-six bus stop. There was a newsstand half stacked with *Metros*. The headline shouted at her from behind the grille. PLAGUE OUTBREAK: EXTINCT DISEASE BRINGS TRAGEDY TO WHITECHAPEL.

Lily picked up a paper and scanned the front page. Seven people, so far. More critically sick. She put the paper back, slowly. *Things are getting worse.* She bit her lip. She wondered where Regan was. *What if more plague demons got through last night ... what if ...* She shook off the thought. *He's fine. He just went back to work, that's all.*

The bus arrived a couple of minutes later. On the long journey up to Stoke Newington, Lily sat absorbed in her thoughts. When, finally, it pulled to a halt at the junction with Amhurst Road, she felt a little calmer. She got off and turned into the street of large Victorian houses converted into flats. Finding the address, she pushed the buzzer for the top flat. And waited. Finally it crackled.

"What?" a male voice said.

"Stedman? Harris Stedman?"

"Christ, keep your voice down! Who's that?"

"I got this address from Regan—"

"Shut it," the voice screeched, making the intercom squeal.

The door clicked. Lily pushed through it and climbed to the top floor. There on the landing, a door stood open and behind it was a brown-haired man not much taller than Lily. He was thin, with a ferretlike face. He jerked his head to the interior of the flat, looking annoyed. Lily walked past him.

The flat was not what she had expected. It was neat and clean, with large white sofas and arty pictures on the walls. Through the glass doors was a roof terrace. In front of the doors was a vast desk covered in paper, scalpels, a printer, and what looked like an improvised laminator.

"Who the hell are you?"

Lily turned. "My name's Lily. My father is representing a client you made fake documents for."

"So?" His eyes skipped to the desk.

"Those documents allowed her to stay in this country as a trafficked individual. While under the control of her traffickers, she was forced to commit various crimes, which she's being charged with. I need to find the traffickers, so we can have them prosecuted, not her."

"And this would be my problem how?" His eyebrows raised.

"You know who they are. And you can't have missed the case in the news."

He stared at her.

Lily folded her arms. "I just need a name, and where to find them."

"And I just need my business and my neck intact, but thanks." He opened the door again.

Lily pushed it closed. "Don't you care about this woman at all?"

He looked at her as if she were stupid. "If I *cared* about other people, lady, do you think I would be in this line of work?"

Lily shrugged. "But I need you to do this," she said simply.

"What have you got over Lupescar that he's giving my name away?" He looked her up and down. "Or is that too obvious a question?"

Lily put her hands on her hips. "Very funny."

He folded his arms. "It wasn't a joke. I need to be able to trust people."

"You can trust me."

"Oh, yeah. In the high court." He snorted.

"There's no reason for your name to come out. I'll make sure it doesn't. But if you don't give me a name, then . . . perhaps it just will. I have you down so far for sixteen fake visas, at least five passports . . ."

"Yeah, yeah. Prove it."

He licked his thin lips, then gnawed at the edge of one, pushing it between his teeth with his thumb. Lily set her chin, looking at him. The phone rang. He reached over and picked it up. "Yes? Right. Okay. I can do it but it'll cost you. Oh, and I have some very interesting merch here that you may want to take a look at. Yeah, I know, but I don't want to hang on to it. Send someone, yeah?" He put the phone down. Then he went over to the printer and pulled out a blank sheet of paper. He handed her a pen. "Write this down. I don't want my hand anywhere near it."

Lily bent over the desk, looking at the neat piles of passport photographs and watermarked paper. She listened and wrote as he dictated a name and address.

"Don't blame me if they're not still there. They come to me, as a rule. And if you value your life, don't go there like you've just come here. They are *not* nice people."

Lily folded the sheet and put it in her jacket pocket. She glanced at the desk again. "How many of these do you do in a day?"

He shrugged. "I'm working toward early retirement." He looked at the iced-over decking on the roof terrace. "Somewhere warm."

Lily turned for the door. "Thank you."

"I mean it—my name appears in that courtroom and I'm a dead man."

"It won't."

She reached the door and turned the dead bolts, finally flipping the latch. As she opened it, he laughed and said, "How does it feel?"

"What?" she asked over her shoulder, seeing him standing in the middle of the room.

"Being one of the good guys?"

Lily never heard the man behind her. As his hand, holding a dirty white cloth, closed over her nose and mouth, she didn't even have time to react as her knees buckled.

Chapter 11

Lily was vaguely aware of arriving at the door of a locked-up shop with a flat above it. She stumbled, the man's arm hard beneath her armpit. Behind them, a car exhaust rattled off. The metal shutters were down and newspapers had piled up between the shutter's letter-box and the interior, spilling out in yellowing, shredded tongues. The peeling red door to the right had a cheap rusted knocker.

Inside was a foul-smelling corridor, littered with fried-chicken boxes and brittle pizza flyers. Lily stumbled and fell to one knee. On the damp doormat was an envelope with an address. She tried to commit it to her fuzzy memory.

The man, who was wearing an ugly tracksuit with purple-and-gold sneakers and a great deal of gold jewelry, grabbed her and hustled her up the stairs, their feet bumping unevenly on the matted carpet.

They burst through a cheap plywood door into a squalid room on the first floor. At a plastic picnic table sat a hugely fat man in a dirty white undershirt and a greasy leather jacket. In front of him were three old mobile phones. *Burners, by the looks of them. Disposable.* Lily blinked, her brain hazy. The man's meaty head was shaved and tattooed right over the top like a number eight pool ball. He held the same ball in his hands.

"What's that?" he asked in a thick accent.

Tracksuit sneered. "Stedman tipped us off. Said he had some quality merch."

Lily refused to wince at the pain in her arm and met the man's eyes. They were hooded, and sunken in his fat head. He wet his thick lips.

"Very nice indeed."

Lily said nothing, although her gut tightened with panic and her head still spun. He passed the black ball back and forth between his fingers, watching her speculatively.

"Put her in the back room for now," he told the boy. As Lily was pushed away, he looked over his shoulder. "Take her phone."

The boy fished in Lily's pockets, finding her phone and pulling it out. He handed it to the man with the ball. "Billiard?" he said, raising the end of the nickname, looking for approval.

Lily's stomach dropped inside her body as if she were on a roller coaster. *Billiard?* This was Anton Andreyev, one of the men they had been looking for in the trafficking ring, the missing piece of the puzzle from the case the year before. Not the biggest cog in the wheel, but certainly important. He had been working in London for years, but Lily and her father hadn't been able to track down anyone who'd had a face-to-face meeting with him. Or wanted to talk about it.

"Latest model," Billiard sneered as he looked at it, and put it on the table with the others.

Lily was stripped of her bag and shoved into a stinking room full of rubbish, broken cardboard boxes, and a mattress without any sheets. The door locked behind her. She sat on the floor in the corner, where the carpet was cleanest, hugging her knees. *This was not your best move, Lily, not by a long shot.*

She got up and tried to open the window, but the metal frame was nailed shut, the rusted nails hammered in and bent over. In the other room, she could hear voices. More men now. She rubbed her aching forehead. Her grazed chin felt sore.

The day outside was too gray to see the time passing. She looked at her watch obsessively. Beyond the door she heard the telephones ringing almost constantly. Different voices came and went. After a couple of hours, the door opened and the boy was looking down at her.

"Get up. He wants to see you."

Lily got to her feet a little stiffly, and walked after the boy into the other room. Billiard was still sitting at the table, the phones ranged in front of him. Next to them was her phone. He was looking at it.

"How old are you?"

"Sixteen."

His hooded eyes stared at her. "You're English. Glossy little rich girl. You don't need papers. What were you doing at Stedman's?"

"Trying to help someone."

"Keep avoiding the question and I will hurt you. Do you understand?"

Lily said nothing.

"Unlock your phone."

"No."

"Did you not hear what I just said?" He sat forward slightly, menacing her.

"Yes, and I said no." *The only way out of this is to buy some time . . .*

"So, if I call my guy and he unlocks your phone, what is he going to find?"

Good luck with that one. It'll take him a year to get into it. "Nothing."

He flipped through her wallet. Lily had always made a habit of keeping her travelcard unregistered and only carrying cash. She used her bank card online at home, but didn't keep it in her wallet. Nothing in there held her identity.

He closed the wallet. "No ID at all. Anyone would think you really were a criminal. Or a spy. Perhaps you do need papers."

Lily said nothing.

"So, what shall I do with you?" He sighed. "I can't let you go, of course. But I'd rather not waste a pretty girl." He stared at her, making her insides writhe. She forced herself to stand still and say nothing.

Tracksuit cleared his throat, looking up from where he was watching television on a foreign network. "That Battersea mob still needing girls? They liked them her age."

"Everyone likes them her age," Billiard said, not looking away from Lily.

"*Da*, but their money was better than everyone else's. And they no care about the face! Can be pretty, can be ugly, all same price. Like dogs' home." He lifted a shoulder and cocked his head to the side in international sign language: poof! "I not know what business they are running; maybe customers blind."

The corners of Billiard's mouth turned down. "I did not like them. Particularly the young one with the smart mouth. They all had stink of *Securitate*. I can smell officials a mile away."

Tracksuit turned back to the screen. "Put her back in the room," he snapped to one of the henchmen, who pushed Lily through the door and slammed it behind her again, the bolt on the outside ramming home.

Lily guessed about another two hours had passed. She sat, back to the door, her head resting against it, listening as much as she could. There was only the noise of the television and Billiard talking endlessly into one of the telephones, or sometimes two at once. Then the television went off and suddenly the voices were much clearer.

"Battersea no want her. Say they have enough girls now. No matter. It will be easy to find a girl who looks like that a new home."

Tracksuit laughed and then the television resumed its burble.

Suddenly there was a splintering noise and a yelp. Lily's limbs tightened and she pushed herself up, backing into the corner.

"Where is she?"

Regan's voice. Lily's knees went weak and she slumped back against the damp wallpaper.

"Who?" Billiard asked.

"The girl."

"And you are?"

"Irrelevant. Where is she?"

"I have no idea what you're talking about."

There was a crashing noise, just as Lily yelled, "I'm here!"

The door swung open slowly, revealing Regan holding down one of the men, by his head, to Billiard's plastic table. Billiard still sat in the chair, looking unperturbed. The man struggled for breath, snorting against the white plastic. The other two men lay on the floor like discarded toys.

Lily ran out of the room. Her bag was on the floor, papers strewn around it. She gathered them up quickly and shoved them back inside, pulling the strap over her head. Regan hadn't looked at her.

Billiard's eyes were tiny inside his huge head. He was still fondling the eight ball. "You think you can get out of here alive?"

Regan's face was impassive as he held down the struggling man with no effort at all. "You think *you* can?"

"I need my phone," Lily said.

"Take it, then," Regan snapped. "I'm sure this gentleman won't stop you."

Lily grabbed it from the table and sent her father a text with a description of the address and the details for his police contact. She added *Send them NOW.*

Got it. Her father's reply was almost instant. Lily thanked her stars he wasn't in court.

"I'm guessing the police are on their way," Billiard said easily. "This, my friend, is not going to go so well for you, or your girl here. In fact, it may well go worse for her."

Regan held the man into the table until he passed out, then let him slump to the floor. He straightened up. "Why? Because your *boy* behind me has a gun? And he's going to shoot her?"

Billiard didn't even have time to smirk before Regan turned and the boy's hands were empty, the gun a useless, twisted lump smacked down on the flimsy table.

"You," Regan said over his shoulder to the boy, "can leave now if you want to."

The boy lifted his chin. "I stay."

Regan nodded. "Fair enough." He reached over and casually cuffed the boy on the side of the head. Hard enough to send him sprawling onto the filthy carpet, unconscious. Then Regan turned his gaze back to Billiard, who was looking at the hunk of metal on the table.

Billiard's face broke into a broad smile. "My boy, *you* are just what I've been looking for."

"We're leaving," Regan said.

"Wait!" said Andreyev. "I am serious. I can use a man like you."

There was the sound of cars screeching to a halt. Billiard stood up. Regan pushed Lily in front of him toward the door.

"Remember, it was your choice," said Billiard. He hurled the eight ball at the back of Regan's head, his hands already fumbling for the gun at his fat gut.

Regan turned and caught the ball just before it connected. He was back, pinning Andreyev into the chair by his throat in an instant, too fast for Lily to see.

"Drop. The gun."

It clattered to the floor and was kicked away, skittering into a rubbish-strewn corner. Regan weighed the ball in his hand for a second before closing his fingers around it. There was a distinct crack. Billiard's eyes widened.

"Pool, not billiards," Regan said, dropping the two halves of the ball onto the table.

Lily stared at the unconscious figures strewn across the room. She turned back. Regan was gone, and through the door flooded half a dozen Metropolitan Police officers in navy flak jackets, large shields on their breasts and guns across their stomachs. Regan was nowhere to be seen. They halted inside the door and almost had a pileup as they saw Lily, Billiard, and the unconscious men on the floor.

It was dark outside when Lily managed to extricate herself from the scene inside the building. It seemed that the line "looking for a friend" wasn't going to cut it with the Met detectives either, who questioned her repeatedly as soon as they found out she was indeed Ed Hilyard's daughter. She managed to keep Harris Stedman out of the equation, but only through some very cagey answering.

The detective, a tall man with pale hair and a sharp face, kept his eyes on her. "Well, Miss Hilyard, you may be called as a witness, but we've been looking for Mr. Andreyev for a long time. He's not the top of the tree, of course, but he's good enough for me."

"Just one more thing . . . what would really be great is if I weren't called as a witness? My father will be standing for the defense in the Kalhuna case," Lily explained. The detective, called Evans, looked at her even more closely. "I was just trying to help," she said a little desperately.

He reached into his jeans pocket and handed her a card. "These are my details. Call me if you think of anything else." He grinned. "Or if you're ever considering a job on the force."

Lily took it with a smile, reclaimed her wallet, and skittered down the steps and out into the road. She looked left and right. The Met cars and a van were still parked on the pavement, but other than that, it was an ordinary London evening. She walked quickly toward the bus stop, finding her father's number in "recent calls" and dialing.

"Hey, Dad."

"Lily." He breathed a sigh of relief. "I knew Detective Evans would be there, but I didn't know what else was happening. He told me he'd gotten you and to stay put here and wait."

"I found Anton Andreyev."

"You did what?" Her father's voice was sharp.

"I know. I didn't mean to. Things sort of got out of hand—"

"What sort of 'out of hand'?" her father snapped.

"I . . . it wasn't bad. They just took my stuff and put me in a room for a while."

There was a silence. "Come straight home. You and I need to talk."

The phone went dead. Lily looked at it in her hand. Her father had never hung up on her before. She couldn't even remember him ever raising his voice.

A cab pulled into the curb, exhaust rattling. It was weighted down on the driver's side. Stanley sat clutching the wheel, eyes straight ahead. The rear door swung open.

Lily clambered inside, thumping into the seat as the cab lurched into the road. Regan sat beside her, fists clenched on his knees, jaw set.

She fiddled with the zipper on her jacket. "How did you find me?" she asked, after a long silence.

"Stedman. Wanted to know why I was giving out his address."

"Oh . . . did you have to hurt him to find out where I was?"

"Yes."

"Oh. Well, thanks."

"You are welcome," he said, pronouncing each word clearly.

They sat, not speaking. The atmosphere was unbearable. As they arrived back in the City, Stanley answered a mobile phone with huge keys and a plastic West Ham mascot hanging from it. He reached back and slid open the window. "Lucas. For you."

Regan looked at the phone as if it smelled bad before leaning forward and taking it from Stanley. "Yes? Did they say why?" He nodded, looking out of the window. "No. No, I understand. I'll go now. Then I have to take Lily home before I go on watch. Yes, I cleared them out of Whitechapel. No, I'm fine. I'll stop by later." He tapped the phone against the glass, putting it into the hand Stanley held up without looking. "Change of plan," he said.

"The Needle?"

"Please."

Stanley nodded. Regan didn't look at or speak to Lily.

"Where are we going?" she asked.

He didn't answer. The anger was flooding off him, filling the back of the cab. Lily bit her lip and looked out of the window. "Where are we going?" she asked again when he didn't reply.

"I've been summoned by the River Guardians," he said, his voice flat.

"*Who?*"

He ignored her. Soon afterward, they rattled under Waterloo Bridge and past an abandoned pier before arriving at Cleopatra's Needle. The carved stone obelisk sat on the edge of the river, flanked by two bronze sphinxes. On the wall a ragged black cormorant dried his wings against the night, beak raised. His scaly eyelid closed slowly over one dark eye, then flicked open again, fixed on them. The gulls began to wheel and cry overhead. Lily looked up as she got out of the cab, Regan unfolding himself behind her.

Stanley drove away toward Westminster. Lily watched the cab recede, tail lights bright in the dark, then turned back to the river.

No. Way.

On the back of each sphinx, staring out at the river, was a smooth-skinned, beautiful woman with night-black hair. One wore her hair short, curled close to her head. Her skin was a deep black. The other had her hair in a thick oiled braid, trailing down past her hips. Her skin was a deep olive color. They wore cotton loincloths, and heavy beaded collars hung from their throats, covering their chests down to their waists. One stood, fists clenched at her sides, staring west. The other, darker woman gazed east, sitting on the bronze rump of the sphinx, one leg pulled up, feet shod in leather thong sandals.

"You come only now?" the black woman said, not looking at him. "The Clerks give us word that our prophecy has come true and *we* have to summon *you*?"

"There was a plague demon loose in the City, Misrak. I trust you to send word if any slip through. We trust each other—we have to. And I dealt with seven today in Whitechapel. *Seven.* There's a hospital ward full of dying people because you didn't send word soon enough. *That's* why I haven't been here."

The other woman hissed, turning to them. "There were dozens. Maybe hundreds. We have never seen so many."

"You should have told me, Delphine."

The black woman shifted, and in a second was standing in front of him. "Do not presume to tell my sister what to do." A gull's cry knifed the air. She looked up and stepped back slightly.

The other woman jumped down onto the pavement. "We have stopped more than a hundred in the last week. There are other demons too. Larger, more dangerous. Our time has been taken. Our attention diverted. It is the vermin that slip our nets."

The two women crowded in on Regan. They were both taller than him, Amazonian.

Delphine straightened up, folding her arms across her beaded chest. "A tanker moored out in the estuary. Hundreds of them came off it. Pouring across the water like locusts. Two days. We scoured it clean. But some got through. Our defenses are breached." She looked down at Regan. "As we hear are yours, warrior."

Regan nodded. "Yes."

"They say the dragons are waking. Is it true?" Misrak's cat eyes narrowed.

"Yes."

Delphine gave a piercing shriek. Lily winced. The movement drew Misrak's gaze.

She moved closer. Her voice softened. "This is her?"

Regan stepped to Lily's side. "Yes."

Delphine turned, her gaze also on Lily. The women walked toward her as one, stooping to stare into her face. Lily looked between them. Unconsciously her fingers reached out and found Regan's. He locked their hands, his touch reassuring. "It's okay, they just want to meet you, that's all."

"Why?" Lily's voice wasn't altogether steady. They still hadn't looked away. Misrak raised a hand and pulled a curl of Lily's hair very gently, then watched it bounce back as she released it.

"This is the blood girl?"

"Yes," he said.

Delphine straightened up. "She is very . . . small," she said finally. "I am not sure she will restore the balance."

"Restore *what* balance?" Lily asked, looking up at them.

Regan put his hand on her shoulder. "Remember, what we talked about? That something in the City threw out the equilibrium a long time ago, and started to let in the Chaos?"

"Yes. I remember."

"Well, there's kind of this idea that one day someone will come along and find out what it is."

"Really, sister," Delphine said to Misrak, "is it possible we could be this wrong?"

Regan cleared his throat. "Either way, first we have to find out exactly why the balance is being upset."

"And why *is* that, brother?" Misrak was still peering at Lily.

Regan took a breath. "I think it's the Agency."

Delphine pulled a face. "You speak of the government? Governments come and go. They are not our concern."

"The Agency is. They're doing something. Taking Eldritche. Mothwings are missing in droves, and now Mona. They may be experimenting on them. It's disturbing the balance even more . . . it's what's going to cause the war."

"What are these experiments of which you speak?" Misrak asked, taking Lily's other hand and holding it between her own. She looked at the palm, then turned her hand over and examined the back.

Regan shrugged. "I don't know. To find out what we are, so they can use the information for their own gain, I assume—though I don't yet know why or how."

Both women made a noise of contempt. The traffic was limited to the odd 388 night bus now, and a few taxis zipping by. Lily no longer wondered why no one saw two half-naked seven-foot women on the pavement.

Delphine's gaze returned to Lily. "So, you are come."

"I am?"

"So war is coming too," Misrak said, looking out over the water.

"Yes," said Regan.

"We remember when wars were invaders, distant tribes under distant kings." Misrak's tone was soft, and Lily realized she wasn't looking out over the Thames, but over thousands of miles, back to the desert. "Now some *department* upsets the world." The contempt was plain in her face.

"Perhaps afterward we should claim her as our tribute? Our payment from the City for all our hard work. This little blood girl."

Regan snatched Lily back. She stumbled into him before recovering her balance. Misrak watched them, then laughed at them.

"Fear not. My sister jests. You keep her, brother. For now. We will tell the water and she will be watched over. It is our way."

The two women leaped back up onto their perches. They settled cross-legged, elbows on their knees, and returned to gazing out at the river, dark and silent. The gulls split into two packs and wheeled out east and west, their cries rending the night air.

Lily and Regan walked back toward the Temple, both with their hands in their pockets. Regan didn't speak.

"What was all *that* about? *Blood* girl? If this is the moment where you tell me I have some sort of superpower, I want a better name than Blood Girl."

He said nothing.

"And the war? The war is definitely coming?"

"Yes," he said dully. "That's what they foresaw. Your arrival—"

"Wait, my *arrival*? I haven't arrived anywhere; I've always been here. And what have I got to do with anything anyway?"

"I don't know. I didn't make the prophecy. It's a war that may destroy the City, if we don't win it." He shrugged, voice flat. "Then again, it may destroy it if we do."

"Should I tell Dad to leave?"

"What would you tell him?"

"That he has to go! Somewhere, anywhere."

"And he'd go without you?"

Lily halted. "No."

"Then there's no point, is there?" he bellowed, exasperated.

Lily stood, shocked. No one ever shouted at her. "Are you still angry with me?" she asked slowly.

"Yes."

"Please don't be."

He seemed about to walk away, then he rounded on her. "I went to get breakfast for us and you left."

She stood still, mouth open, trying to form a sentence. "I didn't know. I thought you'd gone back to work. Or something," she said finally, awkward.

"So you go to the East End to try and get yourself sold as so much . . . why would you do that?" He hissed between his teeth in frustration.

"I was trying to help Dad with the case." This didn't appear to make any difference to how angry he was. "Look, I get that I made a mistake. I won't put myself in that sort of danger again."

He pulled a face. "You don't understand, do you?"

"Understand what?"

"I live by a set of rules. You're changing them. I don't like it. And I don't want to be involved in human problems. The *squalor* of that place . . . of what you people do to each other." He cursed, disgusted.

"Fine," Lily snapped and hurried to get ahead of him. "If you can't stand us so much, then you shouldn't have bothered getting me out of there."

She heard his growl of frustration as he caught her easily. His fingers wound into the strap of her bag and pulled her to a halt, turning her around to face him. "I wasn't going to leave *you* there, was I?"

Folding her arms, Lily looked out at the gray churning water, dangerously high against the Embankment wall. The traffic flooded past them on the other side, yellow lights beaming through the icy air. "I don't know. You obviously think I'm a problem."

"You are!"

They stood, not looking at each other, neither of them willing to move.

Lily bit her lip. "*You're* the one giving *me* magic marbles." She held up her wrist.

He looked away. "It's a talisman. It's supposed to keep you safe from any Eldritche that might try to hurt you. But it buys you nothing in your world, and I didn't realize you liked to put yourself in danger quite so much." He bit out the words.

"I told you I'm sorry!"

"And it's not a marble," he said hotly, "it's rock crystal."

Lily looked at it on her wrist. "It's lovely, thank you."

"It's not meant to be *lovely*. It's meant to save your life."

She tutted, batting that away and pushing her hands in her back pockets. "When you've quite finished sulking, the government offered my mother a job. When she was pregnant. She didn't take it. Said their ethics weren't clear. They were setting up some amazing new lab or something."

At the sulking comment, he'd straightened up and folded his arms, looming over her, but as she went on he became intrigued. "Where?"

Lily shoved her hair back behind her ears, the talisman sparkling. "My father doesn't know."

"He needs to think, then."

"I know! But how can I get it out of him? 'Oh, by the way, Dad, I think Mum was abducted by the government, so let me ask you a million questions about things you say you don't remember.' He'd think I'd lost my mind. And they could have moved ten times since then anyway."

"Did he say anything else?"

She shrugged. "Only that she'd been abandoned as a baby. At Wood Street police station."

Regan looked at her sharply. "Wood Street? You're sure? The one with the old St. Alban church tower outside?"

"Yes. That one." Lily looked up at him, anxious. "Why?"

"That's right by where Cripplegate used to stand. It was the oldest and strongest of the gates." He swore. "Perhaps she wasn't left at the police station—perhaps she was left at the gate itself, for protection."

She pushed her hands through her hair again. "What does it mean?"

He shook his head. "I don't know. Yet. Let me think. I'm missing something."

They turned into the Temple by the south gate and passed under the gatehouse. Lily thrust her hands into her pockets. "So Misrak and Delphine guard the water?"

"Yes."

"Like you guard the Wall?"

"Sort of. Though they weren't born to it like I was. But, like me, they're in limbo. They're desert legends, obviously, born to guard the tombs of the dead from grave robbers, yet they've ended up on the bank of the Thames. So now they're not of the earth, and not of the water, just like I'm a halfbreed."

They passed the guardhouse and walked up toward the flat.

"I can go from here," Lily said.

He shook his head.

"You don't trust me?"

"No." Regan saw her to the door. "I want you to stay here. Stay safe. I'll have enough trouble keeping myself alive tonight."

She fiddled with her keys. "Are you going out again? To the Wall?"

Watching her, he nodded. Then he turned and walked to the stairs, making it down the first couple.

"Wait!"

He stopped and turned, just as the door to the flat opened. Her father stood in the doorway.

"Dad, I just need a second."

Her father looked between her and Regan, but didn't move.

"Dad, just a second, *please*."

He left the door open and walked away into the flat.

Lily crossed to the stairs and put her hand out, tugging the button on Regan's coat. She ducked her head. "I really am sorry. Please don't stay angry with me."

"Lily!" her father shouted. "In here. Now."

She looked over her shoulder for a second. When she turned back, for the second time that day, Regan was gone.

Chapter 12

Lily closed the flat door and leaned against it for a second. Then she came into the sitting room and put her bag down.

"So. I'm hoping Regan didn't have anything to do with you chasing to East London to take on a bunch of men who traffic in young girls," her father said. He was sitting at the counter with a glass of wine, which was not standard behavior.

"No," said Lily meekly. "The opposite. He's furious with me. And he came and brought me home, if you want to know."

Her father sighed, turning the base of his glass. "I'm not sure I do, to be honest. I don't think I'm ready for you to rely on someone else before me yet. Or this quickly."

"I wasn't relying on him!" Lily protested. "He . . . I can't explain. It's stupid."

"The stupid thing, Lily, is you walking into the dragon's lair on your own."

"It's not a dragon's lair. I wouldn't walk into one of those on my own," she said, imagining a smoking drain off Bishopsgate.

Her father looked at her sternly. "But you did. Detective Evans said you were there alone. You know what these men are. You know . . ." He put a hand over his face.

Lily took a breath, but didn't answer.

He got up. "Look, well done for finding him. But never do it again. Ever. Do you understand?"

She nodded.

He rubbed her hair, then the side of her face, with the back of his hand. "You're too precious. And obviously not just to me."

She pushed his hand away. "Don't overreact, Dad. And he's just mad at me for being an idiot."

"Lily, I may be out of the loop with relationships, but I know what people look like when they've been worried sick about someone they care about." He shook his head. "I have to work."

He went into his office. Lily pulled off her jacket and sat down in one of the comfortable chairs, letting her head drop onto the back. Her thoughts skipped back over the day and her skin crawled again. Feeling filthy, she got up and took a shower.

Back in the kitchen she worked through the hard copies of the medic's e-mails. He had been thorough in his observations, and it was clear that he thought Mona was an important find. Lily opened her computer and searched for as much detail as she could about Mona's father. Most of it had to be translated, and came out fairly mangled on the other side, so that it just seemed like rubbish. There was a lot of stuff about regeneration, or maybe reincarnation. It was hard to tell. Lily pursed her lips, then remembered something. Snakeskin. *His hand—the agent's hand.*

She tugged up her sleeve. The bruise where he had grabbed her was clear, the pattern mottled and strange. *It's snakeskin.*

Not for the first time, Lily cursed the fact that Regan didn't have a phone. Then a thought struck her. Her fingers hovered over the keys . . . *Halfbreed. London. London Wall. Guardian.*

She scowled at the fruitless search results, then tried a few Boolean strings. *Yes! Wait, no way . . . The Guardian, bringer of punishment, protector of the weak.*

The telephone in her father's office rang. She glanced at the time on her computer. It was almost ten. She frowned.

"I'll be there," Lily heard her father say. She looked up as he came out of the study. "I've got to go to Heathrow. Border Control wants me."

"Again?" Lily sighed. "Isn't there someone else who can do it? You look tired."

"I *am* tired. Worn out from worrying about you today," he said, pulling on his coat and putting things in his briefcase.

Lily got up. "Sorry," she said again.

"Hmm." He nodded.

She handed him the tie that was discarded on the back of the sofa.

"Thank you. Don't stay up late. I'll see you in the morning."

"Dad?"

"Yes?"

"Mum—"

He looked at her, sad. "Don't dig through this, Lily. I want to save you the years of unhappiness I've had."

She summoned a smile. "Night, then, Dad."

"Night." The door closed behind him.

Lily turned on the television and checked her e-mails. There was one from her best friend, Sam, asking if she wanted to meet up the following day. Sam was also bringing half their class with her on a trip to St. Paul's. Lily bit her cheek, fingers hovering over the keys, then hit "reply."

I've kind of got something on.

It only took another second for Sam to e-mail back.

What? Chat. Now.

Lily signed in, regretting having not made something up. Sam was already online.

lilyh: Hi.
Samsays: Hi. Tell me u've met someone . . .
lilyh: Sort of.
Samsays: OMG. Sum1 finally meets Lily Hilyard's standards?
lilyh: V funny.
Samsays: :) Go on then!
lilyh: Not much 2 tell.
Samsays: Where? When? How old? Guy? Girl?

Lily laughed as she typed a reply: Guy.

Samsays: Just checking. ;-) Has Ed met him?
lilyh: Yes. Embarrassing much? He wants him 2 come 4 dinner.
Samsays: Excellent. Name?

lilyh: Regan.

Samsays: Cool! Photo?

lilyh: No.

Samsays: Take 1 and SEND IT. Sleeping with him?

lilyh: **Stop it or I'm going!!! Dad's bad enough.**

Samsays: I'm ur best friend, U R spsd to be able to talk 2 me about EVERYTHING, u idiot.

lilyh: **We r NOT talking about that.**

Samsays: I'll take THAT as a YES then. :)

lilyh: **Can we change the subject?**

Samsays: Can I meet him?

lilyh: **He's kind of private.**

Samsays: Just like u then. Mum wants me to help her downstairs. Got 2 go. SO EXCITED. LOVE U. XOX

Sam disconnected without waiting for a reply. Lily breathed a sigh of relief and rolled her eyes. *Perhaps I should have just dropped it into the conversation that he's not human. But then again . . .*

Her phone chimed, informing her of a voice mail. Reception was often hopeless in the flat. She tugged it from her jacket and looked at it; it wasn't a number she recognized. She touched the screen.

"It's me. Meet me on Blackfriars Bridge when you get this."

Regan? But he hates phones. Lily listened to the message again. It was awkward and stilted. She got to her feet and grabbed her keys. *He doesn't have a telephone.* She listened to the message again. *Maybe he's sorry he was angry. Maybe he's not okay, like last night.*

She let herself out of the flat. It only took ten minutes to reach Blackfriars Bridge, but when she got there it was empty. A truck grumbled past, heading toward Smithfield Market. Lily checked her watch. *Almost eleven.*

She looked around, then examined the bruise on her arm again. A breeze had picked up, whipping her hair across her face. She shivered inside her jacket. A taxi went by, a man asleep in the backseat, papers open on his lap, illuminated by the interior light.

Lily walked out into the center of the bridge. She leaned against the parapet for a minute, but the cold iron chilled her flesh through her jeans. Straightening up, she pulled out her phone, listened to the message again, and then pushed the "call back" button. Behind her, a telephone rang.

She turned, and caught her breath.

A man almost identical to Regan was standing twenty feet away. His hair was slightly shorter and neater, and his neck was bare. He was dressed in black motorcycle leathers.

"Hi, Lily, I'm Ellis."

"You . . . you're his brother. And . . . you're David Smith." *And I am a colossal idiot.*

"Yeah, well done." He smiled, but there was no warmth in it. "I wondered if you'd get that one."

Lily's brain burned with questions, but fear was gripping her gut. She took a step back. "You tricked me. Why am I here?"

Ellis folded his arms, the icy wind ruffling his hair. "Well, that's the thing. We need you."

"Why?"

"Come with me and I'll show you."

"And Vicky Shadbolt? Mona Singh? The mothwings? I'm assuming that's all down to you too." She took his silence as confirmation. "What did you need them for?"

"You haven't worked it out? Maybe you're not as clever as I thought. I'd have expected you and him to have worked it out by now."

"Regan?"

His mouth twisted slightly at the name.

"Why do you look like that? He's your brother," Lily said slowly.

He rolled his eyes. "He's a crusader, as outdated as those asthmatic shopkeepers."

"He's trying to do what your father did."

"What? Die for nothing because he won't recognize the world has moved on?"

Lily swallowed. "Is that what happened to your father?"

He said nothing.

"And your mother?"

Ellis turned away, then looked back at her and shook his head. "Sorry to have gotten you here under false pretences. But we're running out of time. The project needs to move ahead. Now."

Lily pushed her phone into her pocket and zipped it up carefully. "I'm sorry too."

"You must come with me—you see that, don't you?"

"No. Why?"

"You're part of the project. We need you."

"I'm not part of any project." Lily shook her head.

He smiled, this time looking genuinely amused. "You are."

"You talk as if you know me," Lily said warily.

"But I do," he said.

"No, you don't."

He folded his arms. "I know your height, your weight, your blood type. That you broke your wrist in the playground when you were seven because you wanted to play with the others instead of waiting on the sidelines like you were supposed to. I know that you like Italian food and eat salted popcorn while watching old films. You've a knack for coding and hacking, but you've never let on to anyone apart from your father how good you really are. And that little scar under your chin? You got that when you slipped rock-climbing in Scotland two years ago, *which* you shouldn't have been doing, as you well know. Putting the whole project at risk on a stupid whim."

"Project?"

"Yes." He paused. "Want me to go on?"

Lily swallowed and nodded.

"I've been watching you for almost five years."

"For which you should seek help," she said immediately, then paused. "Wait. You're apache85."

He nodded eagerly. "Fantastic proxies, by the way—and that digital steganography skit you ran on Transmedia was something else. You've given me the slip more than a few times. That layered Caesar cipher on the Noble forum was you, wasn't it?"

Lily hesitated, then nodded slowly.

He smiled, satisfied, punching the air. "I knew it. They said it was impossible that a sixteen-year-old girl was using hexa-decimal characters like that, but I *knew* it was you."

They looked at each other.

"The blood-banking. Is that even real?" Lily asked.

"Your blood type is exceptionally rare, and we do bank your blood in case you need it. But, yes, we test it too."

"Test it for what?"

"Everything. We thought the bandogge incident may have changed the nature of it, but it appears not. His blood hasn't affected you at all." He shrugged. "It's as pure as ever."

"Pure?"

"Yes. That's one of the things that's remarkable about it. No free radicals, no heavy metals, despite living in one of the most polluted cities in Europe." He shook his head, as if in wonder.

"The blood tests, the blood drive. It's you, isn't it?"

Ellis grinned. "I can't take all the credit, but yes, that's us."

"What is it for?"

"Operation Harvest. The first large-scale identification of any remaining Type H females."

"So far, so gross. And a harvest doesn't sound much like identification to me."

Coming over the bridge from the south was a black lowrider van. Lily turned to him, dismayed. They regarded each other warily.

"Why do you want us? Why me? Why Vicky?"

"You'll understand soon."

"You made her believe the two of you were in a relationship."

He shrugged.

"What about Mona Singh?"

"Mona is already proving valuable to the project, even if the results are rather more . . . unpredictable than we had imagined. Three limbs, one too few, five limbs, one too many, you understand? But we're making real progress. And that's why we need you now. You're too important to the project to put yourself at risk the way you have been doing. If only you could have stayed home with your daddy, playing your little online games. Safe and warm in the safest place in London. But no, now you're on the streets almost getting yourself killed. And it has to stop." His tone was final.

She edged back.

"You can't outrun me. You know that."

"I don't know anything about you," she said.

"Why not just come quietly?"

She looked past him, seeing the van pull over on the curb. Below the bridge, the Thames surged. "He's tried to find you. For years. He—"

Ellis's jaw clenched. "He's living in the past, like my father—who threw his life away trying to rescue me."

"So what's the future? The Agency? You?"

He laughed. "You do know a lot, don't you? But not quite enough. Not yet, at least. You will soon, though. Because you're part of it, Lily. Part of the future."

"You sound like someone from a cult. You need to get out more."

Ellis stepped forward, his face suddenly intense. "You should come with me—please—try to understand."

"You killed that man Jack, at Bank station. I saw you do it."

He made a frustrated noise. "He was putting all our work at risk. You don't understand. We can change the world!"

Lily drew back, shaking her head. "Not like that," she said, her voice not as strong as she had hoped.

The van door slid back, and a pair of high-laced black boots swung out as the man who had tried to take Lily before eased himself onto the pavement using the handrail. He straightened up, looking at her. He grinned.

"You," she said.

"Hello again, trouble. Going to come quietly?" His voice had taken on a lisping quality, and patches of mottled skin were visible at his neck.

"What are you doing here?" Ellis snapped.

"You sent in for backup."

"No, I sent in for transport. I don't need backup."

They watched each other. Ellis looked more than slightly angry.

The agent's eyelids flickered and he shrugged. "I don't take my orders from you yet, kid."

"I said I'd bring her in alone."

The agent cast a cold glance at Lily. "Doesn't look as if she's going anywhere of her own free will any time soon."

"Not now, obviously," Ellis ground out.

Lily glanced around again. *There must be a way. Nothing. No way out. Except the river.* She took a step toward the parapet.

Ellis guessed her intention and took a step toward her, hand out. "Don't you want to see your mother again?"

The man in black made a lunge for her, but Ellis knocked him out of the way easily, catching Lily in an iron grip as she tried to dodge away. He restrained her without effort, pulling her against him and turning on the agent. "Touch her and you won't touch anything else for a very long time."

The agent said nothing, his cold snake eyes regarding Ellis. His lip curled slightly.

Ellis dragged Lily to the back of the van. She put up a fight for about two seconds, until he held her so hard her ribs creaked and a squeak of pain escaped her. He pushed her onto a bench seat lining the interior wall of the van.

"My mother's dead," she gasped, holding her side.

He sat down opposite, long legs bent. The snake-eyed agent had climbed into the passenger seat in the front of the van. It drew away smoothly and performed a U-turn, heading back south of the river.

"Are you so sure of that?"

They watched each other in the flashing lights of the streetlamps. The van took a right turn. Lily played with the talisman nervously.

"Did my brother give that to you?"

"Yes," she said, sullen.

"So you believe in the fairy nonsense?"

She ignored him, because she didn't have an answer. Through the grille at the front of the cab, Lily could see Vauxhall approaching. They were by the river again.

"Where are you taking me?"

"The lab."

"But where is it?"

He watched her, weighing her up. "Battersea. The old power station."

Lily frowned, thinking. "Battersea." Her eyes met his as the realization hit her. "You've been buying trafficked girls. From Anton Andreyev."

He raised an eyebrow. "You *have* been doing your homework."

"But you've stopped. Why?"

Ellis folded his arms as the van paused at a traffic light. "Because the girls weren't suitable test subjects, although they were cheap and plentiful. Already full of pollutants, shit dentistry, and a lifetime of bad diets. Useless."

His flat, irritated tone made the bile rise in Lily's throat. "Human life's so cheap to you?"

He raised a black eyebrow. "Cheap? You should see what he charges."

She looked away and swallowed, determined to keep calm. The headlights passed over their faces in flashes. Overhead, the brief whirr of helicopter blades as a pilot came in to land at the heliport. Fear settled in her gut.

"That's why you took Vicky. You were already watching me through the doctor's office. Easy to pick another girl from the same dataset."

He nodded.

"How many girls have you got in this lab?"

"You'll soon see." The van slowed, pulling into the curb. Ellis reached over and drew the door open, looking over his shoulder at Lily. "I have to make a stop here. Pick something up."

"More hostages?"

His winged eyebrow kinked upward, but he said nothing. He got out and slid the door closed. "Watch her," he said through the passenger window.

Lily looked inside her bag, wondering if there was anything at all in it that she could use. The two agents up front were talking, not watching her. In the side pocket of her satchel she had a box of matches and a Swiss Army knife. Because her father had taught her all about how to survive after Lily decided, aged ten, that the Girl Guides were sexist.

She unwound the scarf from her neck and made a miniature firebomb by pulling out four matches, striking them, and stuffing them into the box. They flared instantly. Lily piled her scarf on top of the matchbox in a small bundle, and moments later the black wool crackled into life. The flames took hold and she threw herself against the grille.

"Help, please!"

The snake-eyed agent was out of the seat immediately, cursing her. He flung open the sliding side panel and grabbed her arm. The talisman burst into fiery life as soon as his hand touched her, almost blinding them both. The man fell back as if burned. Lily jumped from the van, sprinting for the Embankment.

"No!"

The shout behind her, the voice so familiar, brought her to a halt. She turned. Ellis stood in the middle of the road, in his arms a blanketed bundle, pale hair spilling free over his left arm. A car rushed the amber light heading toward Southwark and the horn blared. Ellis leaped out of the road, arms full, bellowing in frustration.

Lily. Lily. The river. Jump. A soft voice like mercury slid into her ears. *Do it. Do it now. It's your only chance. RUN.*

She spun around and ran. Ellis ditched his burden and sprinted after her. She hit the parapet, vaulted, and landed in the freezing water with a bang, tide raging. The shock knocked the breath from her. The current was flowing downstream, fast toward the sea. It swept her beneath Lambeth Bridge, eastward, deep below the water.

Lily was a strong swimmer, but she knew that survival in the Thames was measured in multiples of seconds rather than minutes. She surfaced beneath the bridge, gasping. Her brain was already blurring with cold. Something grabbed her, an arm beneath hers, crossing across her chest.

"Don't fight, I have you!"

They sped through the water. The current created rough waves that smacked the breath from Lily, burning her with salt. They were moving almost impossibly fast. Westminster Bridge, then a minute later, Blackfriars. Beneath the modern steel of the Millennium Bridge was an ancient wooden staircase. Crouching just above the angry high tide was Regan. The arm that was holding Lily slackened.

Gripping on to the railing with one hand, Regan bent out over the water, catching Lily and hoisting her into his arms. She was almost frozen and half-drowned, her head lolling against his neck. She saw a naked girl in the water—young, perhaps no more than seventeen. Her thick, matted hair was a dull white, spilling over her chest, full of shells and old pieces of broken glass. In the water, a shining tail glowed orange and blue.

"Eleanor, thank you," Regan said.

"My pleasure, halfbreed! We are all square now, yes?"

Regan nodded. "Yes."

They shook hands. "So now I go," she said. "Rachel is missing."

Regan straightened, Lily still in his arms. "Missing?"

"Yes. Since this morning. I thought she had gone out to the Thames Barrier. She likes to watch it work. But I've been out beyond Gravesend . . . I need to find her. And you need to get *her* inside, before that precious blood freezes solid." Eleanor reached up, grasping Lily's trailing hand. Her mercury voice slipped through Lily's brain again. *Good luck, blood girl. Good luck and a fair wind in your sails.* Lily tried to speak, to thank her, but nothing came out. Eleanor reeled back into the water with a quick salute, her tail sparkling orange and blue, the broad fin disappearing under the glowing lights of the bridge above.

Regan turned, climbed the steps, and began to walk northeastward, back toward the Rookery. He moved fast, without ever seeming to break stride. Lily couldn't speak, her jaw locked with cold, her teeth unable even to chatter. A couple of late-night drunks in crumpled suits staggered past toward the last train to somewhere or other, but their expressions were uncomprehending and no one stopped Regan.

He strode through the alley into the Rookery, his boots clattering on the wooden treads, which glistened with frost. Inside the flat, he pushed open the bathroom door and sat Lily down on the single wooden chair, turning on the taps. Water crashed into the enamel tub, echoing in the freezing hall.

"Come on, up."

With his typical efficient movements he stripped off her jacket. Beneath, her clothes clung, sodden. She was shuddering in waves.

"Your brother. He's alive."

Regan's hands stilled. "You saw Ellis?"

She took a breath to speak. He held her face, looking into her eyes.

"Lily, focus. You saw him? My brother?"

"He asked if I wanted to see my mother again. Does that mean she's alive too?" Her teeth clattered.

He ignored her question and kept talking, hands against her face. "Listen to me. Listen to my voice. Think. And start from the beginning. From when I left you."

"How did you find me?"

"I told you, the talisman. It connects us. I can kind of *see* where it is, when someone touches you who means you harm. The quickest way to get someone to you tonight was Eleanor. She's the fastest thing in or on the water."

"But . . . how do you find her . . . ?"

He pulled a face. "She doesn't take calls. I went to the river and yelled. She owed me, big-time, so she was honor-bound to come."

"Owed?" Lily put a hand to his, covering his fingers.

"It doesn't matter, it's done. We're even now. Just tell me what happened."

Bewildered, Lily struggled free and pulled her phone from her pocket on the chair.

He stepped back. "Doesn't water kill those things?"

She pressed the menu button with trembling fingers. It blinked into life. "It's the case. They call it 'lifeproof'—it's waterproof and shockproof. Dad made me buy it as a condition of him getting me the phone."

Regan nodded impatiently. Lily's hands were so cold that the phone didn't register when she tried to unlock it. He took it from her and looked at the screen, swiping his thumb across it.

"Touch the phone icon. And the little reel of tape on the right." Her teeth chattered so loudly she shut her mouth with a snap. "Press the last message and listen," she said through gritted teeth.

He listened, then took the phone from his ear and looked at it. "I didn't leave that."

"I know. It's your brother." There was a long pause. "You're twins, aren't you? Identical."

He looked at her warily. "So what?"

"You didn't tell me."

"Does it matter?"

"S'pose not."

"Yes. We are. It's the first time it's ever happened to my kind. We're only children—sons—always."

"But not this time?"

He shook his head.

Lily caught sight of herself in the mirror. She looked like a drowned animal, her skin stark white, a blue line around the edge of her mouth. Regan walked out, taking her phone and leaving the room without closing the door. She almost fell, twice, taking off her boots. Increasingly shaky, she dropped her things into a wet pile and clambered into the steaming water. It felt painfully icy, the nerves in her chilled skin so confused they didn't know hot from cold. She sat shivering, hugging her shins, chin on knees to stop her teeth chattering.

By the time she felt clean and a little warmer, the water was cooling. The door creaked a fraction and a shirt flew through the gap, puddling on the floorboards. Clambering out, Lily pulled the only towel from the hook on the back of the door and dried herself carefully from head to toes, skin prickling. She picked up the shirt and pushed her hands through the long sleeves, fumbling with the buttons down the front. It came almost to her knees.

There was no comb on the sink, but there was a toothbrush and a tube of toothpaste. She brushed her teeth thoroughly, spitting white foam into the sink, glad to be rid of the taste of Thames water and fear. Then she looked in the mirror and ran her fingers through her damp hair, pushing it behind her ears. There was still a bluish tinge to the edge of her bottom lip, but her cheeks were flushed with color from the heat of the water.

Cautiously she opened the door and went into the hall. Regan was in the bedroom, putting a match to the fire. Her outer clothes were ranged over an old wooden rack near the hearth. A candle burned on the bedside table, next to another crooked tower of books and her phone. Regan had taken off his wet shirt and replaced it with a tight white T-shirt with just a ragged hem where the collar had once been. The long sleeves were pushed above his elbows, showing his tattooed arm. He crouched with his left leg bent, foot bare on the floorboards, a black flicker behind his prominent ankle bone, and Lily saw the last of the flames creeping over the top of his foot.

He watched the fire kindle. She came closer and he straightened up as it took hold. He was suddenly too close. She stepped back. "Ellis is working for the Agency," she told him. "He took Vicky Shadbolt, made her think they were in a relationship. And I think she's with Mona Singh, and who knows how many more."

"But where?" He pushed his hand into his hair, scowling.

"Battersea, the old power station." She hugged herself, rubbing her arms for warmth.

"And you know this how?"

Lily took a breath. "Your brother told me on the way there. It's the perfect cover. Far enough away from Westminster for the government to have plausible deniability. Derelict for years, always supposedly under development—though nothing ever happens—but still close to the City. Heliport a stone's throw away. All very convenient."

Regan went into the kitchen and returned with an inch of tan liquid in a glass. He offered it to Lily. She took a sip, coughing slightly, and grimaced, shivering at the same time. "Cold?" he asked her.

She nodded. He shook out a blanket from the end of the bed and wrapped it around her. She huddled tightly inside it. "So cold. Can I get into bed?"

"If you want to."

Lily climbed in, sliding her legs beneath the covers, still wrapped tightly in the blanket. Regan sat on the floor, his back to the old whitewashed plaster.

"What are you sitting down there for? Why would you?" Suddenly, to her surprise, she sniffed and a tear splashed on her cheek.

He frowned, his face confused.

She pushed her hand across her cheek. "Ignore me. Overload, that's all. Sit where you like. I don't care."

He got to his feet and came to sit next to her on the bed. Another tear tipped onto her cheek. She brushed it off. He watched her again carefully, then held out his arm. Lily slid under it, burrowing into his chest and absorbing his warmth like a drug. She breathed a sigh of relief, reassured by the physical contact, rubbing a last tear away on the material of his T-shirt.

"Are all human girls like you?" he asked after a long silence.

"Meaning what?"

"Impossible."

"Only the best ones."

He huffed a laugh, relaxing slowly. His arm curved around her shoulder and he rubbed her cheek with the back of his fingers. "Tell me what happened."

Lily took a breath. "Ellis appeared on Blackfriars Bridge,

and there was a van. A black one, like the van in the alley today. Well, yesterday now."

Regan nodded.

"They took Vicky. Your brother is the 'David Smith' from the message app. And he pretended to be you to get me to the bridge. *And* he's the one who's been following me online. He told me I would understand soon. That I was part of the future. And then the man who tried to take me yesterday arrived, and he . . . well, I forgot to tell you yesterday, what with everything . . ." Lily pushed up the cuff of the shirt she was wearing, revealing the talisman and her bruise. "His skin, it's turning like snakeskin. Look at the pattern his hand left on me last night. And tonight it's gotten worse. It was all over his neck."

"You think they could be experimenting on him? Using Mona?"

Lily nodded. "Yes. Ellis said Mona had been valuable to the project already."

"Then what happened?"

"Then Ellis pushed me into the van, but he got out in Vauxhall to see someone and I set my scarf on fire. Snake Man opened the door and grabbed me, and the talisman either burned him or . . . well, it flashed really brightly anyway, and he let me go and I jumped into the river. Eleanor told me to."

"Ellis didn't stop you?"

"He'd gone to get another girl, from the fire station, but none of that is the point. I'm part of a project, Ellis said. I have been since I was born."

Regan's face became set.

"They're testing us. Me. They're looking for more like me. This blood drive—it's not just testing, it's a harvest. He called it Operation Harvest. It's about our blood." Lily ran out of breath and started again. "But it's not his fault. They took him ten years ago, and he's your brother, and—"

He put his hand over her mouth. "Okay, enough. And now Rachel, Eleanor's sister, is missing too."

Lily tugged his fingers away. "I think Rachel might have been the girl Ellis went to get. I only saw her hair, but it was very pale. Perhaps they're experimenting on her too, right now. And the mothwings. On all of us!" She ran a hand through her hair, wincing at a new bump she didn't remember getting.

"What's the matter?"

She pointed behind her right ear. "Bang on the head, that's all."

His fingers slid into her hair.

"Ow! Don't." She tugged her head away. "Pro tip, when a human tells you they've got a bruise, don't start pressing on it."

He ignored her, his finger grazing another knock on her brow bone. "We need to find Rachel, and soon. If the Agency is messing around with her, things are going to get seriously out of control. Their father might get involved."

"Who's their father?"

"The Thames River God. In the Rock Lock. The one I told you about."

"Oh," said Lily. "One of the Ancients."

"Oh," he agreed. "He's dormant at the moment, but—"

"Asleep like the dragons?"

"Not asleep, but yes, something like that. Beneath the south end of London Bridge. Has been for over a thousand years. But he could rise up and destroy the City, turn the river against it, if he wanted to."

"Great," said Lily with feeling, closing her eyes for a moment.

"Speaking of sleep, you should try to get some."

"I *should* go home. Dad will worry about me. Although he's not there right now."

He thought it through. "Then stay, for now. Safer here than being there on your own." He shifted slightly, as if he were about to get up.

"You're leaving?" she asked, surprised.

He shrugged and got to his feet. "I'll go to the lab tomorrow, but tonight I've got a job to do." He picked up the book from the floor and placed it on the bedside table with its gold-covered spine facing out.

"What's that?"

"A grimoire. They're books of our history. I killed something I've never seen before, and I wanted to look it up."

She took a breath. "I looked *you* up."

"You did?" He stared at her. "In what?"

"Archive dot org. Someone had put one of those . . . grimoires . . . online."

"Right." He looked none the wiser, then wary. "And?"

"A bringer of punishment and a protector of the weak. A guardian."

"Yes."

Lily swallowed. "What did Misrak and Delphine really mean, about the prophecy?"

Taking a breath, he looked at the fire. "Ten years ago they predicted I would save a girl—a human girl, like you—who was destined to restore order to the City." He shrugged. "But before that, there will be a war. The Chaos War. I'd always assumed it meant a war between us and the demons. But maybe it's a war between the Eldritche and the Agency. Prophecies are pretty non-specific."

They were silent. Regan took a step, turning away.

"Don't go."

He turned back. "You don't want me to?"

Lily shook her head, unable to speak. He seemed to consider for a long moment, then he sat back down, resuming his former position smoothly. Far too smoothly for a human. Lily sat opposite, looking at him. "I want to ask you some questions."

"Okay," he said slowly. He tucked a curl of her hair behind her ear and ran his finger down her jaw to the point of her chin. Her heart kicked up, thumping loudly in the silence, and all her questions went out of her head.

"Can you hear my heart beating?"

"Yes."

"Sorry."

"I prefer it to the alternative," he said soberly, dropping his hand.

She looked away. "What's going to happen now? Now that it's war?"

"Tomorrow we find the lab and get them out."

"Just like that?" Lily rearranged the blanket on her shoulders.

"Well, I'd imagine there'll be some pretty heavy security, firepower, things like that."

"Ah, right. But we'll be okay?"

"Very possibly not."

They looked at each other.

"Aren't you frightened?" Lily said at last.

"I'd be an idiot if I wasn't."

She looked down. "I think you should tell a girl about things like blood and war prophecies." She shook her hair back, turning her face to the fire that spat and muttered in the hearth. "Because I had all these criteria about boys, you know. Must not have annoying habits or be a sports bore. This kind of stuff wasn't on the list."

He was watching her again, trying to work her out. "What about tattoos, working nights, and killing things?"

Lily thought about it. She wrinkled her nose a little. "No deal breakers so far."

He looked down. "Lily, there's something—"

She leaned across and pressed a quick, soft kiss to his mouth. He took a breath, surprised. She broke away and they looked at each other, unsure.

Lily shrugged. "Okay, fine. Just wanted to try it, before we get killed or eaten by dragons and London gets flood—"

The room tilted as he pushed her back into the pillows, trapping her beneath him, his mouth on hers. She wrapped around him, fingers sliding into his hair. He kissed her until her bones ached and she was struggling to breathe.

Somewhere, far off in the dark outside the bedroom window,

something shrieked. Regan tensed. Kissing beneath the corner of her jaw, he murmured, "I have to go."

Lily slid her hands up beneath the back of his T-shirt, pulling him down.

The shriek sounded again. Regan looked toward the window and swore. He kissed her abruptly, once. "Stay." Another kiss. "Here."

She started to protest as he got up from the bed. He ducked back and kissed her into silence. "I'll be back. Promise."

Then he was gone, pushing to his feet and disappearing through the door. It banged behind him.

Chapter 13

"Lily, I'm back. Wake up." He shook her gently.

She woke, lifting her hands in alarm.

He caught them. "It's just me."

Shoving herself up the pillow, Lily threw her arms around Regan, holding tight. He sat on the edge of the bed, clothes hanging from him in shreds, and buried his face in the crook of her neck, breathing her in. His coat, draped over the iron end of the bed, was covered in black streaks. His T-shirt was burned away from his shoulder, his jeans ruined. He was filthy and his hands had left charred marks on her wrists.

She pulled back a little. "Are you hurt?"

His dirty face was as beautiful as ever. "No. But I *am* over-run. I can't hold them for another night. I'm not sure I got them all tonight anyway."

The built-up fire flared merrily in the grate, giving a loud crack. Lily jumped.

"We need to go somewhere," said Regan. "Get dressed." He left the room, already stripping off the ragged remains of his T-shirt.

"To the power station?" she called after him, climbing out of the bed.

"No," he shouted over the sound of the bath running. "Can't hope to make it into there in daylight. We'll have to wait until tonight. There's other stuff we need to do right now."

"Like what?"

"Drink your tea."

It was only then that Lily noticed the steaming mug next to her. Her clothes were cold and gritty. She grimaced as she pulled them on. The flat was freezing, a chill radiating up from the bare floorboards. She looked out of the window, over the tiny St. Mary-le-Bow churchyard and the narrow lane beyond. It wasn't yet light, and the streetlight was haloed with mist. Lily checked her watch. Five thirty. She slumped a little, then straightened and took a gulp of the tea.

Slipping from the room, she walked into the hall, straight into Regan as he came out of the bathroom. He was wearing nothing but a towel wrapped around his hips. The toothbrush stuck out of the corner of his mouth.

Lily stared, wide-eyed. The black flames snaked up from his left foot, coiling around his long, perfect leg, disappearing into the towel and emerging just above his left hip bone. They curved around his waist, burning up his muscle-quilted ribs and over the right side of his chest, across his back and the wing of his shoulder blade. He was almost thin, but not quite, muscles smooth and sharply defined. The flames met over his right shoulder before coursing down his arm, curling to a finish on the edge of the hand reaching up to grip the toothbrush.

He turned to face her, very slowly.

She looked away, shy.

"That bad?"

"What?"

"Tattoos," he said through the toothpaste.

Lily shook her head. "I like them."

He eyed her uncertainly. "You do?"

She nodded. Walking over to him, she took his left hand in both of hers, her thumbs stroking over the rooks picked out across the back.

He looked down at their joined hands, then pulled her into the bathroom, keeping hold of her hand even as he quickly finished brushing his teeth and drinking from the tap. Leading her back into the bedroom, he sat her down on the bed, looking serious.

"Sit there and finish that." He pointed at the tea before walking over to the old chest of drawers and dragging them open, pulling out clean things and dumping them on the top, his back to her. Lily took a sip of the sweet tea, just as he let the towel fall. She spluttered into the cup. He ignored her, yanking on his jeans and socks and pulling on yet another battered Henley, jerking it down, the muscles of his back twisting under the skin. Stalking out, he returned in his boots and pulled on the coat, holding out his hand.

"Come on."

"Where are we going?"

"You want to know about the prophecy?"

She put down the mug. "Yes."

"So do I."

Outside, the fog seemed to bite her through the damp material of her clothes. They walked north, over Cheapside. Lily struggled to keep up, but Regan wasn't slowing down much, keeping tight hold of her hand.

"Where are we going?" She jogged alongside him.

"Smithfield."

Smithfield was London's meat market. A vast set of Victorian hangars decorated with green, red, and yellow-painted wrought ironwork. Lily had been once, and remembered feeling intimidated by the porters, the loud men clad in white coats, white porkpie hats, and yellow rubber boots, who rushed about, sometimes carrying half a pig or sheep carcass, shouting and swearing at each other.

"And why are we here?"

"There's a man here. A diviner, Micky Marsden."

"Diviner?"

"Yes. Most Eldritche have a talent. Or more than one. Diviners have talents for discovering or seeing things ... I don't know, finding money, seeing emotions ... there's lots of different ones."

"And what's Micky's talent?"

"He can divine the true nature of things. Through fire."

Lily looked at him. "He's not setting me on fire," she said definitely.

They approached the market through the mist. At each of the great doors sat refrigerated trucks, engines running to keep the cooling units working, headlamps lighting up wedges of swirling yellow vapor. The café on the corner opposite was brightly lit. Some porters had already finished their shift and were eating fry-ups with pints of lager in thick glasses, despite it being before six in the morning.

Regan looked down at her. "Did they ever tell you how many people have your blood type? Roughly."

Lily shrugged. "No idea. I looked on the Internet once. Point zero zero zero zero four percent of the population or something. More zeros. I don't know of anyone else in this country."

"And other blood types are toxic to you?"

"Yes."

"But not mine?"

"It doesn't look that way, does it?" She shook her head. "But let's not make a habit of that transfusion business."

He looked at the sky as though despairing. "It's a last resort, not a hobby. I might be a freak, but I'm not that sort of freak."

Lily dug her chin into her coat collar, then winced at the clammy coldness.

They came to the large glass-fronted entrance of the market. Inside, Lily looked around at all the booths selling every type and cut of meat. The inside of the building was unheated, and as cold as outside.

"This way."

She followed him through the gangways, dodging the porters and edging out of the way of customers dragging wheeled trolleys stacked with coolers, destined for restaurants and cafés across the city. Regan stopped in front of a shiny meat counter beneath an old painted sign declaring MARSDEN'S QUALITY MEATS. A young man was weighing and wrapping joints.

"Hi, Joey, Micky around?"

The young man grinned. "He's in the back, as usual."

"Great, thanks."

They walked behind the counter and Joey returned to his tasks. In a walk-in refrigerator behind the booth was a man in a white coat, his back to them. His cropped hair was almost as dark as Regan's. He turned without looking up, writing on a clipboard, a pen in his gloved hand. He had a harelip and a squashed boxer's nose. The air was freezing, their breath clouding. Lily shuddered inside her clothes.

"And what can I get for you? The fillet of beef is top-notch today, even if I do say so myself."

"Micky?"

The man laughed. "Regan! Long time no see, mucker. How's tricks?"

Regan smiled, a touch awkwardly. "So-so. I'm looking for some help. Well, advice, maybe."

Micky put the clipboard down.

"This is Lily."

Micky whistled quietly. He went to the fridge door and poked his head out. "Joey, no visitors."

"Right-o," said Joey cheerfully.

Micky pulled the door to, immediately dropping the temperature. Lily closed her eyes in despair for a second, then she clenched her jaw to stop her teeth chattering.

Micky walked over to her, looking at her in exactly the same way Misrak and Delphine had. It was a mixture of curiosity and satisfaction. Lily looked back at him, glad that Regan was still holding her hand.

"Why are you all being weird?" She edged away a little.

Regan tugged her to his side. "We're not."

Micky glanced up at Regan. "There's another dragon on the rise."

"I know. I met it behind St. Sepulchre's last night."

He nodded. "Joey and I dropped off a couple of cow carcasses for them around the back of Crutched Friars on our way in this morning. Let the van splatter some blood around the streets as we left. Saw one of them heading in a few minutes later. Should keep them busy for a bit."

"Thanks, Micky."

"What are friends for? I got word about it all, but me and Joey've only got each other, so we thought we'd stick it out, watch the show." He was still looking at Lily. "So, this is her." It wasn't a question.

"Yes," Regan said.

"So the war's coming, all right."

"Maybe as soon as tonight."

"And what do you want from me?"

"Divine for us. The prophecy. You know what it says."

Micky nodded, his face serious.

"I need to be sure. That it has to be that way."

The butcher studied him, then nodded. "Okay."

"No setting me on fire," Lily chipped in.

Micky laughed. "Been telling you our secrets, has he?"

Lily ducked her face, then regretted the cold scrape of the zipper beneath her chin and jogged her knees in a vain attempt to keep warm.

Micky winked, taking her chill for anxiety. "Don't worry, petal, it's not painful."

"Will you do it?" Regan pressed him.

"Of course I'll do it." Micky nodded, then sighed. "Shame it has to be here, though—plays havoc with the health and safety." He began to strip off his gloves. "But I'm guessing time is of the essence."

"What do you need?" Regan asked.

Micky looked Lily up and down. "Some of that pretty hair should do it."

Lily stared at both of them. "You *are* joking."

Regan drew a large carving knife from the block on the bench. Lily took a step back, scowling at him. He reached out and, before she had time to protest, had snicked off a single curl.

"See? Painless."

She narrowed her eyes at him.

Micky rubbed his hands together, then opened them. A pool of bright flames lay in his palms. At first they flickered yellow and orange, then rapidly deepened to a bright red. Micky's fingers glowed. He smiled at Lily. "This was a real nuisance before fireproof gloves. And walk-in freezers."

She watched as he concentrated on his cupped hands.

"Now," he said to Regan.

Regan dropped the curl into his hands. It burned immediately with a little flash, filling the refrigerator with the stink of singed hair. Micky frowned as the flames lessened. They receded until his hands were only glowing and smoking gently. "Nothing, mate, sorry."

"You're missing the point," Lily said.

They looked at her.

She raised an eyebrow. "The Agency is taking my *blood*, not my hair."

"Hair should work just as well." Micky shrugged. "It's part of you."

Lily pulled up her sleeve and picked up the knife. Regan caught her hand. "No."

She stepped away, shaking him off. "Micky?"

Micky looked at Regan, one eyebrow cocked. "Game bird, this one, eh?" He rubbed his palms together.

Regan stepped forward, frowning, putting himself between Micky and Lily, facing her. He looked conflicted. Micky side-stepped him, looking up. "Mate, it's all right. I know you're not supposed to let her get hurt, but one little scratch isn't going to make any difference now, is it?"

Lily flinched as she drew the knife along the underside of her wrist, well away from the veins. Blood ran instantly down her fingers. She let it drip into Micky's flaming hands . . . and found herself on the floor, shielded by Regan's body, as a fireball engulfed the refrigerator.

Micky swore loudly as the flashover blew the door wide open. A few seconds later, Joey's curious face appeared.

"Micky?"

"It's all right, Joe. Shut the door, there's a good lad."

Lily lay, winded, in the cage Regan's propped arms had formed around her, one hand protecting the back of her head from the hard metal floor. "You okay?" he asked, his gray-gold eyes looking into hers, worried.

She took a breath. "Yep."

He was on his feet now, helping her up.

"Well, I think we can safely say that's a yes," Micky said, getting to his feet.

"A yes to what?!" Lily looked between them.

"Yes, you are the girl from the prophecy, and, yes, there's a war coming," Regan said, buttoning his coat. "Anything else?" he said to Micky. "About the outcome of the prophecy?"

Micky looked at him sadly. "I'm sorry, mate, I really am—"

"Thanks, Micky. It's okay, really." Regan's smile was tight.

Micky pulled his gloves back on and leaned on the butcher's block. He looked around his scorched refrigerator; shreds of singed paper blew gently on a corkboard and black marks streaked the white roof and walls.

"Sorry," Regan said.

Micky waved his gloved hand. "Don't be daft. What's a fireball in the workplace between friends? Now that there's a war on." He looked at Lily. "I suppose, soon, it won't matter anyway."

Lily mopped the congealing blood from her wrist with the piece of blue paper towel that Micky passed her.

"Thanks," Regan said.

"Any time."

Lily ducked her head, mumbling her thanks. Micky picked up his clipboard again, then frowned at the order form, now reduced to ashes, still attached to it. As they reached the door, he spoke. "You know Hori's back, don't you? You should see him, if this is it."

"What do you mean, this is it?" Lily looked up. "You make it sound like there's no hope."

Regan turned. "Back from Japan?"

"Yeah. Saw Jake in the street the other day. Apparently the old man couldn't hack it there. He remembered it all as wooden palaces and those girls with the socks and the flip-flops."

"Geishas," Lily and Regan said at the same time.

"That's them." Micky shook his head and chuckled. "Senile old coot. What did he expect?"

Regan grinned. "Thanks, Micky."

Micky saluted with one gloved hand. "Good luck."

Outside they walked down to the Farringdon Road. "Who's Hori?" Lily asked.

"You'll find out."

"Why the big mystery?"

Regan smiled. "This one you need to see for yourself."

The number seventeen bus drew into the stop just ahead of them, heading for King's Cross.

Lily sat on the bus feeling uncomfortable inside and out. Her clothes were creaky and the bus was crowded. She was sitting above the heater, hot air pumping out against her legs, making her jeans muggy. Regan had led her to a seat at the back of the bus but then remained standing, leaning against the window, his hands in his jeans pockets and his coat swept behind him. Most of the time he looked slightly down, his face unreadable. Lily tried not to watch him, and failed. People made space around him for no apparent reason.

She had hated Micky's fatalism, and knew Regan was avoiding discussing it. *"This is it"? How can this be it?* Lily looked around her at the people making their way to work on an ordinary January morning. Cold, gloomy, preoccupied. She shook her head to herself in defiance, and looked out of the window at the gray, frozen streets.

At the top of the Gray's Inn Road, Regan pushed the stop button. The once run-down area of King's Cross had been smartened up with the rebuilding of the station, but pockets of the old seediness remained. The freeze took hold of Lily's clothes again. She followed Regan without speaking. On a street between a shuttered fried-chicken shop and a betting place sat a tattoo parlor, the windows blacked out with bubbled, peeling film. A large pink transfer on the glass announced BEST TATTOO.

"Are they open at this time of day?" Lily asked.

Regan pulled the door for her. "They're always open."

Inside the shop were large padded chairs and a massage table, its padding cracked and split. An array of tattoo equipment was lined up on a bench. In a corner a plastic fountain in the shape of a Zen rock pile trickled water noisily. A young man with a round stomach was sitting on a stool near the table, blearily drinking coffee from a paper cup. He was at least half Japanese, and tattooed on every visible part of his body with koi carp swimming in elegant circles, rising to the surface of the water. Even the ripples were perfectly visible. Lily stared.

He got up. "Regan." He grinned as they shook hands and bumped shoulders in a complicated fashion.

"Hi, Jake. Is Hori up yet?"

The boy yawned. "Only been back two days and hasn't gone to bed yet. Just sits and waits for the right customer." He pointed to Lily. "Candidate?"

Regan shook his head. "No, but I was hoping Hori might be able to do some divining for us."

Jake shrugged. "You know what he is. Maybe, maybe not. Should warn you, he'll try to persuade you to have more work. He's never gotten over the experience. If he wasn't such an old git I'd have sworn he'd fallen in love."

The corner of Regan's mouth kinked in a smile. "He's out of luck, but I'm flattered. How's business?"

"Pretty good, thanks. We are—y'know—the best."

"I know."

"Got to be, when the old man won't take a penny for his work. Got to make a living."

Pointing to a door at the back, Regan asked, "May we?"

Jake waved his paper cup languidly. "Go ahead," he said through a yawn.

Regan led Lily down a long corridor hung with rice-paper lanterns. "Horiyoshi. He's a Tenome," he explained. "A Japanese version of the divining spirit."

"And he did your tattoo?"

"The big one, yes. The rooks are by Jake."

"How long did the big one take?"

"A long time."

"Time to change your mind, then."

"Half a full-body tattoo would look even worse than a

whole one. Besides, he decides what you get and if you get it. This is what I got."

"He decides?"

"You'll understand when you see."

They arrived in a light and peaceful room with very simple furnishings, including a large table padded with white leather. It was as clean and Spartan as the front shop was shabby and cramped. An ancient, bald Japanese man in a silk robe was seated at a wooden workbench, gnarled fingers arranging a set of long bamboo-handled tools with sharp tips.

"Master Lupescar." He did not turn around, but continued to run his hands over the tools, straightening them gently.

"I didn't know you'd come back," Regan said. "Had to hear it from Micky."

"Glad to hear the news of my return has filtered down to the very bottom," Hori said sourly.

Regan laughed. "He's glad to see you back, I think. Perhaps he likes the competition."

The old man sniffed. "I had thought to live out a quiet retirement. Perhaps a little work now and again, if there was a fitting candidate. But the place was so busy. Noodle bars and nightclubs. Too much rush." He sighed, still fondling his tools. "And then word got out and I couldn't move for Yakuza wanting to be tattooed like their heroes. Silly little boys, most of them, wanting to look like men. As if a pattern on their skin could make it so." He tutted. "You must be very busy at the moment. I hear the dragons are waking."

"Yes."

"Too busy for more work?" the old man asked hopefully.

"I don't need any more, thanks, Hori. I just brought some-one to see you, that's all."

"Shame," the old man said, not looking at them. "He is my favorite canvas, you know. One of my finest *irezumi*. Beautiful. Powerful. A true meeting of subject material and design." He made a graceful motion in the air.

"You're forgetting the bit where you neglected to tell me exactly how big this design was going to be."

Hori shrugged without remorse.

"We need you to divine for us."

"No work?"

"No, not this time."

He sighed. "But subjects are so few and far between these days. I have not had a decent candidate in almost two months."

"Maybe you're too picky," Regan laughed.

The old man's hands stilled on the tools. "I do not waste my work. Any of it."

"Sir," Lily piped up, "there's something in my blood. Something the Agency wants. We need to know what it is."

"What did the butcher say?" Hori sniffed. "As you went to him first."

"I only went to him because I didn't know you were back. He said we should come and see you. After Lily's blood set the place on fire."

"Did it indeed?" He turned, suddenly interested. Lily was shocked to see his eyes were completely clouded over. "She is surprised, your little friend," he said to Regan.

"I forgot to say, Hori's blind."

"Well?" His blank eyes stared straight at Lily. "What do you think of my work on Master Lupescar here?"

"I-it's very . . ." Lily stuttered. "I've never seen anything like it."

"I should think not," the old man said haughtily. "Would you like one for yourself? Yours, of course, would be different. It would reflect your own qualities."

"No! Well, I never thought . . . but no. Plus I'd rather not be grounded until I'm forty-seven. But thank you."

Hori turned to Regan. "What is she talking about?"

"Human stuff."

The old man's worn eyebrows rose in crescent moons, stretching the folds of skin over his eyes. "Come, child, come here to me," he said abruptly.

Lily walked over. He reached for her hands. On each of his palms was tattooed a large eye. He grasped her fingers in his own. A shock ran up Lily's arms, into her shoulders, rendering her unconscious instantly. As she slumped toward the floor, Regan caught her.

"Hori—"

"She is like a tuning fork!" Hori said gleefully, turning away and picking up a tool before pulling a stone dish of ink pigment toward him.

"I don't think—"

"Place her on the bench. It is the work of a moment." He rubbed his hands together.

"We just—" Regan protested.

"Place her on the bench, my boy. We can talk as I work. There is so much to tell you! So much." The old man slipped from the stool like an otter into water, an array of tools clutched in his knotted hand. "Just a little *kakushibori*, a hidden carving, nothing obvious." He smiled, eager and toothless.

Lily shook her head to clear it. Regan was sitting on a low table in front of her chair. She turned over her wrist to look at her watch; fewer than fifteen minutes had passed. The movement made her aware of something on the inside of her left elbow. The sleeve of her top was pushed right up and a gauze bandage was stuck to her skin. Over the cut on her wrist was another large bandage. She saw the screwed-up paper wrappers in Regan's hand.

"Oh, please. You *are* joking," she said in dismay.

"It was sort of part of the deal for him telling us anything." He lobbed the wrappers at the wastepaper basket.

"You didn't say I'd end up tattooed! Knocked out and *tattooed*," Lily groaned. "Dad will kill me. I mean *kill* me." She began to pick at the edge of the bandage inside her elbow.

He stilled her hand. "They look awful just after they're done, even on me. Come on, we'd better get back to your place."

"What did he tell you?"

Regan hesitated.

Lily caught his hand. "What?"

"I'll tell you. But later."

She dug her heels in and held on to his hand, even though it made her head spin. "Tell me now."

He opened his mouth. To the sound of crashing glass.

Dragging Lily to her feet, Regan hauled her from the back room. As they reached the room with the bench, he pulled her into a cupboard containing Hori's few possessions and clothes. He had to stoop to fit the space, curving his long body over hers. Still dizzy, Lily could only watch through the slats as men in black combat gear spilled through the long corridor, invading the peaceful space. Hori, who had been resting on a white reclining chair in the corner, attempted to get up. The agent Lily was now becoming familiar with grabbed the old man by the scruff of his robe like a bundle of twigs. Lily took a breath in protest. Regan's hand clamped over her mouth.

"What did you do?" the agent hissed. "What did you do, old man?"

Hori cowered, holding up his tattooed hands.

"Where is she?"

"I don't know. They went. I fell asleep. The . . . work tires me," Hori managed.

The agent glanced around. "Look at this place." He glanced at the tools on the workbench. "Like something from the Dark Ages. What did you use on her? These?"

"They are bamboo and the finest Japanese steel," Hori said proudly.

Another agent began packing the tools into a bag.

"No!" Hori said. "You do not understand. They—"

"She's probably septic by now," the first agent sneered. He glanced over his shoulder. "Bring the inks too. Just in case."

Hori made a grab for the bag. The agent struck him across the temple with huge force, and the old man collapsed into a heap on the floor, clearly dead.

Regan burst from the cupboard, felling the nearest agent, then another who came from the corridor behind him. But the agent who had killed Hori was faster, his reflexes superhuman. He pulled out a knife and a gun from a shoulder holster, and squared up to Regan. Faster than Lily could see, he'd landed a blow on Regan's chest, a swift stab. Regan was already responding, but scarlet bloomed across his torso. The agent raised the gun and shot him, point blank in the chest, three times.

The sound thundered through the small space and Lily covered her ears with a cry. The agent ran to the cupboard as Regan fell. He caught Lily's arm, then recoiled from the talisman. The flesh of his snakeskin-covered hand was actually smoking this time.

She stood taller, lifting her arm. Behind him, Regan got to his feet and silently drew a slim, curved Japanese sword from a black lacquer sheath. He spun it once for balance. The next spin detached the agent's arm at the shoulder. The man fell to his knees.

Lily jumped back, out of the blood spray, and watched in horror as the arm began to regrow, tiny budlike fingers emerging rapidly from the gore. The radio strapped to the agent's combat vest crackled.

"Six. Report," a familiar voice said.

The agent's snake eyes blinked.

"Try regrowing this," Regan said and, backhanded, detached the agent's head. For good measure, he lodged the sword in the man's spine, and kicked the body away. The arm stopped regrowing, stunted and grotesque.

Lily covered her mouth with both hands, trying not to gag. Then she saw ahead of her a tiny pile of clothing covering a withered body.

"Don't look." Regan put his hand on her shoulder.

She spun around, seeing his blackened, gunpowder-burned clothes and the blood staining his T-shirt. She threw her arms around his waist and hugged him. He held her head to his chest.

"I'm fine. But he was fast, caught me off guard. That *never* needs to happen again."

In the outer shop, everything was in disarray. The little fountain was overturned, spilling water across the floor, still trickling. The front window lay in one shattered sheet over everything, held together by the blackout material. Jake sat in the wreckage, blood pouring from a cut in his head.

Regan helped him up. "I'm so sorry," he said.

Jake looked at him, dazed. "What?" Then, sudden anguish in his face and voice. "No!" He turned for the back room, but Regan grabbed him.

"No. Don't go back there. Not yet."

There was the distant wail of a police siren. People stood outside on the pavement, looking in. Some of them were on mobile phones. Lily put her hand out to Jake.

"Don't," he said, stepping back. "Just get out of here." When they hesitated, he bit his lips together. "Go on, just go." His eyes gleamed with unshed tears, but his voice was hard.

Lily and Regan walked back toward the station to the taxi stand. Regan buttoned up his coat, covering the mess beneath his clothes. He was quiet and preoccupied as they climbed into a black cab. Lily fumbled in her jeans pocket to make sure she had the fare.

"Temple, please," she said to the driver.

Regan looked at her questioningly.

"I need to get a shower and some clean clothes. And Dad will be going crazy."

He nodded. They sat in the back in silence.

"How are they following us, do you think?" he asked after a while.

Lily sat, thinking. "I bet it's facial recognition through the CCTV."

"Those cameras can recognize faces?"

"The software behind them can, yes."

He looked troubled.

Ten minutes later they were walking across the courtyard in the Temple. Regan stopped outside the main door.

"So I've been tattooed, and it cost an old man his life." She pushed her hand to her forehead.

"He gave it willingly."

"And it was for nothing."

"It wasn't for nothing."

"But Hori . . . why would they do that? It just seemed so pointless."

"Yes. But that agent, he seemed to think that the work the Agency is doing was at risk because of you having a tattoo. Why? Septic, he said."

Lily rubbed her forehead. "Blood poisoning, maybe? Maybe that's why they intervened like that—in broad daylight."

Regan nodded slowly.

"Poor Hori." Lily bit her lip.

"I know. But he told me something before."

She leaned against the wall, cold and exhausted. "What?"

He scrubbed his hand through his hair, exhaling slowly.

"What?" Lily persisted.

He put his hand to her bruised face. "If we stop the Agency, we can win the Chaos War."

Lily looked up at him, her face full of hope. "That's good . . . isn't it?"

He looked away, biting his lip. "Yes. That's good. He also said that you already knew what you had to do . . . what the answer was."

She frowned. "What?"

"To restore balance to the City."

Throwing up her hands, she exclaimed, "But I *don't* know!"

"Maybe you do and you just—"

"I don't!"

He nodded. "Okay, okay. Look, can you go on from here? I

need to see Lucas and Elijah. I'll meet you at my place in half an hour and we'll make a plan. I don't want to leave you, but I need to speak to him. And I'd better change my clothes too. If things carry on like this, I may outlive my wardrobe." He gestured to his shirt, bloody and ruined beneath the buttoned coat.

Lily rolled her eyes.

He studied her face. "You're pretty bruised. Looks like the transfusion has worn off completely. Will your dad be upset?"

She took a deep breath. "Probably. I'll handle it."

Lily let herself in and went up to the flat, pulling her keys out of her jacket pocket. Inside, her father was sitting at the counter, staring into a cup of coffee. Behind him, the television on the wall was running a news item about unprecedented high tides along the Thames. Wapping was flooded.

"You went out early," he said. "Or did you not come in?"

Lily kept her head down and said nothing. *He's testing me, to see if I lie to him. Well, I won't.*

"So, all night, then," he said, mouth set in a line. "I tried calling your phone."

Lily pulled it from her pocket and looked at it. "Ah, yes, sorry. Dead battery," she said. "How long have you been in?" she asked, plugging the phone into the charger by the toaster, keeping her head down.

"The call-out was a total red herring. When I got there no one even knew why I'd been called out. Or *who* had called me out even."

Ellis. Again.

"But then I got talking to the duty manager and . . ." He rubbed his eyes. "But that doesn't justify you spending the entire night out and not even calling to let me know you're okay."

"Yes, I'm sorry. I'm going to grab a shower." Lily walked toward the bathroom.

"Stop *right* where you are."

She froze.

He walked up behind her. "Turn around and look at me."

Lily kept her head down.

"Turn. Around."

Lily turned. Her father lifted her chin. "What in God's name happened?"

"I fell."

His face hardened. "Again?"

Lily closed her eyes and took a long breath.

"If he's done this to you, I'll see him prosecuted to the full extent of the law."

Lily knocked her father's hand away from her face. "He never, *ever* would."

"How long have you known him?"

Lily met her father's eyes. "Someone else did it."

"What the hell does that mean?" he asked, angry.

"It means I am getting into the shower now."

She went to her room and examined the bandage on her

arm, but decided to leave it. Through the gauze she could see a dark patch, roughly the size of a bottle cap. She sighed and pulled on her robe, tying her belt tightly. Ten minutes later she was showered and dressed warmly in a long-sleeved white T-shirt with a loose knit over it, her usual skinny black jeans, and sneakers.

In the kitchen, she looked at her phone, which was still charging. It had moved from its previous position. Her father didn't know the code to get into it; he'd never asked, and it had never been a topic of conversation. She placed it back down and looked at him, frowning at the idea that he would start snooping. He was pouring himself some more coffee and avoiding her eyes.

"Lily, we need to talk."

"Fine. Coffee first, though, please?"

He poured her a cup. Lily added milk and sugar and made herself some toast, packing a spare sweater and her wallet into her bag. She didn't look at her father as she did it.

"Going out again?" he asked, noncommittally.

She nodded, a triangle of toast in her teeth as she buttered the next one.

"To meet Regan?"

Lily took the toast from her mouth. "Yes."

"And what if I told you I didn't want you to go?"

"Non-negotiable, Dad. Sorry."

Her father rubbed his face. "What's so important that you have to go out again right now?"

Trying to thwart a government conspiracy, find two, possibly three abducted girls, restore the balance between a community of mythical creatures and humanity. Not get dead.

"No big plans."

"Doesn't he have to work?"

"He works nights mostly." Lily pushed her sleeve out of the way and picked up her mug. Her father frowned and reached out, touching her arm.

Hurriedly putting her mug down, Lily tugged at her cuff. "It's nothing. I cut myself, that's all."

Her father caught her wrist, pushing her sleeve up. "You don't mean you actually cut your own arm? Not deliberately?"

"Not like *that*," she said. The dismay was plain on her father's face as he saw the other bandage.

"What in God's name have you been doing to yourself?"

"That's not a cut—"

"Oh, Lily, please tell me that's not a tattoo."

Lily took a deep breath. "It's a tattoo."

He stood up, throwing his coffee into the sink. "What on earth were you thinking? You haven't even got your ears pierced, for goodness' sake. You've known him five minutes and he's already talked you into—"

"He didn't talk me into anything!"

"I am so disappointed in you."

"Why?!" Lily exploded. "For having a tiny tattoo? The world won't end."

"But it might make it harder to get a job, people might judge you—" Her father ticked things off on his fingers.

"Like you've judged him, obviously," Lily snapped back.

He put his head in his hands. "I'm trying not to. But . . . staying out all night . . . your face? And . . ." He shook his head, gesturing at her arm. "And I thought perhaps to start off with you'd have a boyfriend more your own age."

"Dad, please. We've been over this. It's not like he's thirty or something."

"But he *is* older than you."

"Three years? I'm sixteen, not twelve."

Her father sighed. "He just seems older than nineteen."

"He had to grow up early, that's all."

"It's not drugs, is it?"

"Drugs? Are you *insane*? I doubt he's taken so much as an aspirin in his whole life."

"I'm sorry, I just worry. I see so many young girls who are exploited every day."

Lily almost stamped her foot. "He isn't exploiting me!"

"That's what *they* say—"

"But 'they' aren't me, with you for a parent. And he isn't. He wouldn't."

"It's—"

"Dad, stop. He isn't . . . easy, I know. But he's not some console-obsessed idiot who only thinks about one thing when he's not gaming."

Her father held up his hands. "Okay, I'm convinced! I wouldn't want to come up against you in court!" He dropped his hands. "Look, perhaps you'd like to invite him around? Or we could go for dinner. Tonight, maybe?"

"The next few days might be busy."

"Why? What's happening?"

She picked at the seal around the stovetop. "Nothing definite that I know of. His work is kind of demanding." Lily felt the familiar burn in her cheeks. "Dad, will you trust me if I tell you that I'm trying to do the right thing? And that there are people he needs to help, who don't have anyone else to help them, apart from him? And maybe me."

"Lily, are you in some kind of trouble?"

Only massive, possibly fatal trouble. She shook her head. "Nothing for you to worry about."

"Does that mean yes but you're not going to tell me?"

She gulped down the rest of her lukewarm coffee. "I have to go."

"I'm asking, as your father, that you stay here."

"I have to *go.*"

"Go to your room."

"No. And you won't physically make me. I will hate you for the rest of my life if you try."

He studied her for a long time. "That's emotional blackmail, and I have taught you better than that."

She pouted and said nothing.

He sighed. "Lily, you look absolutely exhausted. You're thinner than you were a week ago. You're covered in bruises and bandages. Your clothes are torn as if you've been in a fight. And all this is happening since you met a young man who appears to be straight out of every father's worst nightmare."

"Don't say that about him. None of this is his fault."

Her father went on as if she hadn't spoken. "And it's quite clear whatever's going on between the two of you is serious. The way he looks at you . . . I've never seen anything like it—which is a point in his favor. I can't let it put you in harm's way, though. I won't."

Oh God, how can I ever explain? Lily took a breath. "Dad. You're right. You *have* taught me right from wrong. And you've raised me to make my own choices too. And today, this is my choice."

He turned away, hunched on the stool. Lily hugged him from behind, wrapping her arms around his neck and kissing his cheek. "Let me go. I need to."

Her father held her hands tightly in his own, pressing them against his chest. He sighed. "You were always going to be trouble. I just always thought I had time."

"You do." *I hope.*

"I love you, Lily."

She pressed her cheek to his. "I know, Dad. I love you too."

Lily hurried back toward Ludgate Circus, her head down and her hoodie pulled up over her hair. Heading out of Temple Gate, she saw a figured slumped on the frozen pavement.

"Gamble?"

He sat up suddenly, uncoordinated. Lily saw the dark stain seeping out from his crotch. The stone slabs beneath him were spreading with wet.

"I bin waiting for you," he slurred, trying to put a hand to his face and missing. He stank.

Lily watched him. "What is it?"

"The . . . the . . . it's not where it should be. That's the . . . the . . . s'why iss all wrong. S'what brings th'Chaos."

"What does?"

He squinted up at her. "Cahn remember."

Lily looked at the sky and swore. "Come on, Gamble, try to think."

"I AM THINKING," he bellowed from the pavement, sitting in his own piss.

"Oh, for God's sake." She walked off, leaving him shouting incoherently after her. As she passed the dark mouth of a parking garage on Bouverie Street, a manic chattering noise caught her attention. She ventured inside, her eyes adjusting slowly to the dark. In the corner sat a mothwing, hugging her knees and making inconsolable noises. Lily walked over cautiously.

"Are you okay?" *Do they even understand language?*

The mothwing began to sob. Lily hunkered down on her heels and reached out, patting her shoulder carefully. She saw that one wing was broken and painfully torn.

"Look, I have to go. But maybe you could come with me?"

The mothwing buried her face in her filthy knees and carried on crying. Lily unshouldered her bag and opened it out, putting it on the ground. When the mothwing ignored it, Lily shortened the strap and then pushed her into the bag. After a few shoves, the mothwing understood and curled into the canvas. Lily stood, slinging the bag across her chest and carefully holding the little body against her, avoiding the damaged wing concealed beneath the flap of the material. She looked like any other teenage mother on the street, she realized. Apart from the mothwing's dirty hair.

She hurried away. Five minutes later she arrived at the bookshop and let herself in. Lucas was sitting behind the counter, reading. He looked up.

"Miss Hilyard?"

"It's just Lily." She smiled.

"Lily," he said. "How may I help? You've just missed Regan. I believe he was on his way back to the Rookery. To meet . . . you."

She came and perched on the edge of a hard wooden chair near his desk, putting her bag between them. "Yes, I know. I'm on my way there now. But look what I found. I thought you might be able to help."

His eyebrows rose fractionally as the mothwing emerged from the bag. He clicked his tongue. "You poor thing."

Elijah emerged from the corridor that led to a group of shelves marked *Grand Tour, Italy.*

The mothwing looked disoriented. Lucas's thin hands took her shoulders, examining the torn wing. "I wonder how this happened. They do fight sometimes." He said something to the creature. Miserably, she looked up and chattered back.

"What's she saying?" Lily asked.

"That men came. With nets and wheels." Lucas shook his head. "They're very simple creatures. But at least now we know that it is men taking them. It must be the Agency. The mothwings are disappearing so quickly now."

Elijah frowned. "But what use are mothwings? They can't even fly."

"This will heal," Lucas said absently, thinking.

"Good," said Lily.

"As will your face, I assume," Elijah said.

"I'm hoping so," Lily told him. "Or my father may never let me leave the flat again."

"That would be a shame. You have the most remarkable face."

She looked at him, surprised. "Thank you."

"Most welcome. We imagined you would be beautiful. The ones they end up with always are. We hadn't expected you to be quite so fragile, but . . ."

"Will you people please stop telling me I'm too small and breakable?" Lily exclaimed. "It's getting really old."

Lucas watched her for a moment. "Regan told me about Hori. His death is a sad loss to the community, but I am glad, at least, that we know the Guardians' prophecy is real."

"I don't understand."

"Hori." Lucas frowned. "That's what he—oh, he hasn't told you."

Lily set her chin. "Told me what?"

"There had been predictions, of course," he went on, "little more than rumors. The chance that you would end up, quite literally, on his doorstep, seemed remote. But such is the way of things in our world. What is meant to be, is."

Lily frowned, suspicious. "What do you mean, 'meant to be'?"

"The two of you. You and him. The prophecy." Elijah's voice was quiet.

Lily held up one hand. "Whoa, okay, just stop. Prophecies are starting to pile up here. That he would save my life, yes.

Got that one. That we are about to start a war—that I like less, but got it." She looked at them, wary. "You're telling me there's *more*?"

"He's told you about your blood?"

Lily nodded. "Yes. His blood and mine are compatible, which is weird, as my blood isn't compatible with anyone else's at all."

"What else did he tell you?" Lucas spun the globe gently, his eyes on her.

"I . . . er . . ." She looked at him for help.

He sat forward, steepling his fingers. "He's a halfbreed, Miss Hilyard."

"Yes."

"Half Eldritche and half—what, do you think, exactly?"

"Human?" Lily perked up. "He's half human?"

"Yes. He's viewed as a bastard by most of our community. The halfbreed."

Lily raised an eyebrow. "Something's telling me you didn't get the memo about bigotry being very uncool."

Elijah ignored her. "His kind are the only Eldritche who take human wives. Women with your blood type."

"Go easy! We've only just met. No one is getting marri—"

"No, you are not. Because he will give his life to save you, in blood and fire, so that you can restore the City's balance and end the Chaos War. The final two parts of the same prophecy. They're not different—they're all parts of the same one."

Lily pushed to her feet, slamming her fist down on the table. "NO!" The talisman jumped on the leather. Lucas pointed to it.

"The fact that he gave you that proves that he knew," he said, his voice tinged with sadness. "He can give it only once."

"We're just teenagers." It was all Lily could think to say.

Elijah patted the little mothwing's head. "And we were dead at twenty, Miss Hilyard. We must all play the cards we are dealt. Regan has accepted it. His tattoo—the fire consuming him—do you know how long it took?"

"Three weeks."

"Three weeks of having his fate printed onto his skin."

"Please. Stop. You're making out as if this is it! Have we no choice in any of this?"

"There's always a choice," he said, making it sound as if there were really no choice at all.

"I have to go." She shook her head.

Lucas got to his feet as well. As Lily reached the door, he spoke again, almost hesitantly. "Neither of us had the chance to have children of our own . . . never had the chance to try, even. Many of our kind think that he cannot be hurt. Over the years we have come to know only too well how hurt he can be." He tried to smile. "Be kind, Lily Hilyard, in what time there is left."

Lily began to run.

Chapter 14

She pounded to Bow Lane, head down, slamming through a group of office workers gathered outside the old wooden pub in the heart of the street, shouting apologies, running on and hooking left into the alley. Bursting through the gate, she ran up the switchback stairs, grabbing the worn wooden railings. On the second floor, a door stood open.

Lily stopped, heart thumping, and pushed at the frost-rimed wood. It creaked back on its hinges. Inside, a large flat spread out, echoing with cold. There was a bright kitchen off to the right. Lily could see a row of mugs hanging from hooks. One missing. Closer, a round table with three chairs, and space for one more. There were photographs on a sideboard. To the left, a beaten-up old sofa, covered in faded but once brightly knitted blankets of woolen squares, sat in front of an old gray television. Regan was sitting on the sofa, staring at the screen as if there were something playing on it. He was wearing clean clothes but was totally immobile, as if he too were frozen.

Lily took a step forward. He started, but didn't look back. Instead, he leaned forward over his knees for a second. When he stood up and turned, his eyes were bright.

Lily hurtled into the room, leaping over the sofa arm onto the seat and throwing herself into his arms, wrapping her legs around his waist and her arms tight around his neck. He hoisted her up, so that she was slightly above him.

"*No.*" She pressed her hot face against his, breathless, feeling wetness against her cheek. She kissed him hard, kissed his mouth, his sharp-stubbled jaw, his face, the edge of his beautiful, winged brow. His hand came up to her hair, the other tight around her waist. When she couldn't breathe she broke away.

"I won't let you do this. I *won't.*"

For a long moment, he looked up at her. "What is meant to be, is."

She shook her head. "No. You don't believe that."

"Lily, of all the girls who could have ended up bleeding to death in my courtyard, it's you." He let her down slowly. "And the gathering dark, it's stronger than I've ever seen. Ever felt. It's coming. I can't control it anymore. The river is rising; it's the start. This is the Chaos War. It's here. Maybe today, maybe tomorrow. I can feel it."

She buried her head against his chest, sliding her arms around his waist inside his coat. He held on to her for a long time, his cheek pressed against her hair.

"Don't cry," he said at last.

"What makes you think I'm crying?" she sniffed into his tight top.

He laughed.

"This is where you lived," she said. It wasn't a question.

"Yes." There was a long silence. "So. You know. Lucas and Elijah?"

"Yes. There was a mothwing. She was hurt. I took her there and they told me. But you've got a choice. There is always a choice. That's what Lucas said."

He tipped up her chin. "I already made it."

She bit her lip. "When?"

"When I chose to save your life rather than let you bleed out in the courtyard."

She grimaced. "So much for romance, huh?"

He smiled. "I think that's pretty romantic."

She bit her lip. "You never wanted anyone else?"

He took a deep breath. "After they told me about the prophecy, a few years ago, I looked at human girls. Sometimes I *really* looked—"

Lily punched him in the chest. He pretended to flinch, laughing. "Hey, I *am* half human." Straightening up, he put his arms back around her. "But I never *saw* them. And then there was you." He said it like a simple fact. "And now you're all I see."

She put her forehead against his chest, unable to look at him. "And the talisman. It's a one-time-only deal?"

He rubbed his face and linked his hands behind his neck, breathing out. "You can take it off. If you want to. I don't expect you to . . . it's fine if you don't . . . I mean, my job is to keep you safe."

Her phone chimed loudly in her pocket. Lily tugged it out. Her breath caught.

**If you want to see your mother again
go to St. Alban's Tower, Cripplegate.
NOW.**

Lily turned the screen to Regan. "From an unknown number."

He read it. "Sounds like a trap to me," he said.

Lily took his hand. "Please? I'm willing to take the risk."

He sighed. "This prophecy thing. It doesn't mean I'm going to give in to you all the time, you know."

"All the time before we die, you mean?" Lily corrected, stuffing her phone away.

They left the Rookery. Felix was leaning on his cart outside the coffee shop, sipping from a white cup. Despite the day being a dull pewter, he was still wearing his sports sunglasses.

"Look if it e'nt jubee and de big mon."

"Not today, Felix," Regan said.

"Oh, not today, says he. Den Felix naw give you he news." Felix sucked his teeth and folded his arms.

"Tell us, please," Lily said when no one spoke. Felix looked increasingly obstinate.

"Huh," Felix huffed. "Is a good ting you have jubee now, for she got *all* de charm." He made them wait a little longer. "Two more dragons did wake in de night."

Regan swore with feeling.

"Yes." Felix nodded. "Dem some big trouble now. Dey lookin' mighty hungered."

"Where are they?"

"I see dem on de roof of some office in Portsoken. Near de Tower. Dey keepin' warm on de heatin' unit. Lookin' still a likkle sleepy. But who kno' how long dey stay dere? Perhaps only till dey is feelin' some besser."

"You need to tell the Clerks. They should know. People will be going to them for information."

"Already taken care o' dat," Felix said haughtily.

"You should go, you know. Leave the City. The next few days—"

One of Felix's black brows appeared over the plastic edge of his sunglasses. "I no leavin'. Dis not yous fight alone. Dis *my* city. My *streets*. You tink you above my help?"

Regan turned to him, frowning. "It's not that. I just—"

"Tell it to da man." Felix held up his hand, palm out. "I's out of here." He walked away, his usually rolling gait stiff and awkward.

"You think he should leave?" Lily asked, when he'd gone.

"Yes."

"And go where?"

"Anywhere."

"But . . . he wants to stay and help."

"How can he help me?"

"I don't know, but—"

He turned on her, angry. "How can any of them help me? Lucas and Elijah can't move from the bookshop. Felix is human and too easily hurt. I don't want him involved. Lilith . . . well, she hasn't stayed alive and as successful as she is by getting involved with things like this. She'll just move on, to another city. And Gupta's got enough on his plate right now. If he's even survived Amanvir's visit."

"But they're your friends."

"I told you, I don't have friends. Who needs a friend with a death sentence hanging over them?"

She frowned at him. "That doesn't stop people caring."

He pushed his hands deep into his pockets. "They shouldn't. It'll just make it harder on them."

Lily blinked back the tears that burned behind her eyelids. Stuffing her hands in her pockets, she walked a pace behind him, head down. In another few minutes they turned into Wood Street. Before them stood the lone spire of St. Alban. To the right was Wood Street police station, the City of London Police Headquarters, its brutally modern pale stone facade bearing two old-fashioned lanterns.

Regan walked to the church tower and tried the door. It opened easily and swung on oiled hinges. They looked at each other, and went in.

The ground floor was dim and looked like little more than a storeroom. Rolls of packing material and old cardboard filled the space. They looked around. In the corner was a stone stairway, leading to the floors above. But beneath the stairway was a metal door panel, out of place in the old church tower. To the right, a red button glowed dully. They looked at each other, then Regan shrugged and pressed the button.

They stepped inside and the door slid shut, swooping them downward. Seconds later, it opened. Beyond the door was a vast, empty space, lit by low-level lighting. They walked out into it. Doors led off in all directions, but to the right was a corridor, lit at ground level.

Regan held out his hand behind him, causing Lily to stop. He walked on, silhouetted against the light. Then he halted, seemingly stuck to the spot.

Lily frowned. "What is it?"

"Is she there?" asked a quiet voice. The hope in it was unmistakable.

Lily came forward, into a stunningly modern though dark

room, part office and part clinic. In the center was a table, with a metal-and-leather chair next to it. On the chair sat a small, frail woman in an immaculate gray skirt and jacket. A woman who was undoubtedly Lily's mother.

Lily looked over her shoulder at Regan for reassurance. He put a hand on her back, nudging her forward.

"Lily?" Caitlin said softly.

Lily fell to her knees at her mother's feet and took her cold, pale hands, staring up at her. There were so many questions forming in her mind that she struggled to speak. Instead, her eyes took in every detail of her mother's face greedily. Hooked around Caitlin's ears, beneath her fading golden hair, were the tubes of a cannula supplying her with oxygen.

"Mum?" she managed, at last. "What have they done to you?"

Closing her eyes and shaking her head, Caitlin Hilyard took a breath. "They've kept me alive. After the blood transfusion, I was dying, slowly. It's called a hemolytic reaction. The other blood was killing my red blood cells and stopping me from making more. I don't get enough oxygen."

"Dad never said . . ."

"Your father never knew. The Agency. They came to me, in the hospital, and they told me I could stay alive if I went with them, I could continue my work. Find out how to stop it ever happening to you."

Lily frowned. "So you left us?"

Caitlin's eyes closed for a second.

"She can't have had a choice, Lily," Regan said from behind them. "She was dying, leaving you anyway. And besides, that must be why they set up the blood-banking." The realization was clear in his voice, his eyes on Caitlin. "It wasn't because Lily might need the blood, it was because *you* needed it. She's been keeping you alive."

Lily looked up at her mother unsteadily. Her eyes shone. "Is . . . that true?"

Caitlin nodded. "Lily, I'm so sorry. It was the only way. They keep your blood too, in case."

"But they do test it, don't they?" Regan said.

Her mother swallowed. "Yes."

"And what have they found?" Lily's grip on her mother's fingers loosened a little, although Caitlin's hold remained tight.

"Your blood . . . it's the vehicle by which the properties of the Eldritche can be harnessed." Her mother's voice was low and becoming more breathless.

Lily sat back on her heels, tugging her hands free. She looked over her shoulder at Regan, then turned back to her mother, forcing the confirmation. "You mean they can use it to mix Eldritche and humans."

"Yes." The words were gasping now.

Pushing to her feet, Lily walked a few steps away. "So we were right. That's why they're taking the other girls. You're trying to combine all Mona's reflexes, Rachel's ability to—what, breathe in water?—and what about Vicky Shadbolt?"

"Human control subject." Her mother put her hand to her chest. "Expendable."

"*Expendable?*"

"I don't have much time," Caitlin said, her voice becoming fainter. "My alibi, it won't give us much. I've sent the driver for extra medication. I've come to inspect the new facility here—"

"You've just created this place?"

"Yes. It's less than a week old. We're moving here to Cripplegate from our old headquarters. We move every couple of years."

"The Cripplegate dragon, it was the first to wake," Lily murmured to Regan.

Her mother shook her head. "It's something more than that. Eldritche activity is exploding and we don't know why. Nothing we've done so far has created a surge of Chaos like London is currently experiencing. Not even when their father died." She nodded toward Regan. "The dragons are waking because, as of three days ago, the City has been under siege."

Regan stepped forward. "My father. What about my family?"

Caitlin's eyes closed again, as if she were in pain. "I'm sorry. Your father breached the facility. We had no choice. He was destroying everything we'd worked for."

"They killed him? How?"

"Radiation chamber. All blood products are tested using radiation. It exposes weaknesses and can be used to fix the properties, or enhance them—"

"And my brother?" Regan's voice was impossible to read as he cut her off.

"He joined the program as soon as he was acclimatized. He's exceptional. The best operative anyone's ever seen. Espionage, tech, medicine. He's unbeatable. Been in the field for five years already. He was too young, but we couldn't hold him back. He'd already finished his traditional education."

Lily looked over at Regan, but his face was unreadable.

"He's running the new project," Caitlin managed, gasping on the last word. "We've been working together, but he will have to start reporting directly to the Ministry now. They know I haven't got long."

"No!" Lily burst out.

Her mother tried to get to her feet. "I'm keeping you. I need to go back. But I'm trying to tell you." She took a breath. "They don't know, but I think—the increase in the Chaos that's com-ing—it's the two of you. It's because you've met. We thought it was nonsense. A fairy story. It . . . I think it's true."

Regan watched her, judgment in his eyes. "The things I see, every night . . . they're not fairy tales."

"You knew about the prophecy?" Lily burst out, tears in her eyes.

Her mother looked between them both. "I didn't think it could be true—"

"So you know the war is coming, then?" Regan said, his voice flat.

Caitlin looked down and nodded. "I'm sorry," she said. "And we predict—well, Ellis predicts—he's been tracking all the incidents reported to us in a computer program, and devised an algorithm to calculate when it would happen—that the rise in

Chaos tonight will be the tipping point. The Ancients will start to wake."

"But how can *I* restore the balance, or whatever it is I have to do to end this?" Lily asked urgently.

Her mother shook her head. "I don't know." She paused, taking another labored breath. "But I have an idea what it might be."

"So tell us," Regan urged.

"Tomorrow we present our findings to the Ministry. If we've proved, irrevocably, that Lily can harness the qualities of the Eldritche and transmit them to humans, Operation Harvest will roll out across the country and"—her chest heaved—"in the various nations where we have interests. Africa, some other developing nations. The hunt for Type H girls will commence."

"We're going to be lab rats?" Lily's voice was filled with outrage.

"I'm sorry. I'm here to warn you. There's a conference being held in Docklands at the beginning of next week. It's called FutureMed. All of the multinational companies attending are aware that the Ministry is on the verge of a breakthrough. On Monday, the Ministry will make a presentation and reveal its findings. The rest of the week is supposed to be a conference, but it's not. It's an auction."

"They're going to *sell me*?" Lily said, backing into Regan. He put his arms around her.

"And girls like you. When, and if, they find any others. At the same time, a wholesale roundup of the Eldritche will begin. There's already a holding facility in place just outside London. There, they'll be tested for potential—"

"Potential?" Lily was aghast.

"Let me *finish*," Caitlin panted. "Transmittable qualities, stability, IQ."

Lily looked between her and Regan. "How many people are we talking about? How many Eldritche are there in London?"

Regan shrugged.

"We monitor just over seven thousand Eldritche in London alone," said Lily's mother.

"You're going to round up *seven thousand* people, just because they don't fit in?" Lily snapped. "And use them to make expensive drugs that will only be available to those who can afford them?"

"Don't be naive, Lily. Genetic engineering is rife in the Far East. Africa is the largest medical testing ground for Big Pharma in the world. I thought I could make a difference here, but it wasn't meant to be like this." Lily's mother put a hand to her head. "You have to believe me."

"I *believed* you were dead. That's what *I* believed. My whole life."

Caitlin reached out a hand to Regan, speaking only to him. "Listen to me. Just listen. I thought that if they had me, my work, they would allow her to live a normal life, or as normal as it could be. They lied. It's all been a lie. Please, take her away, keep her safe. If anyone can, you can. You're resourceful enough to go anywhere."

Regan said nothing, his gray eyes unreadable.

"But what about you? You're not going back, surely?" Lily shook her head.

"I must. Lily, my time between transfusions is so limited now. They manage it deliberately. I need injections and treatments every few hours. It keeps me dependent on them."

"And working for them." Regan's voice was hard.

"Help her!" Lily exclaimed, turning to him. "Help her like you helped me."

"They've already tried that, I'm sure," Regan said.

Caitlin nodded. Her breathing was shallow. "It worked for a while. For a long time. A mixture—your blood and Ellis's. But it always wears off, and I'm too weak now. And a straight transfusion would kill me. Please, you need to go."

"Mum, you can't go back! I won't let you! What about Dad?"

She smiled sadly. "Your father believes I am long dead, Lily. The woman I was *is* dead. Let it stay like that."

"How can I?!"

Regan caught her hand. "Lily, we have to go. They'll be here any second. Your mother's right."

"One last thing." Caitlin's voice was almost a rasp. "Ellis. He watched your parents die. His life has been one long series of tests, tasks, and experiments. The Agency, they use him relentlessly. He was just a little boy. I tried to stand in for his mother. He needs friends. Don't judge him. *Now go.*"

"No!" Lily urged.

Regan caught her wrist.

"I'm staying," she argued.

He pulled her to him. She struggled, but it was impossible to resist.

Caitlin took a grateful breath. "Thank you. Make her go. Keep her safe."

Regan hesitated. "I thought you wouldn't want that. I'm everything the Agency is trying to use up and then eradicate."

"Never. Nothing is that simple. Go! Take her with you. Get out now."

He hauled Lily back into the corridor, then through the giant hall toward the elevator, even as she kicked and struggled. He held her against him inside the metal box.

"Get off me! We have to take her with us."

"No. She has to go back. And we need time."

She was still struggling when they arrived in the church tower. Outside, the street was empty, apart from a police riot van with a driver sitting nearby. He wasn't looking at them, but reading a newspaper. Regan pulled the door closed behind him and tugged up his hood to obscure his face. He held Lily firmly by the hand. She was no longer struggling.

"Time for what?" she asked as they crossed the road, walking south back into the heart of the City.

"Time to work out how to stop this. And"—he glanced over his shoulder—"time to lose the two agents who are right behind us. We need to get somewhere public. Find as many people as possible. Now."

A moment later, they were heading for St. Paul's.

"But if they know we were with her, we need to go back. She'll get into trouble!"

"Going back won't help your mother," he said, his hand tightening on hers. "She took a calculated risk."

"But—"

"They're still behind us," he said. "Two men on foot."

Lily's head turned.

"And there's a van on the road, like the other one. Just keep moving." He walked between her and the road, herding her farther into the pavement.

"What are we going to do?"

"I'll think of something. We need to stay in plain sight for now."

The west door of St. Paul's Cathedral rose up before them, vast and beautiful. It was teeming with people walking to and fro and waiting for their friends on the huge set of steps.

"Lily!"

Lily turned. Her friend Sam was running down the steps. Tall, with masses of thick brown hair, she enveloped Lily in a warm hug.

"You changed your mind! Are you coming around the cathedral with us? We can get coffee afterward."

"Yes," said Regan definitely. "Let's do that." He put his hand in the small of Lily's back, pushing her forward unceremoniously.

Sam looked up at him, eyes wide, as if seeing him for the first time, as if she hadn't known he was there. Although Sam was tall, he was still taller. Lily turned hurriedly, taking his hand and pulling him toward the steps. "Sam, this is Regan. Regan, Sam."

"Hi," he said, flashing her a brief white grin. Sam was walking up the steps sideways, still staring.

At the top of the stairway, a dozen of Lily's classmates were gathered, chatting in the freezing air. The conversation died as

Lily and Regan arrived. Most of the girls stared openly. Most of the boys sneaked glances at him while pretending he wasn't there. Regan appeared not to notice any of it, looking out toward the square. Inside, he kept hold of Lily's hand as they passed through the ticket barriers, pulling folded notes from his hip pocket and handing them over.

"*How* much?!" he said in her ear as she picked up the tickets in her free hand.

"Probably a bargain if it means we stay alive for another hour."

"We're not staying here for an hour," he muttered. "And who *are* these people?"

"I go to school with them."

He rolled his eyes.

Sam was standing at the edge of the group. Most of them were still staring at Regan. As the others dispersed a little into the huge church, Sam approached them cautiously. Regan was looking over his shoulder toward the doors. His tattoos were stark in the vee of his collar. Sam's eyes widened again.

"So, how did you and Lily meet?" she asked brightly.

He pushed his hood back from his dark head and looked down at her. "I saved her life."

Sam's mouth fell open. Lily elbowed him. "He's such a dramatist," she told Sam. "He saved me from a dog. Outside his work."

"And what do you do?"

"Security." He glanced over his shoulder toward the doors again.

"Do they need advice here?" she teased.

Looking at her gorgeous friend flirting mischievously with Regan, Lily felt an unwelcome pang of jealousy. *Don't be ridiculous*, she scolded herself, nerves still jittering.

"Everyone does." He smiled. "They just don't always know it."

"So, what advice would you give me?" Sam teased.

"Always look before you leap," he teased back and squeezed Lily's hand. "Come on, Lily, let's look at this place."

She tried to pull her hand away but he held on. They wandered the cathedral, tagging along with Lily's school friends, who eyed Regan curiously but mainly stayed away. Except Sam, who walked with them most of the time, making it impossible to discuss what had just happened with her mother and the fact that at least two government agents were trailing them. Matt MacGregor, Lily's biology-class partner, also hung back, making sarcastic comments that were out of character. Sam chatted animatedly to Regan, who responded in a friendly if abrupt way, keeping firm hold of Lily's hand. He ignored Matt.

Then Laura Mason wandered over, flicking her long blond hair and spinning a mint on the tip of her tongue provocatively as usual. "Hi." She flashed Regan a huge grin. "I'm Laura."

He smiled. "Hi, Laura."

"Cool tattoos."

"Thanks."

"Have they got meanings?"

He shrugged. "They meant something at the time."

"That one." She pointed to his chest, where the unbuttoned neck of his top let the flame tattoo show across his collarbone. She raised an eyebrow, the corner of her mouth turned up, poking her tongue through the center of the mint. "Is it . . . all over?"

There was a silence.

"Yes. It is," Lily said, irritated. Then she realized everyone was staring at her. She turned bright red. Laura blinked.

Lily tugged herself free and walked away, examining Wellington's tomb with great care. Sam came over, unable to control her giggles. "Sorry, but that was so funny."

Lily folded her arms. "Not that funny," she muttered.

"Hey, what's the matter?" Sam chucked her lightly on the shoulder.

Jaw set, Lily looked away. "Nothing. Just not having the best day, that's all."

Sam gave her a hug and a bolstering smile. "Well, FYI, when you said you'd met someone, I thought it was going to be some bionic geek you'd met at the library, not a smoking hot—"

"Oh, don't." Lily rolled her eyes. "He'll hear you."

"He can't hear me. He's miles away."

"Don't count on that," Lily grumbled.

"So, he saved you from a dog? That's so cool."

"It wasn't, not really. It was pretty awful actually."

"Is that what happened to your face?"

"Oh . . . er. Yes."

"Still"—Sam flexed her biceps—"heroics are seriously hot. Where does he live?"

"Not far from here."

"Great! Maybe a few of us can go back to his place afterward."

Lily glanced toward Regan. Their eyes met briefly, then he turned away as Laura caught his arm. Lily shook her head. "I don't think so. Like I said, he's kind of private. And there's stuff, things, going on."

"Oh, okay." Sam looked a little hurt.

Lily put out her hand. "Don't take it like that. He's just . . ."

She shrugged. "No, I get it. I'd want to be on my own with him too. Or at least, I *think* I would." She looked over toward where Regan was listening to Laura, his head cocked on one side, gray eyes on her. "He's pretty intense."

"You could say that," Lily agreed awkwardly.

"How do he and Ed get on?"

Lily looked at her friend. "Dad's managing to stay fairly chilled, considering he wants to lock me in the flat right now." *And he doesn't even know what's really happening.*

"Come on, let's get over there before Laura actually tries to see this tattoo." Sam turned back and whispered, "Does he really have it all over?"

Lily ducked her head and nodded.

"Good work." Sam nudged her shoulder, smirking.

Back on the edge of the group, Regan was visibly tired of being sociable. He pulled a tight smile at Sam and Lily. "This is what you like doing on your time off?" he said. "Coming to places like this?"

Sam shook her head. "We're not that square. We've got a

project based on the history of the City. Today we're coming here, then going to see the London Stone on Cannon Street and the Bevis Marks Synagogue."

"What's the project?"

"It's about the different types of religions here. Christianity and Judaism and—well, no one really knows what the stone's for, I suppose. They say it was part of a temple that was here way before the Romans, Brutus of Troy or something. Old gods and all that classical stuff. Anyway, we're going to look at it and write about it."

Regan looked down at Lily. "You have to do this too?"

"Yes, but I haven't even looked at it yet. Heavy week helping Dad," she explained.

He nodded, looking nonplussed, then glanced toward the doors again.

"You don't like it here?" Sam looked around at the milling tourists and the wedding-cake interior of the cathedral.

"Churches aren't for people like me," he said after a while.

"Are you an atheist?"

Regan looked at her for a long time. Then he glanced down at Lily. She bit her lips together and turned away, stifling a giggle. He burst out laughing, his joyous boy's laugh. "No, no. I'm not an atheist. At least, I don't think I am."

"What's so funny?"

Lily shook her head. "Nothing. Honestly, Sam."

Matt rejoined them and the four of them walked the cathedral in companionable silence, although Lily knew Regan's eyes remained on the door at all times. In a corner he leaned down and spoke quietly to her. "They're waiting outside, at the taxi stand. And they're covering the other exit."

"What are we going to do?" she whispered.

"It's fine. There are ways out of here."

"How?"

"In the crypt, there's a—"

"Coffee shop!" Sam appeared behind them.

Regan raised an eyebrow. "That's what I meant to say."

Sam grinned. "Shall we go? I think everyone's pretty much down there already."

Regan looked at Lily and shrugged. "Okay."

"I don't think I can get used to this new easygoing you," she muttered as they went down the dark stairs into the basement crypt.

"Shame. I quite like him. Although he'd probably be a bit more easygoing if *they* weren't out there."

Lily rolled her eyes.

Downstairs, half the class was already taking up three wooden tables among the monuments and tombs. All the seats were taken. Regan leaned against a marble sculpture of a woman reclining on a stone coffin and pulled Lily between his boots so her back was against his chest, his hands crossed over her waist at the front. Lily's friends were all watching again, looking at his coat and his tattoos and his angular, impassive face as he stared at the busy doorway. After a few moments, he frowned and leaned to the side, looking at Lily's face.

"What's the matter?"

She shrugged, gnawing on the inside of her lip.

He turned her around to face him. "What is it? I won't let them hurt you. Ever."

She took a shaky breath. "No, I know. It's not that."

"Your mother?"

She nodded, tears in her eyes. He put his arms around her, gathering her up against him like something fragile.

Her friends crowed encouragement and insults from the chairs and tables. Someone threw a balled-up piece of paper that bounced off Lily's shoulder. Regan caught it and bolted upright, turning on them. The café fell silent.

Lily grabbed his arm. "They're only joking."

But he was already looking away, toward the door, distracted. "We have to go. They're here."

Lily turned, trying to find Sam. She and Matt were sitting a little distance away. Lily pulled Regan over to them. "We have to go."

"Oh, right," Sam said, not looking too impressed.

Matt scowled. "What, you're going, just like that? Because psycho says so?"

"It's, um, complicated."

Regan was already moving, pulling her after him. Lily waved apologetically. Sam raised her hand in surprise.

"Where are we going?" Lily hissed as he pulled her into a service storeroom, dragging over an enormous set of metal shelving and pushing it up against the door. "My entire class now think we're . . . in a closet!"

"We are in a closet."

"But—"

"But what? Did you see their faces? They think I'm a freak, and they don't even know what I *really* am." He kicked a mop bucket out of the way and knelt down, tugging up the grating in the floor. "In you go."

"What?!"

"In. Now!"

Lily sat on the edge of the square hole and looked down. "How far is it?"

"Put your hands on either side and let yourself drop. It's not that far."

She eyed him dubiously.

"Go."

She pushed off and hit the ground below. It wasn't far, but the blood rushed painfully to her toes. "My God, it reeks down here."

Regan landed like a cat beside her. "I know. It's the dead stuff in the walls."

"Grim."

Reaching to his left, he flipped a switch and lights illuminated the tunnel ahead of them, stringing away into the distance. He pulled the grating back over their heads.

"Come on."

A short distance down the lit tunnel there was a massive iron grating in the wall. Regan moved it, seemingly without effort. They climbed through the hole into a stone chamber with pillars and grille-covered gateways ranged along the walls. Regan replaced the grating. Lily looked around. "What's this?"

"Underground network. Helps me get around at night." He

lifted a metal portcullis between a pair of grand pillars, straining a little to hold it as Lily scrambled beneath. She looked up at him as he boosted it up, ducked beneath to the other side, and then caught it and let it drop back into place.

"What do they weigh?" she asked.

"I don't know. They're pretty heavy—they're supposed to be. Saved my skin more than once."

They kept walking. At the end of the passage was a short flight of steps and a door. Regan unbolted it and opened it for Lily, flicking the switch off as they walked out—straight into another church, this time small with a black-and-white marble floor. Lily looked around in amazement.

"Another church?"

He nodded. "This one is particularly handy for our purposes. You'll see why."

They crossed the floor. In contrast to St. Paul's, the place was deserted and filled with scaffolding. Almost a ruin. Regan opened the wooden outer door and checked outside. "Coast's clear," he said.

They went out onto a set of stone steps. Their breath steamed in the air.

"St. Nicholas Cole Abbey. It's disused. Handy for me." He pulled the huge door closed behind them. Lily's phone buzzed an alert. It was from Sam. **U OK? xx**

Lily typed a reply. **Y. Explain l8er. xx**

Huh, explain, she thought. *Like I could.*

He watched her. "So they're your friends?"

"Yes." She pushed her phone into her pocket.

"But they were laughing at you."

She rolled her eyes. "Duh. They were messing around. Well, maybe not Laura, but you can't have everything."

"Your friend is very pretty, isn't she?"

Lily frowned. "Sam? Yes. She is."

He looked thoughtful. "Not like you. But pretty."

"I'll be sure to tell her."

He glanced at her, brows drawn together. "I was just saying."

"Right." Lily felt her chin sharpen.

"What?"

"Absolutely *nothing*. Where are we going?" she asked as they arrived on the river path and Regan headed east.

"Back to the Rookery."

"Why?"

"There's something I need to do there."

"Oh, right, of course. Very mysterious," Lily muttered under her breath.

He hauled her after him by her sleeve.

"Okay, okay! I'm coming!"

"Can you check your phone for news?"

"Yes." Lily pulled it out and checked the updates.

Oh, no.

Rioting had broken out in Islington again, and in Deptford. A man in Mayfair had killed his family, then himself. The canal in Little Venice had flooded dozens of gardens, then frozen solid, turning the area into a skating rink with lethal railings sticking out of it. There had been sightings of a huge black hound on

Hackney Marsh, and a man was found dead from terrible injuries.

She passed the phone to Regan. His face became increasingly set as he read the screen. Then he found a number and dialed. "Lucas? Yes, me. Look, the Agency—they know about us. About all of us. Across London. Probably everywhere. You need to put the word out. Get everyone out. No, all of them. There's going to be some sort of roundup. I know. It's hard to believe, but believe me." They spoke further, discussing practicalities, then Regan handed Lily her phone.

Back at the Rookery, they banged into the flat and Regan shut the door behind them. He dumped his coat over the chair and turned, arms folded, watching her. "Are you okay?"

"With . . . ?"

"Your mother. With all this." He swept a hand toward the window.

Lily blew her cheeks out. "Short answer? No. But for now I'll just not think about it. Focus on the plan. Er, what *is* the plan?"

He put his hand against her face, his thumb stroking over her cheekbone. "Well, it's two hours until nightfall, which will be the earliest we could hope to get into the power station with any kind of cover. But I'll have to try to hold the Wall until dawn. I have to at least try. So, dawn. That's when we'll go in. That still leaves us time to get everyone out before the meeting with the Ministry." He took a breath. "If we can hope to get everyone out."

Lily was staring up at him, mesmerized. After he stopped

talking, she shook herself. "Out of London or out of the power station?"

"The power station. The rest, they stay or go, their choice. I can't decide that for them."

"So what do we do until nightfall?"

He let his hand drop, looked away, and sighed almost imperceptibly.

She blushed. "Oh! Right. *Yes*. Sorry, was still in *plan* mode. I just . . ."

He kissed her, gentle at first, then less gentle, catching her waist and pulling her up against him. Lily slid her arms around his neck, adoring his mouth and the scrape of his stubble. She stumbled slightly as he pulled her into the bedroom and onto the bed, his body breaking her fall. Kneeling over him, sitting on his hips, she shoved up his Henley. With a careful finger she traced the path of one flame over his ribs, then ducked and kissed the curling black shape. His chest heaved as he hauled in a breath.

She laughed. "So that's your weakness? You're ticklish?"

He smiled. "I am, but that's not my weakness." He traced the edge of her lip with a fingertip.

She sat up, sobered. "Me? *I'm* your weakness?"

"You know you are."

"I'm sorry."

Reaching up, he touched her face. "Don't be. Today, tomorrow, it doesn't matter. I'll never be sorry."

She caught his hand and pressed her lips to his palm, closing her eyes for a second. Then she grabbed his other wrist and pinned his hands above her head. He looked up at her, letting her hold him down, eyes full of light.

"Got you now," she teased. Leaning down she paused, her mouth an inch from his.

Without effort, he rolled her into the rucked bedding, still unmade. "You had me anyway. From the moment I saw you. Close your eyes."

Less than a second later, the key turned in the lock outside the bedroom door.

Chapter 15

"No!" she yelled, scrambling from the bed to the door, twisting the old iron handle. She rattled it in fury. "No! You utter, *utter bastard*. You let me out of here right now!"

"Felix will come for you. I'll arrange it. You can go with him, get your dad, then leave the City. Go, Lily. Go for me." His voice, calm and resigned, came from the other side of the door.

"No!"

"I can't let you come with me. I was never going to. I have to keep you safe, remember?"

Lily shook the handle. "What about you?"

"This is my fight. I have to stop the Agency. Whatever comes afterward, I know you'll be amazing." The door creaked slightly, as if he were pressing his hand against it. "Maybe I'll be there to see it, in one way or another."

There was a scrape of a boot on the boards. Then silence. Lily kicked the door, hard, hurting her toes. She put her fingers to her kiss-bruised mouth and then thrust them into her hair despairingly. *Think, think, think, Lily.* She went for her phone, but her pocket was empty. *He's taken it.*

She screamed in frustration, kicking the door again. Running to the window, she looked out at the sheer drop. A four-story drop into the churchyard. *Impossible.*

She tried the window. It slid up, rattling in the old frame. Poking her head out, she peered down over the deserted graves.

She looked back at the bed, with its rumpled bedding. *Well, it works in films . . .*

Ten minutes later, she had knotted together two sheets torn into strips. Her teeth and arms ached from pulling and ripping. She only hoped it was long enough, and that the knots would hold. She tried them all again, then tied one end around the bed frame. Hitching her hip onto the window ledge, she climbed out and began to let herself down.

She knew before she was even halfway down that she wouldn't be able to hold on much longer. Speeding up, she slipped, her boots scraping against the plaster and timbers. Then, miraculously, her feet touched the churchyard wall. Cautiously, Lily looked over her shoulder. Still a good fifteen feet to go. She scurried down the rest and landed hard in the crisp white grass of the churchyard, heart thudding. Straightening up, she looked around and, seeing the metal gate, she ran for it, her only thought to get to the power station.

Her feet ground to a halt. *No. That's not the way.*

Hands on the top of her head, she counted to ten, eyes closed, working through the possibilities in her mind. Then, she sprinted for the gate.

Three minutes later, she banged through the bookshop door. Lucas was at the desk, not reading for once, just spinning the globe and looking morose. Elijah was sitting on the top rung of the ladder again, reading.

"I need your phone," she gasped.

Lucas looked surprised, but opened a drawer and took out a shiny new mobile phone. "Of course. But what for?"

"I need to call the others." Lily searched for Lilith's number on the phone's Web browser and hit "dial." It was answered on the second ring.

"Hello?" a voice said.

"Is that Lilith?"

"No. Who's this?"

"I need to speak to her. It's Lily. The girl who came in with Regan."

There was a click as the phone went down and another was picked up. "Yes?"

"Lilith, he needs your help. *All* our help. He can't do this on his own."

A long pause. "Isn't that all part of the prophecy? That he has to sacrifice himself to save you—"

"He's not saving me. Not like this. He's just doing it because he thinks he has to. And as far as I know, there's nothing in the prophecy about him not being allowed some help, is there?"

"Well, no, darling, I suppose there isn't."

Ten minutes later, Lily hung up the last call. No one was answering at the Singhs'.

"I'm going up there."

"Is that quite wise, Miss Hilyard? Colonel Amanvir and his guard are not known for their sympathetic natures." Elijah climbed down the ladder.

"I think we're beyond wisdom now."

"But the prophecy—"

"Doesn't say anything about me being wise, does it?"

"No," Elijah conceded.

"Didn't think so."

Elijah and Lucas stood side by side as she went to leave, manners still perfect. Lily headed for the door, then ran back, throwing her arms around their necks and hugging them.

"Thank you," she said.

They both patted her back cautiously. "For what?"

She pulled away. "For looking after him."

"It was . . . a pleasure," they said in bewildered unison as the door closed behind her.

Lily ran to Artillery Lane as fast as her feet would carry her. She was operating on adrenaline and by the time she arrived outside the newsagent's she was trembling. The door was closed, but the lights were on inside. The sign said OPEN but when she pushed it wouldn't give. She hammered on the glass, knuckles ringing.

"Colonel! Colonel Amanvir, are you there?"

A slim figure emerged from behind the plastic-strip fly curtain at the back of the shop. His eyes were dark beneath his red turban, but as he came closer Lily could see the narrow slits of his pupils, marking him out as a child of the Serpent King. He stared at her through the door, then unbolted it and opened it a little.

"Be quiet! What do you want?"

"I need to see Gupta. And Colonel Amanvir."

His breath came out as a hissing sound. "No one *wants* to

see Amanvir. Most people spend their lives trying to escape his notice."

"I want to see him."

"The council is sitting." He looked over his shoulder, toward the back room. "They are deciding the fate of Gupta Singh. His failure to guard our sister will cost him dearly."

"Let me in. Let me speak to them. Please. I know where your sister is."

The man studied her, then pulled open the door and stepped aside. Lily came into the shop and hurried through to the weapons room. Inside, Gupta sat on a chair, the Serpent King's guard ranged around him, all wearing beautiful navy suits, setting off their red turbans. A tall, slight young man held a wicked-looking curved dagger beneath Gupta's chin. The point had already drawn blood, which had trickled and dried on his neck. Gupta looked tired and terrified; they had clearly been there for some time.

Lily looked around. The guard was a mix of generations, and all of them had the same strange eyes. Opposite Gupta, in another navy suit, sat a man who had to be Amanvir. He was tall and slim, like all the others, with a prominent nose and a gaunt face. His startling eyes were hooded as he sat, poised and severe, looking at Gupta.

Lily ran over to him, skidding to her knees in front of him, hands by her sides, head bowed. "Colonel."

He looked down at her. "What is this interruption?" he asked the soldier who had allowed her in.

"She says she knows where our sister is."

The colonel looked back at Lily. "Then tell me, child."

"It wasn't Gupta's fault. He wasn't to know what the Agency was planning."

"That is for this council to decide, not a little girl."

Lily clenched her fists. She bit her tongue.

"Where is our sister?"

"I will tell you, if you promise not to hurt Gupta."

Amanvir gave a hissing sigh. "You will tell us anyway, child."

Lily looked up at him, eyes narrowed. "You just try me. I've had enough of being ordered around and threatened in the last few days to last a lifetime. My blood is what's gotten us into this mess, and it's going to take all of us, together, to get Mona out of it."

They stared at each other. Finally Amanvir spoke. "I give my word Gupta Singh will come to no harm. Despite his *incompetence*." He stressed the last word.

Gupta shifted on the chair in relief as the dagger was taken from his throat.

Lily pushed to her feet. "Mona is in Battersea Power Station, in a laboratory somewhere inside. She was taken so that she might be experimented on. There are other Eldritche there too. It will be well protected, by humans who are not what they seem. Some of them have your powers, and the government has discovered how to harness them. Regan Lupescar will be there."

"The Guardian?"

"Yes. He's waiting for dawn. Then he'll try to stop them, to get Mona and the others out. Find him, time your attack together, and your chances of success will be higher."

Amanvir stood, his suit perfect. He nodded. "We must act quickly. Guard, to the transport!"

In the sudden flurry of silent movement, Lily slipped out into the street and headed back into the City. There was one last thing she had to do.

She followed billboards advertising the blood drive to a quiet, cordoned-off street where two large mobile medical units stood. Lily walked up to the first one and climbed the stairs. The interior was brightly lit. There was a large man sitting in a padded seat, hooked up to blood-giving apparatus, and a young nurse perched at a desk filling out forms. There was a spare donation chair.

"Hello," the nurse said cheerfully. "Are you here to donate?"

Lily nodded.

"Excellent." The nurse picked up a clipboard with some forms on it. She handed them over to Lily and gestured to the spare padded chair. Lily sat down and looked at the forms. "If you can just fill those out, we'll get everything sorted."

Lily studied the first form and began to fill it in with fake details. Any doubts she had had about this being the Agency's work evaporated; there was no way this could be a real drive. She was too young and too small to give blood voluntarily.

The nurse opened a sterile packet with a cannula. "You look like you've been in the wars," she said cheerfully.

Yet another reason for you not to take my blood. Lily said nothing, but handed over the forms and stripped out of her jacket. She tugged up her right sleeve. "This is the best vein."

The nurse smiled. "You've done this before?"

"A few times." Lily settled back in the chair and ignored the scratch. The nurse arranged the bag on the stand and picked up the clipboard. "It'll take a minute to get going."

"I know. Low blood volume." Lily gave her a tight smile. The nurse went back over to the desk.

The man sitting in the other chair, his donation almost finished, leaned over to her. "Excuse me. I know it's really not my business, but if you've got low blood volume, it's not advisable to donate without medical advice."

"I know. It's okay. My doctor knows I give blood." *Not a lie.* He relaxed. "That's fine, then."

"Yes, fine," Lily said quietly, watching the red thread slip through the tube and start to drip into the bag.

The nurse unhooked the man and gave him a cup of tea and a cookie. He smiled at Lily. "I have a daughter about your age. Bit of a tomboy too, always getting herself into scrapes."

The nurse came to check on Lily's progress. She looked at the bag. At the base were two white sensor markers, both of which were turning a vivid purple as the blood touched them. The nurse's expression changed. Her eyes flicked to Lily.

"If you'll excuse me for a second," she said, her voice high and false. She took a mobile phone from the desk and walked out. It was only seconds before she returned and sat back down at the desk, her eyes shifting to Lily every few seconds.

Lily's head was spinning. She shook it, trying to clear it. Ten minutes later, there came a familiar noise: the sound of a large and powerful motorbike. It thrummed to a halt outside, and the rider jumped off and threw himself up the few stairs in one bound, erupting into the small unit. His face was invisible inside the helmet, but he looked at her for a long time.

Lily stared back at him, determined not to show any fear.

Ellis lifted the helmet off. He shook his head, eyes narrowed. "What the hell are you doing?"

The man put his mug down. "Are you her boyfriend? I have to say, I was a little worried about this young lady."

Ellis barely spared him a glance. "Back. Off."

The man frowned. "I was only concerned—"

"And I told you to back off. Don't you have some-where to be?"

The man got up. "Well, actually—"

"Then go there. Now."

The man picked up his overcoat and edged around Ellis's intimidating figure. "Are you okay?" he asked Lily when he was almost at the door, looking between her and the nurse.

Lily nodded and smiled a little. "I'm fine."

The man looked relieved. "If you're sure . . ."

"Get OUT," Ellis bellowed.

The man scurried down the steps as fast as his frame would allow him, and disappeared.

"You too, get out," Ellis said to the nurse. "Go."

She left, closing the door behind her.

Ellis looked at Lily and swore at her, starting to detach the bag from the cannula. "You fool. You'll kill yourself if you carry on like this."

"What do you care?" Lily snapped.

He taped the cannula down on to her arm, leaving it in place. "What's the reason for this exercise anyway? If you wanted to see me again, you've got my number."

"On what possible planet would I want to see you again?"

His eyes met hers for the briefest second, then slid away.

"You asked if I wanted to see my mother again. And I do. Is she alive?"

"You already know she is," he said, irritated. "You saw her at the Cripplegate facility."

Lily swallowed. "Is she in trouble for that?"

He shrugged, unhooking the half-filled blood bag from the stand and putting it inside his jacket. "We knew we had to watch her. She's compromised by being your mother. It's understandable." He held out his hand. "Phone."

"I haven't got it. Your brother took it. That's why I did this. I want to see her again, and this was the only way I knew I could reach you." Lily got to her feet. "If you promise, I'll go with you."

"You're coming with me anyway." He spun her around and pushed her in front of him, out of the unit and down the short flight of steps. The nurse stood nearby, breath steaming in the cold. Ellis nodded to her and she went back inside. Reaching his bike, he passed Lily a helmet. She pulled it on and slid onto the bike behind him.

"Hold on. Tight."

The bike streaked through the City, heading west. Speed cameras popped and flashed behind them. Lily held on to Ellis just as he had ordered, fingers frozen against the hard black leather of his jacket. The power station loomed into sight, dark and forbidding on the opposite bank, its white cooling towers pale against the night sky.

Ellis pulled up at the lights, one booted foot striking the ground. Lily flexed her fingers, feeling them creak with cold. The next moment he had taken them both in his warm grip and pushed them into the unzipped pockets of his jacket. They began to thaw instantly. The lights changed and he made a sharp left turn over Battersea Bridge. On the south bank, he wound his way through a couple of back streets before arriving at the beginning of the waste ground on which the derelict power station sat.

He slowed. The bike splashed through puddles and bumped over the rough ground around to the river side of the vast building. Ellis brought it to a halt, and Lily slid off and removed her helmet. He looked at her for a long time. His gray eyes were familiar, so similar to Regan's. But Lily knew she didn't know him at all.

He straightened up and dismounted the bike. "Come on, then," he said, holding out his hand.

It was a curious gesture, inviting trust. Lily put her fingers in his, unsure. He led her inside the building.

They walked through the derelict turbine hall, boots crunching on broken glass and brick fragments, crossing the vast space until they came to the other side, and a bank of doors. Ellis pressed his hand against a black glass plate to the right of one of the doors and it opened immediately, revealing a laboratory beyond. As Lily and Ellis entered the lab, another agent with snake eyes slid down from a wooden stool. Other male agents in black combat clothing stood across from each other at a bench, arranging weapon components on the worktop. All of them appeared to be under the influence of some form of Eldritche blood or another, with strange-colored skin or eyes. Some had the snakeskin effect on their neck and hands, but one man's hand appeared to be developing orange-and-blue scales. An assistant in a white lab coat worked at another station, entering data into a computer. The place felt compact, but busy. The new snake-eyed agent—presumably a replacement for the man Regan had killed at Hori's—blocked Lily's view.

"Well, well, look what we have here."

She looked up at him, determined not to show fear.

His third eyelids blinked briefly. "Brave little thing, aren't you?"

"Not particularly."

The eyes flicked to Ellis. "This the girl you got the call about?"

"Yes. She went to give blood. Decided she wanted in on the project."

Lily raised an eyebrow, pulling her hands into her sleeves. "I said I wanted to see my mother. I don't want anything to do with"—she looked the agent up and down—"this."

The agent's unpredictable temper flared and he grabbed her arm. There was a crack, as the talisman, hidden inside Lily's cuff, reacted. Ellis separated them instantly, just as the agent was already jumping back.

"You stupid idiot!" he raged, tugging up Lily's sleeve. "Now you've told him exactly where she is." Ellis pulled her away, pushing her roughly into an adjoining corridor. "Bet you think that was very clever, don't you."

Lily said nothing, just walked ahead of him, into another room. In it was a series of glass boxes—cells—all of them empty except one, in which a girl with short, dark hair sat on the bed, looking exhausted. Her bare arms were covered in bruises and flecked with bloody scabs.

Lily halted. "Vicky?"

The girl stared at her, then got up from the bed, coming to the window and pressing her hands against the glass, her face stricken.

"Help me! Please help!" she shouted, her voice deadened by the thick glass.

Ellis immediately dragged Lily into a long corridor lit with strip lighting and with pipes running over every surface, closing the door behind them.

She turned to him and shoved him hard in the chest. He didn't move. "You are a grade-one shit, you know that, don't you? She trusted you."

Ellis folded his arms, staring her down. She shook her head at him, refusing to be cowed.

"You want to see your mother? Then zip it." He sidestepped her and walked away down the corridor. Lily ran to catch up. He put his palm to a glass plate by an industrial door.

A light passed over it and there was a bang as internal bolts slid back.

They walked into a small medical facility. There was a sink, a medical refrigerator, and a counter with a computer and printer beneath it. Pharmaceuticals were in racks on shelves, all stuck with little white labels covered in neat printed handwriting. The only sign that it wasn't an ordinary treatment room was a padded chair fitted with Velcro restraints. Ellis buzzed an intercom.

"Take a seat," he said.

"I'll stand, thanks."

A man of about Lily's father's age came into the lab. He had immaculate brown hair in a side parting and severe spectacles with tortoiseshell frames. He wore a lab coat and had a stethoscope around his neck.

"Ah, Miss Hilyard. We have the pleasure of your company at last." He held up the stethoscope. "May I? It's just a check over, to assess your condition."

Lily glanced at Ellis. He nodded, indicating that her compliance was part of the deal. She sat, thumping into the chair with bad grace.

The man listened to Lily's heart. She glared at Ellis, who stared back, impassive. The doctor looked in her eyes and inside her mouth, and checked her pulse.

"She's fine. She's just tired and her blood pressure is low, for the obvious reasons."

"*She's* sitting right here," Lily snapped.

The man looked at her, then at Ellis. He raised an eyebrow. "I'll rig her up with some IV fluids. And she should eat something." Ellis nodded. "And it might be an idea to give her some of the refined plasma, just to get rid of that bruising. If we have to take her to the Ministry in the morning, we need her in better condition than this."

"I'm not an animal!" Lily protested.

They both ignored her. The man disappeared the way he had come, and Ellis pulled up a stool and tore Lily's black jacket and T-shirt up from the wrist.

"I could have just taken them off," she said sarcastically.

"You won't be needing them again. We have clothes here for you."

"I am so not wearing anything provided by you."

"Your mother chose it all."

Lily was silent for a few moments. "She . . . she's very sick, isn't she?"

"Yes. She's very sick," he said finally.

"And you can't fix her?"

"No. But we keep trying."

"But she's getting sicker."

"Yes."

"Who was that man?"

"Professor Hellier. He's the chief medical advisor on the project."

The doctor returned. He examined the exposed cannula on Lily's arm, then tutted. "These people. No finesse." He smiled at her.

Lily said nothing, just looked away as he pushed a small syringe of something into the port and depressed the plunger.

The instant rush through her arm and into her neck and chest made Lily sit up.

"That's it. Good girl."

She shook her head to clear it.

The doctor examined her face, watching the bruises fade from her white skin. "I never tire of watching this work," he said to no one in particular.

"I want to see my mother."

He began to attach the bag of fluids to the stand. "Your mother needs to get as much rest as she can."

"Why can't you fix her?"

"The original transfusion did colossal damage to her system. Irreparable. We do everything we can to keep her as healthy as possible."

Lily bit her lips together.

"How are you feeling?" Lily refused to look at him. She just nodded. He got up and looked over at Ellis. "I'll be back in an hour to check on her."

The doctor left. Ellis took hold of the metal stand, pushing it on its casters and maneuvering it around the chair. "Come on." He led her through a maze of smooth sheet-metal corridors, then pushed open a door into a large communal kitchen. Pulling the stand over to a table, he pointed. "Sit."

Lily sat on the shiny white bench. Ellis went to a fridge emblazoned with a large biohazard sticker and opened the door. The bright light from inside threw his features into sharp relief, reminding Lily almost unbearably of his brother. She looked down.

"I'm not eating anything from in there," she said, her voice not quite as steady as she'd hoped.

She heard him laugh. "Oh, that?" He pointed to the sticker. "It just means it's my fridge."

"Huh. You must be high up the food chain here."

He glanced over his shoulder. "Pretty close to the top." He reached inside and pulled out a plain white carton. Next to the fridge was a microwave. He put the carton inside and set the timer. Turning back to Lily, he crossed his arms over his chest, hands on his biceps. "I'm too young to be the face of the project, as far as the Ministry is concerned, but without me it's sunk."

"What about Dr. Hellier?"

He shrugged. "He's a good doctor. Brilliant, even. But he's not me."

The microwave chimed. He turned and pulled out the carton, removing the lid in a puff of steam. Taking a pair of chopsticks from a drawer, he walked over and put the carton in front of her, sitting down opposite. Lily peered into it.

"Wait, these are the noodles from—"

"Yes. You like them, don't you?" For a second he looked unsure. "You go there with your father."

Lily looked down. "Yes. I like them."

"You should eat."

She picked up the carton and sipped the hot broth.

"You don't eat enough."

"Don't you start," Lily retorted, then shut up abruptly, annoyed with herself at the sudden sense of familiarity between them.

Ellis traced an invisible pattern on the table with his thumb. Lily took another sip. Grasping the chopsticks, she tried to gather up some noodles, but her hands were shaking too much. Her show of bravery wasn't quite as convincing as she'd hoped.

He frowned. "You're not frightened of me, are you?"

She set her jaw. "Of course not. I'm frightened of this place and everything in it. But I'm not frightened of you."

"Good," he said, sounding strangely satisfied. "And you'll get used to it. You're pretty important around here. We'll look after you."

"I don't want to be *looked after*," she snapped.

Ellis got to his feet and fetched a fork. Taking the carton from her, he wound the noodles around the fork and offered them to her.

She looked mutinous. "I can feed myself."

He dropped the fork in the carton and sat back.

"Don't try to be nice to me. It doesn't suit you."

"I can be nice. Maybe you'll find that out, if you want to."

She looked at him for a moment, then gestured to the building around them. "This whole place—it's built on the idea that my blood can be used to mix us up, create new creatures."

The passion returned to his face. "No new creatures. Your blood plasma allows us to transmit Eldritche qualities to humans. We need to learn more about how to pick and choose the desirable qualities and leave the others behind. When we perfect it, it'll eradicate disease and frailty overnight. It's what this whole project is about. Imagine—the cure for cancer, HIV, you name it—here, instantly, easily deliverable. Don't you want that? It'll change the world."

"Don't make me laugh," Lily retorted. "This is the government we're talking about. It'll be like everything else, sold to the highest bidder at FutureMed. Like the traffickers and the drug companies and the arms dealers. Just with an official stamp."

"It won't be like that. We'll be working in partnership with some of the most talented and well-funded people in the world."

She watched him, shaking her head slowly. "And you call your brother an idealist. They will sell it to the pharmaceuticals, who will exploit people desperate for cures. It's all about money. Not to mention the farming of seven thousand of your own people. Seven. Thousand." She shook her head. "I'm not sure which is more disgusting."

He took a breath. "If you worked with me, we could steer it. Make it what we wanted. Welfare could be a priority, if you wanted it to be." His gray eyes were cast down, his strong hands on the carton.

"Me, work with you?"

Ellis nodded, almost enthusiastic. "What would be so wrong with that? We're both brilliant. The work, it would be incredible."

"But it's based on exploiting your own—"

"Let me finish!" he barked, startling her into silence. When she was quiet, he went on. "So far blood products have impressive, if temporary, results. But they need refining. The effect on the user can be undesirable."

"You mean like the snake man out there."

He nodded. "That's exactly what I mean. The idiots. They're all like gym freaks being given free access to steroids. We don't even know what these combinations will do over time, but the Ministry is pushing so hard. And Mona Singh's extract turns them all into borderline psychopaths. If we can just get past this week, I'll stop all that."

"How?"

"I made a deal. Produce the work to make FutureMed a success and I'll get to head the project. Take over from Hellier."

"Who's promised you that?"

"Your mother . . . negotiated it with the Ministry."

Lily eyed him. "Where is she?"

He studied her for a long time. Then he pointed toward the door. "I'll take you to her, if you promise me you'll join the project."

"With you leading it?"

"With me leading it," he said definitely, putting his hand over hers on the table.

Lily's eyes went to the talisman. The shimmering dust within it swirled placidly. She looked at it, surprised.

"See?" Ellis said. "It knows I don't mean you any harm. That's why it never reacts to me."

She frowned.

"And I can see he's got you believing that garbage about a prophecy."

Lily bit her lip.

"Part of his egomania." He held up his hands. "The job has turned his brain, made him think he's the only one who can stop all this. We're identical twins. Perhaps it's me who's going to stop it, through my work."

"You don't believe in it?"

He shrugged. "I believe that there are things out there, the Chaos, that will swamp us if we let them."

"So you do believe?"

"In things I can see. Not in prophecies and fairy tales."

"How can you say that? When you're part of it?"

"You've inherited a rare blood condition. We're genetic freaks, you and I, that's all. Look, people invent stories to make sense of the world, when they should just look at the facts."

"But . . . your parents."

"They died because they couldn't accept those facts."

Lily stalled. "And you're okay with that?"

He drew her after him, walking backward. "No. But it happened. And I have a good life here, work that challenges me. And we will save lives—millions of them. Those seven thousand lives will mean *everyone* suffering from cancer can be saved. That's way more than seven thousand, even in one year."

"But only people who can pay," Lily insisted. "It won't be for everyone."

"You don't know that."

"I know how governments work. It's only taken this one a couple of years to start dismantling the health service. The end of free treatment is coming, and soon. Forget survival of the fittest, it'll be survival of the richest."

They were approaching another metal door. Ellis opened it again with the palm reader. The bolts whirred, the door swung open, and Lily walked inside. Nothing could have prepared her for what she saw in the vast laboratory beyond. On one side, in a small, reinforced glass box, lay an Indian girl, eyes closed. It was Mona, frost creeping over her sleeping body. A blood transfusion unit emerged from the side, whirring steadily as it dripped into a collection bag.

Lily looked up at Ellis. "The cold. Reptiles don't function well in the cold; I saw that on a documentary once. You're doing that to keep her docile?"

"She's dangerous. Killed two lab assistants and an agent on arrival. We had to do something." Ellis's voice was matter-of-fact.

Farther away down the lab was a water tank containing a mermaid, slightly smaller than Eleanor. She was completely submerged and shackled; only her hair floated free. Another transfusion unit was slowly pumping her green blood from her body. Her eyes were large, magnified by the water, and she stared out at Lily. *Help. Help us, please,* her soft voice resonated through Lily's mind, just as Eleanor's voice had done before. Lily put her hand to the glass and the girl responded from the other side. Even though she was underwater, it was clear she had been crying.

Lily looked over her shoulder at Ellis. "This is so cruel. How can you stand it?" Then her gaze snagged on the sight behind him. Against the back wall were large metal crates holding dozens of mothwings. "No!" she shouted, stumbling forward, the drip stand clattering to the floor.

She collapsed to her knees in front of the ranks of cages. Dozens of the small creatures were confined within. Tubes and wires ran everywhere. One cage held a little mothwing whose head was patchily shaved, electrodes sitting over old scars, steel staples holding together the lips of new wounds. Another lay dead, veins standing out blue against its pallid skin, needles taped between its thin fingers.

Lily brought up what little she had eaten. Ellis swore and hauled her to her feet.

"Don't you touch me. How can you do this?"

"It's necessary! They're expendable."

Lily wiped her mouth with the back of a shaking hand. "You're disgusting." She forced herself not to look away from the cages, though her stomach rebelled. She swallowed repeatedly to try to quell the nausea. Ellis dragged her to a sink unit, wetting a cloth and handing it to her. Lily cleaned her face and hands and rinsed her mouth.

Ellis shook his head. "It's vital to our work. They're wholly Eldritche and they respond fast to whatever we give them."

"You mean they die quickly if you give them something that isn't meant to be in their system."

He said nothing.

"I need to get out of here," Lily said. "Take me out of here, please. I can't look at this."

But as they passed the cages of mothwings, Lily couldn't help herself. She crouched down next to them. A little male stretched his hand through the bars. Lily put her fingers around his. She looked up at Ellis. "This is disgusting," she said.

"You'll see."

She shook her head, disengaging her hand with a last stroke of the little creature's fingers and pushing herself to her feet.

Ellis shut down the lab for the night and walked Lily back to the treatment room. She sat on the edge of the padded chair, elbows on her knees, and rubbed her face, suddenly exhausted despite the plasma. Ellis disconnected the cannula and the bag of saline.

"You're a menace with this thing," he said quietly. "You should rest."

Lily looked at him, shaking her head. "If you've watched me so closely, the thing you *must* know about me by now is how good I am at taking orders."

He grunted a laugh and pushed her flopping sleeve aside to look at the cannula. "How is it?"

"Sore. They always are, in the elbow."

"I can take it out?"

She nodded.

He popped the tape and slid it out perfectly, leaving nothing but a tiny, rapidly healing purple dot. By a large computer screen on the side was a spray bottle. He picked it up and pumped it over her elbow and arm a few times. "Magic skin," he explained, putting his fingers over the film, the heat from his hand drying it even more rapidly. He kept it there.

Lily watched him doctor her. "Must be strange for you, not understanding what you're putting these girls through, and them"—she gestured with her good hand back to the mothwings beyond the door—"with these tests."

Ellis's expression became set.

"*They* are vermin. And *they* are not *girls*."

Lily pulled her arm away, examining it. "How can you say that?"

"Mona is an emotionless reptilian assassin. And Rachel has, in case you hadn't noticed, a tail. And they're the most human of what's out there."

"Just because they aren't human doesn't mean they aren't people, with feelings and lives. What about you? And your brother?" Lily straightened up.

"What about us?"

Lily frowned at him. "You're half human."

"Our mother was human. We aren't human at all."

Their eyes met, and held.

"That doesn't mean you don't have to care about things, or do the right thing."

"Lily, stop. Just stop." Ellis sighed. "There's nothing more to say on the subject."

She kicked out at him. He just stepped back, then shook his head. "Don't make me lock you up. And don't judge me. I've done what I think is right. If we find the answers we're looking for, we'll unlock the key to perfecting the human race." His voice had taken on the same passionate note as before.

"You can't *perfect* human beings, it's not how it works!" she shouted, getting up.

"You! *You're* perfect!" he shouted back.

She sat down in shock, staring at him. The silence stretched out.

"Oh," she said.

Ellis turned away, cursing under his breath.

Lily put her head in her hands, then pushed her curls back and hugged the back of her neck. "Right."

"It should have been me. Not him," he said quietly. "You should have met me first."

"That wouldn't . . . it wouldn't change anything," she said slowly.

"You don't know that. It *would* have been different. I mean, it's obvious you find us okay to look at." His voice was half angry, half uncertain. "And *I* know you."

"Ellis, you're a professional stalker. That's not normal."

He folded his arms, hunched, his back still to her. "Who wants *normal*? You don't, that's for sure." His tone was bitter.

She slipped around him and looked up into his gray-gold eyes. He looked away. She put her hand in his. "Look. Maybe things would have been different. I don't know." Tired, she rested her forehead against his bicep. His fingers threaded through hers. "All this has been a lot to take in."

"It was supposed to be different. We were going to approach you. As soon as I was in charge. You could have come here and seen all the good we can do." He sounded defeated. "You would have seen it differently."

Lily took a breath. "No. I couldn't see what I've just seen any differently."

"Life is about sacrifice, Lily. This is for the greater good."

She shook her head stubbornly, looking up at him. Carefully he lifted his free hand and touched one of her gold ringlets, winding it around the tip of his finger.

Holding his gaze, she didn't move away. "I want to see my mother. Please?"

He didn't respond, his thumb smoothing the strands over his knuckle.

"Ellis?"

He sighed. "I'll see if she's awake."

The second he was gone, Lily ducked beneath the desk and turned on the printer.

Chapter 16

A few minutes later, she examined the piece of paper the black box had spat out. The handprint was only partial, but hopefully it was enough. Lily prayed that the advice in the article she'd once read held true, and that if dampened, the surface of the paper would hold enough electrical charge which, coupled with the handprint, would fool the scanner into thinking her hand was, in fact, Ellis's. She licked the handprint, and pressed it against the door scanner, her own hand behind it. The light slid over the paper and the door popped open.

Two minutes later, the door to Vicky's cell opened just as obediently. Vicky was sleepy and confused. And terrified.

Lily took her arm, hustling her up. "Ellis is out of here for who knows how long, and we need to go. Now. And we need to try and get the others out too, okay?"

Vicky nodded. "But . . ."

"No buts. Come on."

"How did you get in here?" Vicky rubbed her forehead hard, as if trying to rub something out.

"That wasn't such a problem." Lily held up the piece of paper. "Magic skin. Turns out, it's magic."

Another minute and they were in the darkened lab. Lily walked straight over to Rachel's tank. "We'll get you out, I promise, but we're going to have to come back for you. Okay?"

Rachel nodded, sad but understanding. Lily pointed at the mothwings and spoke to Vicky, who stood behind her looking frightened. "We need to get them out too, though. This entire system runs on electricity—the cages, the doors—it's the one weakness. If we can kill the circuit, there's only two options: Either the whole thing will lock down, or all the doors will spring." Lily's eyes ran over the cabling. It was hard to tell, beyond the sheeting, where the fuse box might be. She tried to think. "There'll be individual boxes controlling the place. They won't just have one central one. The controls must be close by. First, we get Mona and them"—she pointed to the cages—"and then I'll try to find them."

They headed toward the cold box containing Mona, using the paper to spring the door. Then Lily ran off toward the cages at the back of the room. The film of paper was getting tired, and it was harder to work on the smaller screens set into these panels, but soon the doors hung open. Lily did her best to free the little creatures that were restrained or had wires and probes beneath their skin, her experience with needles suddenly coming in handy. As she worked, the mothwings scrambled out, over her, climbing down her body to the floor. They scuttled instantly for the exit. As they all scattered, Lily ran for the door, licking the paper again and pressing it to the scanner, then pushing her way out into the vast, ruined brick hall beyond.

There, she followed the electric cables over the wall until they led her into a narrow corridor. Pipes and wires ran overhead. She turned again, into a room where the door stood open; beyond, everything was darkness. As her eyes adjusted, she could vaguely make out dozens of brand-new fuse boxes.

Oh, well, here goes nothing. Lily began to kill each box, throwing the large switches. It took a minute to get through them all, then she ran back toward the lab. The light level was low and bluish. *Some sort of emergency lighting?* She quickened her pace; Ellis must be missing her by now.

Vicky was struggling to get Mona up from the bed. Lily helped, tugging Mona up by her arm, wrapping it around her own neck and trying to get her on her feet. The two of them half carried, half dragged Mona from the cell.

"Which is the way out?" Vicky asked, hoisting Mona up higher.

Lily shook her head. "We're not leaving."

"What?!"

"They'll be expecting us to make a break for it. We can't make it out of here undetected. With the power out, someone will be coming to check Mona's cell, like right now."

"Well, *I'm* leaving," Vicky said.

"That's your choice. I won't leave my mother here," Lily replied. "I passed a service closet on my way to the fuse boxes. It might just buy us enough time—this place is like a labyrinth."

They headed out of the lab and across the huge brick hall. On the other side was the dusty, dark storeroom Lily had seen before. They laid Mona down on its debris-strewn floor. She was slightly more awake now, but not fully conscious. Lily went to leave.

"Where are you going?" Vicky hissed.

"I need to find my mother!" Lily hissed back.

Vicky stared at her, then shrugged. "Okay, go. But don't leave me here."

Lily nodded. "I promise."

She crept quietly back toward the lab. Peeping through the door, she ducked back as Ellis and an agent appeared from the other side. The agent saw the empty cages and swore loudly.

"They can't have gone far. Cover the exits," Ellis said, disappearing the way he had come.

Lily and Vicky ducked away and headed back to the storeroom at a run. The corridor was lit only by a thin, bluish light above the piping, making their skin pale and luminous. Lily put her hand on the storeroom door, pushing it open and slipping inside. She gasped and stifled a yelp as pain blossomed across her right side. Mona stood in front of her, one end of a thick shard of broken plastic in her hand. The other end was buried deep in Lily's gut.

Vicky caught Lily as she fell. "What have you done?" she hissed at Mona, trying to stop Lily from hitting the floor. "She was helping us escape, you idiot!"

"I only did what I was trained to do."

Vicky swore. "Come on. Help me get her inside."

Mona and Vicky hustled into the small storeroom and shut the door. It was completely dark as they found the nearest wall and laid Lily down carefully against it.

Mona was unapologetic. "I was protecting myself, that was all." She spoke with a soft lisp, making her sound gentle and calm in the darkness.

Lily's hand closed on the plastic shard. She hissed in pain as she pulled it from her stomach and dropped it on the floor. She could feel blood wetting her clothes. Her heartbeat crashed in her ears, thudding through her head.

"We have to get you out," Vicky said quietly.

They fell silent as boots walked swiftly past the door, heading for the fuse-box room.

"We have to wait," Lily managed finally.

"You haven't got time," Vicky argued.

"I'll be okay. I just . . ." Lily stopped talking, unable to go on.

Regan waited by the wire fencing. He let his head drop back, breathing out slowly, and stared at the power station, dark and barren. The tiny smashed windows were like a hundred eyes, watching him. He listened hard, but nothing reached his ears. His hands clenched. He forced them to loosen.

On the north bank of the river, fairy lights were still strung between the lampposts, a relic of Christmas. The early-morning traffic moved steadily toward the City. Cars and taxis carrying bankers from Chelsea; vans carrying deliveries. Cement trucks heading to construction sites, laborers dozing for a few more precious minutes as the drivers listened to radio phone-ins. Just to the west, a train thumped out of Victoria heading south, the first of the day, lights picking up the steel tracks. It creaked and faded toward Clapham Junction. Out on the river, gulls settled on a barge, the water gray. Watching for Misrak and Delphine. Regan watched the gulls watching him. The sun began to rise in the east, flat and pale across the dirty sheet of the Thames.

He straightened up and turned toward the power station, taking a deep breath and looking down. It wasn't as if he hadn't faced bad odds a thousand times before. *But not quite these odds.*

Behind him came a noise. A white van approached from the direction of Battersea Bridge Road, sloshing through the underpass beneath the railway, headlights bouncing through the icy puddles of the derelict ground. The lights flicked off as it pulled to a halt. MARSDEN ALWAYS DELIVERS was emblazoned on the side. Micky jumped out of the driver's seat, Joey from the passenger side.

"So you're in a spot of bother, mucker?" Micky smiled.

Regan took a deep breath just as an ancient Fairway cab heaved across the open ground, the doors already opening. Stanley lurched out of it, dragging an enormous sledgehammer after him, followed by Felix and then Lilith, who was dressed from head to toe in skintight red leather and red stiletto thigh-high boots, carrying a coiled bullwhip. Jake emerged behind her, a pair of swords crossed behind his shoulders, his long black hair tied back. Regan laughed.

Lilith looked down at herself. "Is it too much, darling? I've been looking for an opportunity to wear it for simply ages."

He looked down, swallowing. "Us against . . . I don't know how many."

Micky rubbed his hands together, palms igniting in the cold air. "Sounds like good odds to me."

Stanley swung the hammer onto his palm. "Just show me where."

Gupta Singh emerged from the scrappy dawn light, carrying a spear and a leather doctor's bag. His face was daubed with paint and he was wrapped in warrior's robes, the belt bristling with knives. Three more daggers poked out of his turban. With him, from the shadows beneath the railway bridge, from the deep dark of the waste ground and the edges of the power station, slipped dozens of young, upright Sikh warriors. They moved without noise, wearing red skirts low on their hips, bands of dark red cloth crossed over their chests and around their waists. Each carried a spear and observed the group with iridescent, reptilian eyes.

"I'm starting to like these odds," Stanley said. "Wot's in the bag, Gupta?"

"Mona's kit." Gupta Singh let it gape open briefly, revealing a long length of chain with a heavy spiked ball at each end, a pair of short swords with braided handles on a belt filled with throwing stars. He snapped the bag shut.

Stanley looked at him with new respect. "Capable piece, your Mona."

"You have no idea." Gupta took a proud breath, staring at the power station. "Is there a plan?"

Regan turned his face to the gulls wheeling overhead, and laughed.

Fifteen minutes later, he had outlined his strategy on the scrubby dirt. "It's not much, but remember—whatever happens to me, it doesn't matter. Wait for the signal. Micky?"

"Electronics. Seek and destroy." Micky held up his flaming hands.

Regan turned to Stanley. "Stanley, I'm relying on you to spring me if they manage to get me in a bind."

"Wot, ain't you strong enough?" Stanley smiled.

Regan smiled back. "Don't worry about that. And you know what to do about Lily?"

"Flower's comin' wiv me, an' no arguments about it."

Regan nodded. "I think she engineered the agent making physical contact with her, so that I would see where she was, but all I saw was the inside of what looked like a cross between a medical facility and a military base, which could be anywhere inside this building. The only way to stop them is to go in and find it."

Lilith pouted. "Darling, I'm not convinced by this lion's-den idea. I saw how that ended in the original, remember?"

"Believe me, if I could think of another way, we'd be doing it."

"For a little human thing?"

"For all of us." There was a silence. He looked around at them. "But yes. For her."

Lilith sighed, her hands on her hips. "Men. So sentimental. It's a good thing you're one of us, Regan, or I'd have to put you out of your misery."

He smiled. "Remember, whatever happens to me—"

"Yeah, yeah," Jake said, "whatever. We'll make sure she's fine. All of us. You know there's people who would pay good money for your pelt? They bind books in it, all sorts of kinky stuff. Can I have first dibs?"

Lilith raised an eyebrow. "*Dibs?* Jake, I was born four thousand years ago and even I know no one says 'dibs' anymore."

"What sort of creep binds books in people-skin?" Stanley looked at Jake, horrified.

Colonel Amanvir cleared his throat. Regan gestured toward the wire fence. They filed through the hole. The Thames was already lapping over the open ground, encroaching on the factory. The word on the water was that the River God had woken.

The others went to their positions and Amanvir's guard disappeared again into the dark as silently as they had come, leaving Regan standing on the open ground with Felix. The Cleaner adjusted his sunglasses. They stood in silence for a while.

"Why you naw come an' acks Felix for he help?"

Regan frowned. "I didn't want to drag you into this. You could get hurt."

Felix tutted in disgust.

"I think if we can stop this, now, then perhaps we can still reset the balance, perhaps the—"

"Is too late, boy. Dey will do as dey please now. Tings has gone too far."

Regan exhaled. "If you say so, I believe you. I'm sorry."

"Sorry dat de end of days is upon us? Or sorry dat you so rude to ol' Felix all dese years?"

"Both."

Felix rocked back on his heels. "Diss prophecy . . ."

"Yes." Regan pushed his hands into his pockets. "It's okay. If that's what's meant to be."

Felix clapped a hand to Regan's shoulder and looked at the power station. "An' you say dey de people who kill you sweet madda and you fine daddy?" He surveyed the huge building, sucking his teeth.

"Yes."

"An' you acks me what I tink?"

"Tell me."

Felix grinned, gold tooth glowing in the early sun. "I tink we gon' take us out some righteous trash."

Chapter 17

Lily pressed her hand to her side as hard as she could, but her strength was starting to give out. "Here," said Vicky, and took over. Lily flinched.

"We *have* to get you out," Vicky said.

"No, we have to wait," Lily ground out. "He'll come for us."

"Who?"

"Regan. Ellis's brother."

None of the others spoke.

"And the others," Lily managed with a slight cough. "They're coming too."

"Gupta Singh?" Mona hissed softly.

"Yes."

"And Ellis's brother. We can trust him?" Vicky asked.

Lily nodded in the dark. "He's saved my life. A few times."

"Someone needs to save it again now," she muttered.

Mona said nothing.

There were voices outside. Agents.

"Any sign?"

"Nothing, sir."

"Keep looking—they can't have gotten far. They're probably still in the building somewhere. Did you check the exit from the main lab?"

"Yes, sir. Not there."

"Fine. Then go back to the holding pen and search there. Report to me in fifteen minutes."

"Sir."

The girls waited in silence until the sound of the agents' footsteps died away. Vicky's hand touched Lily's hair. "How are you feeling?"

Lily grunted. "I've been better. If they've already searched the lab, we should go and try to get my mother. She's in there."

"But we don't know who else is in there, do we?"

She struggled to sit up. "No, but we've got Mona now. Come on, help me up."

Lily kept her hand pressed to her side, but walking was painful and her head had begun to swim. They followed the corridor that led back to the main laboratory. The strip lighting had now been restored. Her arm was around Vicky's neck as she trudged, one foot in front of the other.

"Mona, I don't know exactly where my mother is, but she's resting somewhere in the lab—if Ellis hasn't moved her."

"There's accommodation near the kitchen block. I saw it when I first arrived. If she's resting, she'll most likely be there."

"Could you go? Find her for me?"

Mona's eyes were blank. "Why?"

"Because she's my mother!"

"She started all this." Mona gestured around them.

"Yes. And now we're going to finish it. But not without her!"

Then, from the corridor, agents spilled into the lab. Guns were trained upon the girls instantly. They shifted to the left, farther into the room, keeping a row of benches between them and the men with the guns. Ellis was the last through the door at the end of the huge room and immediately saw the bloody patch on Lily's side.

He swore. "Let me help her."

Lily's legs gave out. It took all Vicky's strength to hold her up.

"You stay where you are." Regan walked through the door from the holding pen, followed by Lilith, Gupta, Jake, Stanley, Felix, and the warriors of the Serpent King. The bodyguard instantly ranged themselves around the vast room. The air they carried with them stank of burning plastic, and suddenly Micky appeared, rubbing his hands together.

Regan didn't look behind him. "Micky?"

"All done, matey. There'll be nothing recoverable from that little lot."

"You idiots." Ellis was scornful. "All our work is stored remotely. Doesn't matter what you destroy here."

One of the agents stepped forward toward Jake. Lilith uncoiled her bullwhip. "No, darling, I don't think so. There's a good chap."

Lily leaned heavily on Vicky.

Regan didn't take his eyes from his brother. "What's wrong with her?" he called over to the girls.

Vicky turned Lily slightly so that Regan could see the huge bloody patch covering her clothing all down her right side. "She got hurt."

Regan's eyes flicked to the bloody shard in Mona's hand. His jaw tightened. "We're leaving here. Now. All of us."

" 'All of us' means my mother too." Lily struggled with the words.

"I don't think so." An agent stepped into the room from the opposite doorway, training a gun on Regan.

Regan raised an eyebrow. "Guns—really? That's all you've got? Against us?"

"No!" Lily shouted, her voice breaking. "Stop it. All of you. I want you to bring my mother."

"I'm here," a quiet voice said.

Caitlin Hilyard was sitting in a wheelchair, looking exhausted from the effort of propelling it herself.

Ellis ran to her.

The agent fired.

Regan dodged, then vaulted a bench, closing the gap between them. The others closed in on him. As more agents spilled through the door, Lilith, Mona, Gupta, and Stanley swung into action and the bodyguard of the Serpent King flooded the room. Mona and Gupta were fighting back-to-back as Lily collapsed to the floor, dragging Vicky with her.

Suddenly Ellis appeared and pushed Vicky aside. Amid the mayhem, he pulled up Lily's top and examined the long, thin wound, which was pumping blood steadily. He glanced over his shoulder at Caitlin.

"If we don't stop this, she'll die. She's nicked an artery, by the looks of it."

Lily shook her head. "Regan will help me. It's okay, he knows how."

Caitlin's breathing was unsteady. "Ellis should do it. We have the blood here. It's all ready."

"No." Lily pushed Ellis away weakly.

"Don't fight him, Lily." Caitlin was gasping, struggling to pull out the small portable oxygen cylinder from the side of the wheelchair.

Ellis caught Lily's face in his hands. "Let me help you."

"Stop!" Caitlin shouted above the noise. "Please stop."

Her voice was lost in the din of the fighting, but Regan and the others, along with Amanvir's men, were rapidly overwhelming the agents. Ellis propped Lily against the wall as the combat began to cease. Only moments later, the bodyguard held their spears to the throats of the remaining agents. It was over.

"My daughter is dying. Please . . ." Caitlin's voice ran out.

Ellis ran to a huge glass-fronted refrigerator, pressed his palm against the front, and hauled it open, sorting through the blood bags stacked inside.

"The Two Fifteen trial," Caitlin said, breathless.

"I know!" Ellis said over his shoulder.

Lily yelped as something cold pressed against her chest.

"Ellis," hissed the snake-eyed agent who had been burned by the talisman, and who had avoided capture with the others to reappear at Lily's side.

Ellis turned.

"I want it. The mythical Two Fifteen. That's your trial, yes? We've all heard about it. Faster, stronger, better. The best strain yet. Enhances every other quality."

Shaking his head, Ellis looked at the agent, the bag of plasma in his hands. "It's not ready."

"But you're going to give it to her."

"Because we know it's compatible with her."

"I want it."

"I know, but you can't have it."

The muzzle of the gun pressed harder into Lily's chest. She winced.

"*Now*, or I kill her. And all your precious work is for nothing." The hand that held the gun over Lily's heart surged and faded with mottled scales, the patterns washing back and forth, as unstable as the agent's mind.

Two of the bodyguards shifted, sliding along the edge of the laboratory. "Any closer and she dies!" he yelled.

Lily lifted her head just in time to see Ellis hurl the bag of blood high into the air and launch himself at the snake-eyed agent. But he wasn't fast enough. The agent pulled the trigger. There was a bang and Lily heard, rather than felt, her heart pop. It exploded messily, flooding her lungs with blood. Her knees buckled and she dropped to the floor like a stone, blood smearing the wall behind her. As Regan caught the bag in midair, Ellis tackled the agent, flooring him, and as they fought mayhem broke out again as the others saw their chance. Regan sprinted to Lily. He grabbed a syringe kit. Skidding to his knees beside her he shoved the syringe straight into the plastic of the bag and filled it.

"It's too late," said Lilith, crouching, her fingers bloody from checking the pulse in Lily's throat.

"Not yet, it isn't," Regan snarled, pulling the syringe from the bag. Lifting it, he used his left hand to find a space between Lily's ribs. "Just a spark left, that's all there needs to be. One spark of life and the will to live." He stabbed down, hard, and pushed the plunger.

Caitlin fell forward from the chair and hauled herself over to them, cradling her daughter. She pulled Lily's head onto her chest, their fair hair mingling. The little group crouched together as, on the other side of the vast room, the guard began to dispatch the last of the agents without mercy. Tears ran down Caitlin's face as she fought for breath, her thin hand stroking Lily's bloodless cheek. Nothing happened.

"I'm so sorry, Lily, so sorry. This was never meant to happen. We were going to take such good care of you." Her voice was little more than a choking whisper, tears dripping from her chin onto her daughter's still form. Regan and Lilith watched as Caitlin's soft words weakened and faded, any will to carry on defeated by the reality of her daughter's body in her arms.

Ellis came over to them, breathing hard. Behind him lay the body of the snake-eyed agent. "Isn't it working?"

Suddenly there was a commotion as one of the last agents broke free from the guard and ran for the exit, his enhanced reflexes making him so fast he caught them all by surprise.

"Stop him!" Ellis bellowed to the guard, pushing to his feet. He looked back at his brother. "Get them out. He's going for the fallback plan. This whole place is rigged, but the power outage means it has to be done manually in the control room. Get them out now!" Then, he was gone, racing through the door after the guard.

Everything was quiet and dark. For just a while, the agony stopped. Then Lily was catapulted back into pain.

Her hands knitted into knots. She gasped a huge breath as

Regan put her down, very gently, on the ground by Micky's van. The river was encroaching on them, the puddles joining up as the water slopped over the embanking walls. Stanley loomed behind him, Lilith hovering nearby.

Regan caught her face. "Don't talk."

Lily's eyes closed again. *Please stop spinning.* The spinning stopped. She frowned, opening her eyes and looking into Regan's gray-and-gold ones.

"Am I dying?"

"Not yet." He smiled. She lifted her fingers to his face and he took her hand, kissing her palm briefly. "And I'd rather you didn't. Here, drink this. It'll speed up the healing." He unscrewed the cap on the bag labeled with Ellis's name and handed it to her, pushing to his feet.

Lily took it and sucked cautiously. The thick, salty liquid filled her mouth, but there was no urge to gag. She drank quickly, squeezing the bag to speed the process. It leaked from the needle hole, spilling down the inside of her pale wrist. She pulled it away, blood spilling over her chin, teeth red. "Where are you going?"

"I have to get Ellis out." He grinned. "I'll be back. Don't worry about me." He sprinted into the seemingly derelict power station, and into the laboratory deep inside it.

Lily pushed to her feet, sick and dizzy. Joey got out of the van and stood by a frozen puddle, hands in the pockets of his hoodie. Lilith checked her hair in the side mirror of the van.

Then they were all blown to the wet ground as the power

station detonated behind them, turning the factory into a vast, rolling ball of fire.

Lily spun onto her back, propped on the heels of her hands. The others were all taking cover as the vast brick building began to collapse. The huge cooling towers toppled inward as a mushroom of dust and smoke rose from the center. The walls began to keel in on themselves, almost too slowly. As they fell, an even bigger cloud of dust rose, spattering them all with hot grit and dirt as the flames burned higher.

Lily sprang forward. "No!" She took a step toward the power station, but Stanley was surprisingly quick to grab her and hold her back.

"No, flower. You can't go in there. It was rigged. The brother, he told us—right after he killed the one who shot you."

"Ellis? Where is he? Is he okay?"

"He went to try and disarm the system so we could get the others out. But the power outage meant he had go and reset it manually."

Me. I did that.

"Let me GO!"

Stanley shook his head slowly, ignoring her frantic struggling.

"But they're still in there! They're still in there! My mother!"

"Gone, flower. I'm so sorry. It was just her time."

The others were staring at the flattened power station, tongues of fire leaping over a hundred feet in the air.

"He's done it," Lilith said in wonder. "His life for yours. The prophecy came true."

Lily fought, kicking out at Stanley. He said nothing, just held on to her grimly.

She began to cry. "Stanley, please!"

Stanley's heavy hand closed over Lily's nose and mouth, cutting off her air supply. She fought harder, her lungs feeling as if they would burst. Then nothing more.

Chapter 18

Lily woke in her own bed. The pillow was gritty and her face felt raw from tears. She rubbed her eyes, the cuff of her nightshirt falling back, showing the bandage on her wrist. And the talisman, swirling gold around the red, as ever.

She sat up and looked around. Her room was neat and quiet, as always, but there was a distinct smell of jasmine. She got up slowly, checking herself over. The edges of her vision felt sharp, and she could hear a tap dripping. She went through to where her father was sitting at the counter. There was a report open in front of him, but he wasn't reading it. He was staring at the television, watching a bulletin on the flattened, still-burning Battersea Power Station.

A reporter was standing on the waste ground, speaking to the camera. "The cause of the fire and subsequent collapse is at present unclear. Observers are reporting a series of explosions just after dawn."

Lily burst into tears.

Her father jumped up, the report falling to the floor. "The City's falling apart. I've heard nothing but sirens and speeding vehicles all night. The Thames has broken its banks as far up as Chelsea. And now the power station. Lily, what's the matter?" He put his arms around her.

She rested her head on his shoulder, exhausted sobs shaking her body.

He held her tightly. "Oh, Lily. Is it Regan?"

Nodding against his chest, Lily sobbed even harder. "And Mum. And Ellis."

"Ellis?"

She shook her head. "Doesn't matter now."

"Oh, darling. I'm so sorry." He held her even tighter. "It will be fine, I promise."

Lily shook her head, agonized. "It—"

"I was so worried when you didn't come home again last night. Sam was calling. Then all of a sudden you were there, in bed, fast asleep."

Lily said nothing, tears running down her face.

"Would you like to talk about it?"

She pulled away, shaking her head.

He nodded, his eyes worried. "Okay."

The news item changed behind his shoulder. "And today, the Minister for Health will make an announcement at the FutureMed convention, which will open this morning in London's Docklands."

So they're going ahead with it anyway. I should have known. They've still got all the research, after all. That in itself is worth a fortune.

"I should get cleaned up," she said, breaking away from her father.

She sat on the floor of the shower, the scalding water drilling holes in her skin, pounding on her head, washing the tears over her chest. She sat there until the water cooled before forcing herself to get up, to get out.

After she dried herself, she looked at her reflection in the mirror over the sink. Still the same pale, sharp girl she had always been. Stuck to her left arm was a white rag. The bandage, wrinkled and wet from the shower, but still clinging on. She tugged it away slowly, revealing a perfect white water lily, the edges of the petals tinged with pink. It rested on a smooth green leaf, beneath which were the slight ripples of the water.

In her bedroom, in warm, clean clothes, she stuffed her old laptop and her fake junior press card in her bag. Tears leaked out through her lashes. Her body felt empty, like tattered rags wrapped around a cage of bones. Even breathing felt insubstantial. But her heart beat steadily, hurting with every strong, sure rush of blood. Her skin was super-sensitive, each brush of fabric or her own fingers raising tingling waves of nerve reaction.

"Lily?"

She didn't answer. Her father stood outside the door, uneasy.

"May I come in?"

She said nothing, just froze. He came over and took her hand. "You're going out again?"

"Yes," she said dully. "There's something I have to do."

"What?"

"It doesn't matter. I just have to do it."

She checked her travelcard.

"Okay. If you feel you need to."

Lily shouldered her bag. "I do."

"Sam called while you were in the shower. I told her you were home and she said not to forget the London Stone. Do you know what that means?"

Lily nodded and left, the door banging shut behind her.

She headed straight to Temple Tube station and got on a train to Tower Gateway, where she changed on to the Docklands

Light Railway headed for Beckton. Getting out at Custom House, she walked up to the front of the massive London Conference Center. Emblazoned across the front of it was the FutureMed banner. Suited delegates were flooding in.

Lily checked her watch. The Health Minister was due to make the opening speech at eleven. She looped the press card around her neck. Walking up to the steps, she went through the glass doors and showed her card to the girls taking names and dishing out badges.

"Katy . . . Evans? No, your name's not down here, I'm afraid."

"It's not?" Lily looked at the list, confused. "My school should have definitely set this up." She gave the name of a school she'd once competed against in a math challenge.

The girl checked again, frowning. "No, still nothing. Oh, never mind." She handed over a card and smiled. "You'd better get in there. They're about to start."

Lily took the card and added it to the other taped around her neck. She climbed the stairs to the auditorium. Her limbs had a new looseness, a confidence she'd never felt before. Life had trained her to be delicate.

She went through the doors into the vast auditorium. It was cool and smelled of ozone. The place was filling up rapidly, and an intern was pouring out a glass of mineral water at the lectern on the stage.

Lily took a seat at the back and opened her netbook, putting it on the desk in front of her. She waited for it to detect the Wi-Fi, then saw the network appear: FUTUREMED. Open network. Public presentation system. 100 Mbps.

Amateurs.

Lily opened a clean presentation document, copied the public presentation into it, and typed, fast. The place was filling up, but she ignored that and carried on working. Then the doors closed and everyone settled into their seats. Lily turned and checked that the cameras she'd seen on the way in were all ready. The auditorium fell silent and the chairwoman crossed the stage, her high heels clicking neatly.

"Ladies and gentlemen, welcome here today for the start of FutureMed, a conference we think will change the world. My name is Fiona Miller and I am both proud and excited to be chairing this event. Research recently conducted in this country, at our best facilities, has yielded startling results. We want to share those results with you today."

Yeah, yeah.

"So, without further ado, I'd like to hand you over to the Minister for Health, Christopher Kitchener . . ." Her voice faded out as Lily stopped listening.

Get on with it.

Lily watched as the gray-suited minister walked out to the lectern, a sheaf of notes in his hand.

"Thank you, Fiona. And thank you all, very much, for coming here today. As my esteemed colleague said, we have reached a breakthrough in modern medical science, one that will have huge repercussions for society, and for all our health care solutions . . ."

Annnd, run.

The words began to splash across the huge screen behind him. Different sizes, different fonts, but all the same word.

LIAR. LIAR. LIAR.

A ripple went through the auditorium. The minister carried on speaking, oblivious. Lily sent the next screen, with the words she had just written. The writing was large, the font slashy. Behind it, genetic code trickled down the screen.

What you are about to hear of is a discovery that could change the future of medicine. Of the human race. This discovery was made at the expense of many lives and the exploitation of some of the most vulnerable members of society, the unseen. To secure it, this government has lied, stolen, kidnapped, and, worst of all, murdered. Today, this government will attempt to sell to you, Those Who Have, what they have taken from the Have-Nots. But they have nothing to sell. As of this morning, the people who created it are dead. Their work died with them.

Do not trust this man. Look around you. Nothing is what it seems.

This is the City of Halves.

#cityofhalves

The minister stood, gaping. "Turn it off. Turn it off!" he yelled at the girl who had poured out the water. She looked lost and rushed away.

The room erupted. Phones were pulled from pockets and bags. The whole thing was all over social media before Lily had zipped up her coat. She left the netbook on the table, grabbed her bag, and walked away from the auditorium.

Outside, she headed back toward the station. Above her, gulls wheeled, knifing the skies. Back in the City, she walked up to St. Paul's. On Ludgate Hill, people surrounded a burned-out shop front that had been petrol-bombed in the night. Lily avoided the gang of boys with their hoods pulled up at the start of Cannon Street. They were looking around restlessly, seeking trouble. The newspapers blowing on the frozen ground reported that all the windows in the Shard had cracked overnight. Lily stopped a paper with her toe and read the front page. Some blamed the architects. Some the cold. Some thought there might be another reason. She walked on.

At Bow Lane she turned into the alley. Tom's was shut up. A sign on the door read CLOSED FOR REFURBISHMENT. The gate to the Rookery was locked. Lily pushed aside the ivy and peered through. The passage had been boarded up at the other end.

She stepped back, looking for another way in. In St. Mary's churchyard, Regan's window high above the gravestones was dark and empty. Back out on the streets, crowds were gathering. A Metropolitan Police riot van flew down New Change, sirens blaring. Lily looked up. High above the City, coiled on the roof of the angular dark glass shopping mall, a silver dragon lay, watching and waiting. A news helicopter thudded overhead. The oversized trash can with the large streaming news screen embedded in one side relayed the footage of the shining, gold-clawed dragon. As Lily watched, it was joined by another, slinking and settling to watch the pedestrians below.

Lily bolted to Carter Lane. The bookshop was closed, the windows covered with patchwork shutters in faded green and red. There were no signs, nothing. She banged hard on the front door, staring through her tunneled hands, pressed against the glass.

"Lucas! Elijah!"

Silence. The bookshop was empty, cleared completely. No books left at all.

Lily set out for Liverpool Street, her eyes scanning the rooftops, looking for more flashes of silver and gold. Nothing.

Liverpool Street station was closed, people milling everywhere. "What's happened?" Lily asked a man standing nearby.

"The signals have failed across the whole city. Not a train moving, above- or belowground. Some people have got a long day ahead of them. And they're saying there are animals loose."

Lily fled, finding herself near St. Botolph's churchyard. There was no sign of Ankou, the old Breton, just an old man in a flat cap raking up leaves. She ran to Lilith's. There was no brass plate and the door was locked, a metal bar in place, secured with an ancient padlock.

She ran, her feet pounding the pavement, hard and steady. Fifteen minutes later she was at King's Cross. Best Tattoo sat, as dark as ever, in between the betting parlors and fried-chicken shops. Lily pushed the door, not even out of breath. It opened straightaway and she almost fell through. Inside was a man in a T-shirt, covered in ugly tattoos, sitting on a stool and drinking coffee with his back to her.

"First customer of the day," he said cheerfully, turning. "Ah. Can't do under-sixteens, love."

"I'm not an under-sixteen. And I'm not here for a tattoo. I'm looking for Jake."

He shrugged. "No idea."

"This is their business."

"No love, it's my business."

In the corner the plastic rock fountain trickled. "This is their shop."

He shook his head. "No, it isn't. It's mine. And you'll be leaving now."

Lily walked the streets back to the City slowly, hands shoved into her pockets, thinking. *The Chaos, it's still rising. We didn't stop it. It was all for nothing.* She bit her lip until it bled, determined not to cry.

She sat on a bench, watching the people, thinking. She did not feel cold, her body still warmed by Ellis's blood. Only her chest felt empty and warped, as if her heart had mended crooked. She grabbed a cup of tea from a street vendor and drank it sitting on the back of a bench in St. Paul's churchyard, watching the dragons high up on the roof. Reporters had gathered beneath, and the police, fire brigade, and news crews were massing.

Another dragon had now joined the others, resting on the roof terrace of the most popular bar in the City. The minutes ticked by, slowly. On the recycling bins, the embedded screens showed a loop tape of the Minister for Health, Lily's proclamation writ large on the screen behind him. #cityofhalves was already viral.

Lily could hear snatches of the conversations going on around her, as if her hearing had become tuned in to a different frequency, clearer than the one she had been on all her life. Her eyes saw different colors, brighter and deeper, even in the drab winter clothes of those nearby. The polystyrene cup in her hands had a texture she'd never felt before, as did her coat, her own skin.

"Lily! I found yer at last."

She looked up. Gamble stood before her. He looked shattered. Worse than she had ever seen him. He was sober, though.

"Gamble?"

"I remembered. I remembered what I'd seen."

"What?"

"The thing I couldn't remember. The thing that's at the heart of the Chaos."

"But what is it?"

He grinned. "It's the London Stone." He pulled from his pocket a filthy piece of paper. "Look, I went to the library and looked on th'Internet. It used to stand in Candlewick Street, inside where Cannon Street station is now. Then it was moved. But, thing was, where it was before, it was where all the ley lines crossed. It was there for a reason. They think, on the Internet, that it was the earliest place of worship in London, before the

Romans even. The original foundation of London. That's it. It's got to be. It's because it's out of kilter, see?"

Lily looked at the printout.

Don't forget the London Stone.

She caught sight of a familiar green uniform and jumped down from the bench, ditching the long-empty cup in the trash and crossing Cannon Street, oblivious to the honking bus. Gamble lumbered along behind her.

The tall black street sweeper was bending over, picking up an empty cigarette packet. He straightened.

"Felix!"

Felix stared at her. "Whatchoo wan', likkle girl?"

"Felix, it's me, Lily!"

He eyed her suspiciously. "I don' know who you be, jubee, I sorry."

"Don't be ridiculous! Jubee, you always call me that," Lily protested.

"No, no, I never see you befo'. I sorry."

"Why are you pretending not to know me?" She frowned.

Looking her straight in the eye, he swallowed. "I seen tings, jubee, dat I never want to see again and I got friends I never *gonna* see again."

He put his brush in the cart and took the handles. Lily put her hand on his arm.

He looked down at her. "You let me gaw in peace now, you hear?"

"NO. You have to help us, right now. It's up to us, the humans, to finish this."

They all put their hands over their ears as the dragons reared up on their haunches and roared.

A bandogge emerged from the trees at the edge of the churchyard, its four yellow eyes searching them out. The gulls wheeled and screeched overhead. On the Cannon Street water fountain, a banshee materialized and began to scream. The gratings on Cheapside began to boil with red-and-black insects, their carapaces shining as they were crushed beneath the wheels of buses. Then the people on the buses began to cough. A strange wind picked up, pulling candy wrappers, coffee cups, and tattered copies of the free papers into miniature tornados.

"Now!" Lily screamed, shaking Felix's arm.

"Where?"

"The London Stone. We have to put it back inside Cannon Street station, restore it to its original site."

Felix, Gamble, and Lily bolted down Cannon Street, leaving the scenes of Chaos behind them.

The London Stone was embedded into the wall of an ugly 1970s office block, an undignified place to rest. It was sealed in by a plastic window and iron bars. The streets were deserted; everyone had rushed up to the cathedral to see the dragons.

"How do we get to it?" Gamble scratched his head.

Lily squared her shoulders. "Okay, cover me." She knelt down as the others crowded around her, facing out. She took a deep breath and grabbed the two nearest bars, praying she still had enough strength left. Gripping tight, she pulled . . . and felt the iron begin to give. Gritting her teeth, she tore the bars, metal squealing, down to the pavement and started on the next two, her shoulders screaming. Then she slammed her hand straight through the plastic window and pulled the stone out through the sharp shards, her shredded skin healing almost immediately.

"Come on! Help me!" she said to the others. Gamble shoved his hands inside and they tipped the large, square block of stone forward, out of its cage. Staggering upright, they carried it between them. Felix ran into the road and stopped the traffic while Lily and Gamble struggled across the road and up the steps of the modern station.

"Can you feel it?" Gamble shouted over the sound of their horns.

Lily, jaw tight, nodded. The stone was getting lighter. By the time they reached the top of the steps, it barely weighed anything at all.

A rail worker walked over to them as they got to the top step and walked into the huge station. Felix held up the dog-eared card on the chain around his neck.

"I wit' da City. Important works, dey is needed here."

"But—"

They ignored him and walked on, to where the original location of the stone was marked on the floor of the station in a mural. The stone seemed to weigh almost nothing as they placed it carefully into its rightful position over the brass outline. Yet they had only just pulled their fingers from beneath it when with a great bang the floor gave way and the stone was suddenly embedded a few inches into it. Cracks radiated out across the station floor, and Lily, Felix, and Gamble, along with the rail guard and the few commuters left in the station, all doubled over at the noise, hands over their ears.

The newspapers reported it the next day as a sonic boom, perhaps from some meteor. It had happened as reporters had been feeding live from the City, where four large illegal reptiles had escaped from a penthouse flat above the new shopping mall, and the noise had frightened the animals away. But one Web site said that they had not fled the scene, but watched, then retreated slowly, heading across the rooftops in different directions. Everyone on a bus in Cheapside had been taken sick, and one man in a Porsche, but they were all expected to recover. A mysterious hound had been seen in the grounds of St. Paul's, and a bloodied woman clinging to the drinking fountain, but someone had been leading a ghost walk at the time and no one thought any more of it. That afternoon, the sky above London was astonishingly beautiful, and the sunset streaked away toward the horizon. People took photographs and posted them across the Internet.

Lily, Felix, and Gamble emerged from the station into the spectacular sunset. Slowly they walked back to St. Paul's. Lily looked around her. Felix's cart lay on its side in the churchyard. He righted it, organizing his brushes. A man on the corner hailed a taxi and the number fifteen bus rumbled past. Nothing was out of the ordinary.

Gamble turned to them. "Well, I got to go. Got a place in an 'ostel tonight. Up north London." Lily gave his arm a hug. He nodded. "Second sober night in fifteen years. I en't enjoyin' it much, truth be told."

"Stick with it." Lily smiled. "After all, the City needs you."

"What, old mentals like me?"

Her smile became a grin. "It needs all of us."

Gamble shook Felix's hand and walked away toward the Tube. Felix was surprised when Lily threw her arms around his neck and hugged him. He patted her back.

"Not enough time," she whispered. "There wasn't enough."

He nodded, looking at her as she dropped back on her heels. "Never enough time, jubee. Never enough."

"But it was my fault. I killed the power and—"

He put a hand on her shoulder. "What will be, is. He always knew." He held up her arm, studying the talisman. "So, de Chaos is beaten, for now. What will be my good fight, hey?" He tugged a curl of Lily's hair, then turned and pushed his cart away.

Lily watched him go. "Felix?" she shouted as he reached the other side of the road.

For a moment he didn't reply, pulling out a brush and making a sweep across the pavement. "Yes, jubee?"

"Will I be seeing you?" she yelled across the traffic as the light turned green.

He twirled his brush, laughing, gold tooth visible even so far away. "Of course, jubee!" he yelled back. "I de Cleaner!"

Chapter 19

Two days later, Lily was lying on the sofa. The television was on, but she wasn't watching it. Her father was working in his study with the door open. Lily's laptop was open on the coffee table, a dozen searches for government conspiracies and the Eldritche in the browser. Lily had even been following local London news sites, but to no avail. They had all disappeared without a trace. However, the #cityofhalves tag had been picked up by the media, and taken on to represent not only the abandoned FutureMed conference, but the social and financial inequality rife throughout the city. *If only they knew.*

The FutureMed story had made the front pages. Apparently a "planted" computer linked to a global group of hacktivists had been found on-site and was being tested by forensics. Lily's lip curled at that. The only prints on it would be hers and Regan's. They knew where to find her if they wanted her, but somehow she knew they wouldn't come. She'd uploaded the entire story, from her own perspective, into a Web site that could be sent public at any time. They were watching her, she was sure of that, but so far it was a stalemate.

Her in-box pinged. She summoned up the enthusiasm to sit up, cross-legged, pulling the computer onto her lap. It was from Sam: *Turn on your chat if you're there.*

Dutifully Lily signed in.

lilyh: Hey.

Samsays: How ru? Been txting u.

lilyh: Lost my phone.

Samsays: Sup?

lilyh: Nothing.

Samsays: Regan?

Tears threatened again. Lily bit them back; her father was concerned by how much crying she'd been doing. She pushed her fingers between her eyebrows, hard.

lilyh: Yes. And some stuff about my mum that I'm working through.

Samsays: What happened?

They died, that's what happened.
Lily's fingers hovered over the keys. The cursor flashed insistently. She could make out each individual pixel on the screen. She was adjusting to her enhanced vision, but the hearing was worse, and she lay awake at night listening to the water rushing in the pipes of the old buildings—flushing, dripping, running away. It was fading gradually, but that made it even worse. Soon there would be nothing left but who she had been before. Small, breakable, alone. She blinked more tears away.

lilyh: It's complicated.

Samsays: I've got time.

Lily sighed. Her father came into the room and patted her hair as he walked past. "Are you chatting?"

"Yes. With Sam."

"Send her my best. Why don't you ask her to come 'round?" He put a glass of water on the table beside her.

"I'll see her at school tomorrow."

"Right." His voice was both cautious and weary. The last couple of days had been difficult.

Lily picked up the glass and took a sip.

Samsays: U still there?

lilyh: Yes.

Samsays: So, ur not seeing Regan anymore?

The glass shattered in Lily's hand, spilling water all over the sofa and slicing her palm messily.

Her father cursed and grabbed a dish towel. Lily pushed the computer onto the table and looked down at the mess of glass and blood in her lap and on the cream sofa. Her father caught her hand in his, turning it over. He frowned. Her skin was clear and unmarked.

"Where did you cut yourself?"

Lily closed her fingers over her palm. "I didn't."

He looked at the bloodstain on the cream material.

"I'm fine," she said quietly.

He held on to her hand when she went to tug it away. She pulled harder, breaking his grip easily. He stepped back, looking at her uncertainly.

Lily got to her feet. "I'm really sorry, I'll clear it up."

"Lily . . . is there anything you want to tell me?"

She sighed. "Like what, Dad?"

"I don't know. I've read that there are drugs that can make you feel very strong, almost invincible."

"Drugs?" She looked at him. "You think I'm on drugs?"

"I don't know what to think," he said slowly. "I thought we were close, but now you barely speak to me. I feel that I don't know you."

Lily took the towel from him and began to load the broken glass into it. "I'm still the same person. Just . . . things happened, and I'm still trying to work it out."

"You know you can talk to me, don't you? About anything you like?"

"Yes, Dad." Lily tried to smile, taking the broken glass to the trash.

The following morning, her father came out of his room into the kitchen holding up two shirts. "Which one?"

"What?" Lily started out of her trance at the kitchen counter.

"Which one?"

"Oh, er . . . the blue one."

"They're both blue." He frowned.

"The bluer one." She pointed. "Since when did you need my advice?"

He disappeared, coming back buttoning up the shirt. "Big meeting today. And the end of the Kalhuna case."

"It's going in her favor, though, isn't it?"

He didn't look at her as he fastened the cuff links. "It is, but that doesn't mean you can ever put yourself in danger again, like you did."

Lily rolled her eyes. "I get it. And wish her luck from me."

"Ready for school?"

"Oh. Yes. S'pose."

"I take it that means you aren't looking forward to going back?"

Lily thought about school. She shrugged. "It'll be fine, I'm sure."

He squeezed her hand. "Do you need to see a doctor, do you think? I could book it, perhaps get you in—"

"No! No doctors."

"Fine, fine. No doctors." He smiled.

Lily slid down from the chair. It was still freezing outside, but these days she barely noticed it. Time was passing in a blur of nothingness and feverish, futile Internet searches. *Three days? Four?*

She shouldered her bag. "I'll get going, then," she said.

He was still watching her closely. "Lily, I know it doesn't seem like it now, but you will feel better. You'll get over him."

She looked down. "No, I won't."

"What makes you say that? You said yourself you barely knew him. I'm just trying to understand."

Lily blew out a deep breath, unwilling to stir through the ashes inside her chest. "Remember when we talked about human rights being your thing? Being what mattered to you more than anything?"

"Anything except you, yes."

She nodded. "Well, he showed me something that mattered to *me*. That there are people out there worth fighting for. And it became the only thing that mattered. Except him. He showed me the world where I belonged, and the person I belonged to. And now he's gone."

Ed stood up, taking her shoulders in his hands. "Lily, what you're feeling . . . it's grief. But no one's dead. You'll get over him."

She shrugged his hands away and turned for the door. "Please stop talking, Dad. I'll see you later."

The journey to school was long, with two changes of Tube and a walk. Outside the gates, Lily looked up at the modern building, weak sunshine bouncing off the large windows. Her heart sank. She squared her shoulders, taking a deep breath.

Inside, she went to the cloakroom and found her locker. She pulled off her coat, and was hanging it up just as a girl called Sarah came up. "Hi, Lily! How are you? Why haven't you been replying to any of my messages? And you've totally disappeared from Facebook. Did you delete your profile? Oh. My. God . . . is that a tattoo?"

Lily looked at her arm where her shirt had fallen back. She pulled her elbows into her sides and yanked the cuff down. Sarah grabbed her wrist, pushing the sleeve back up. "Oh. My. God . . . it so is!"

Lily tugged her arm away.

"It's amazing. Trust you to have something *so* gorgeous. Wait until Laura sees it. She is going to *die*."

"Can we not talk about it?"

"Where did you get it? Did anyone go with you? What was it like? Did it hurt? Laura said you were seeing this hot guy with loads of tattoos. Did he go with you?"

Lily pushed her hair behind her ears, rubbing her forehead. She opened her bag and pulled out her textbooks.

Sarah talked all the way to the classroom door, then left for her own lesson. Lily held on to her books and said nothing, grateful for being able to sit down in silence when the teacher arrived. She opened her book, the figures falling into place in front of her eyes, reassuring her with their certainty.

The time passed quickly. Lily completed the two problems and drew a line under them, her pencil resting between her hands. She began to sketch a vague shape.

The teacher walked down the row of desks.

Ten minutes later, she dropped her head back in relief and pulled her papers together as the break bell rang.

A gaggle of girls waited by the lockers. "Lily!" Laura exclaimed.

The other girls watched her. "Show them your tattoo, Lily," Sarah said excitedly.

Lily reluctantly pulled up her sleeve. The girls gathered around to look. Laura sniffed. "Not very original, is it? A lily? Why didn't you get something cool, like his?"

Touching her thumb to the tattoo, Lily pulled her arm into her side. "I got what I was given."

Sam bowled up. "Hey, guys."

"Lily's showing us her tattoo," Sarah said.

Sam frowned. The other girls moved off. Taking Lily's arm gently, she examined the tiny water lily. "Very pretty," she said at last.

Lily shrugged. "It kind of happened by accident."

"With Regan?"

She nodded.

Abruptly Sam leaned forward and hugged Lily. "It'll be okay, you know."

A single tear streaked down Lily's cheek, quickly brushed off. "I wish you were right," she whispered.

At lunch, Lily pulled on her coat and she and Sam headed out of the school gates to their favorite place for lunch, a tiny café a ten-minute walk away. It was in an old shop, the windows steamed up and the tables covered with black-and-white plastic cloths.

"Now, then, you two." The plump owner smiled through her bright red lipstick. "Same as usual?"

"Yes, please, Margaret." Lily took a seat in the window and waited for her sandwich and tea, lost in thought.

Sam sat down next to her. "Bit bloody chilly, isn't it?"

"I suppose it is. I don't seem to feel the cold much at the moment."

"Yeah, you feel really warm. I noticed earlier. You're not ill, are you?"

"No."

"So, tell me. Everything."

Margaret put two cups of tea in front of them in thick earthenware mugs. Sam picked up hers and blew on it.

Lily pulled her cuffs over her hands. "I'm not sure I can. I don't know where to start."

"Start wherever you like."

"He left and he won't be coming back." Lily bit her lip. "And that's it, really. That's the short version."

"Where did he go?"

Lily shrugged and looked away.

"Wow, you really liked him, didn't you?"

Lily swallowed, then nodded, once.

"He was amazing looking."

"It wasn't that . . ." Lily looked away. "He . . . I can't explain."

"Lily, did something happen?"

"Yes. Something, lots of things. Terrible things," Lily said suddenly, picking at a rip in the plastic tablecloth.

"He didn't hurt you, did he? Because if he did, it doesn't matter where he is, I'll hunt him down and kill him." Sam's voice was deadly serious.

Lily couldn't help but laugh. "He wouldn't. You don't need to hunt him down."

"Good. But I'm still worried about you." Sam frowned.

"I'll be okay," Lily said slowly. *I don't think I'll ever be okay again.*

"You can talk to me, about whatever . . . anything. You know that?"

She nodded hesitantly, still picking at the table.

"So, just try?"

Lily waited as Margaret put their sandwiches down and returned to the little kitchen at the back of the café. Sam took a large mouthful and watched Lily, waiting.

"Would you believe me if I said there was more to . . ." Lily stumbled over his name. "More to him than met the eye?"

Sam chewed and swallowed. "Er, I think that was pretty obvious. To everyone."

"He said you all looked at him like he was a freak."

"Did we? Freaking hot, maybe. I mean, *everyone* was talking about that. Laura literally could not get over it. She's still talking about it now. Keep going, though."

"He worked in his family business; they'd been doing it for generations. And what they did is secret, but really important for London. For all of us."

"Secret like what?"

Lily sighed. "That doesn't matter. But it was sort of like security. And . . ." She shook her head. "I'm sorry. There's just . . . I can't explain."

Sam put her hand over Lily's. "It's okay. Eat something. Have you finished that math assignment?"

Half an hour later, they walked out into the cold afternoon, breath steaming. Sam glanced up at the sky. "Do you think it'll snow? It feels warmer."

Lily looked at the clouds, low and heavy. "Who knows?"

Sam tucked Lily's hand through her arm as they walked back to school.

Chapter 20

Lily dumped her bag on the chair and fell backward onto the sofa.

"Good day?" Her father was standing in the doorway to his study.

Lily blew her cheeks out. "Tolerable. What are you doing home?"

"We won the case, in no small measure due to you. She's free and clear, if you call staying in a hostel in King's Cross 'free.' But I've got her into a program and I think she'll be okay. Thought I'd take the rest of the day off. Celebrate. Spend some time with you."

Lily punched both of her fists above her in victory and then struggled onto her elbows. "Cool. How did your meeting go?"

He put the report on the coffee table and sat down. "Interesting. Went on for a long time. Made me realize a few things."

"Like what?"

He shrugged. "All sorts." He slapped his knees. "Which reminds me . . ." He went to his briefcase and pulled out a small box. It was a new phone.

Lily looked up at him, surprised.

"I know I said I wouldn't replace it if you lost it, but I can't have you running around without a phone, can I? What sort of father would I be?"

Lily stared at it. "Thanks. I mean . . . really, thank you."

He smiled. "No problem. What are dads for anyway? Now, what shall we do? What would you *really* like to do?"

Lily thought about it. "Go for a walk, get a DVD and some Chinese takeaway, and veg out."

"Deal."

It was already dark outside, but they walked for miles along the river. Sometimes they talked; sometimes they just walked in silence. The conversation stayed in neutral territory. At Cleopatra's Needle, her father paused, looking up at the sphinxes. The cormorant on the post eyed them through his scaly lids. Lily watched him, remembering.

"You know they're facing the wrong way, don't you?" he said.

"What?" Lily shook her head to clear the memories.

He pointed. "These sphinxes. To guard the Needle, they should be facing outward, but they were installed the wrong way 'round."

Lily looked up at them.

"And something I didn't know, until recently, was that sphinxes are Ethiopian as well as Egyptian."

Lily nodded. "Yes. I knew that."

Her father carried on looking up at them. "You learn something new every day," he said cheerfully.

When they got back to the flat, it was dark and quiet. Lily turned on all the lights and the television, hating the silence. Her father looked at her, surprised. They unpacked the takeaway and ate on trays on their laps, watching a science-fiction movie about the discovery of a new race on a distant planet. *They should try this one first.*

After they'd finished eating, her father put his arm out. Lily snuggled up to him gratefully, pulling the throw over them. "You know, they say science fiction isn't really about space travel and so on, but about what it means to be human," her father said.

"They do?" Lily said, noncommittal.

"Because as soon as there's something out there that isn't human, the boundaries have to be defined, don't they? Because that changes everything." He sounded thoughtful.

As they watched the credits roll, Lily yawned.

"You should get a good night's sleep," her father said, patting her shoulder. She nodded, but didn't move.

"I thought about what you said, you know. About... Regan."

Lily said nothing.

"I think I understand now."

She looked up at him for a moment, then put her head back on his chest. *Unlikely.*

"Anyway, I just want you to know that I support you. In whatever you want to do. And I'll always be here for you. Always."

Lily drew in a breath, trying not to smile.

"No more tattoos, though," he said, cutting her off before she spoke.

She sat up and laughed before giving him a big hug. "Night, Dad."

Lily woke the following morning to a dark sky in the blank square of the window, snowflakes flurrying past. She pushed back the covers and got up, staring out at the court. A thick white carpet covered the square. Under the old-fashioned street-light the snow was slightly disturbed and a set of footprints led away, under the stone archway. Lily felt a moment's irritation with whoever had spoiled the perfect drifting white.

Soon she was washed and dressed. She was feeling the cold again now. It was wearing off. Soon all traces of their blood inside her would be gone. It made her unutterably sad.

Her father was boiling the kettle in the kitchen. It was still dark outside. "Morning," he said. "Seen the snow?"

"Yes." Lily looked over at the window automatically. Before it sat the wooden table of photographs. Lily frowned. On it were only the few of Lily and her father.

The kettle clicked off.

"The photographs . . . where have they gone?"

Her father made the tea briskly, not looking at her. "I was thinking about what you said, about moving on. And I've decided it's time. I can't live in the past forever. And she's dead. I think we both know that now."

Lily's heart twisted. She reached for her coat. "I think I'm going to go over to the Millennium Bridge and see if I can get a photo before it gets all disturbed. I can get the Tube to school from there."

"Nice." Her father smiled. He picked up the cordless phone

and disappeared into the bedroom, kissing Lily's cheek. "See you whenever."

She slipped out of the door.

Lily did not go to the Millennium Bridge. She halted there, for a few seconds, took some pictures, and watched the sun begin to rise, but then she did what she had done every day since it had happened. She walked to Cannon Street station, sat on the London Stone, and watched the early-morning commuters flood into London. There, for at least a little while, she felt connected to what had happened. To the truth of it.

She listened to her music, hands stuffed in her pockets. The moving of the stone seemed to have almost gone unnoticed. The empty window in the office building had been tidied, but left empty. Someone—Lily put her money on Felix—had lit a candle there, in a jam jar. The cracks in the station floor beneath Lily's feet had been repaired, and the stone had not been interfered with. The authorities had clearly decided to leave it where it was.

Lily was so lost in thought, she didn't notice the tall figure in a long dirty-white coat walking up behind her.

Her playlist ended. And a familiar voice said, "Like I said, you really shouldn't wear those. Anything could creep up on you."

She closed her eyes and swallowed. *One, two, three . . . four. It's just a dream.*

Getting slowly to her feet, she turned around, waiting for the crushing disappointment to hit.

He stood in front of her, the stone between them.

"In fact," he said, unable to keep from smiling, "anything just did."

Her crooked heart thumped. She leaped onto the stone and threw her arms around his neck. They clung to each other. Tears filled Lily's eyes. "How did you know I was here?"

He pulled a shiny new phone from his pocket, holding it in front of her. "Your dad called and said you left fifteen minutes ago."

"Dad? Why would—"

"Met him yesterday. Showed him a few things. Introduced him to Lucas and Elijah. Explained." Regan's face was stained red by the rising sun through the enormous glass windows of the station. He smiled, eyes full of mischief.

"You met him? He met the Clerks . . . ?"

He laughed. "Well, someone had to persuade him I'm not a total loser."

Lily ducked her head, smiling, unable to stop a tear from splashing onto her cheek. It hit his coat and hung there, glistening.

"You made me believe you were dead."

He laid his hand against her hair. "Felt like it. Until now."

They stood, not talking, just breathing. "And everyone disappeared. *You* left me."

"They're still here. Just lying low. And I never left you. Thought I *should* leave you alone, maybe. Now that you're safe." He looked away. "But I've been . . . around."

"Around?"

He sighed. "Now I sound like a creep." He wrapped his arms around her. "I was in that rubble when you did this." He gestured down at the stone. "I felt it."

"I thought you were dead."

"Almost. It felt like I was in there for a lifetime. The world spinning. Time stretching out. Everything." He looked lost.

She reached up and tugged a lock of his hair to bring his attention back to her. "What about the others?"

He came back to earth and kissed her forehead. "Micky, yes. Jake, no. Rachel, no. We just couldn't get her out. Gupta and Mona and some of the bodyguard made it; they're okay. On their way back to India for a while. But they'll be back."

"What about Ellis?"

He breathed in. "I've searched the rubble. Every night. No sign."

"So he's alive." Lily breathed out.

He looked down at her. "You're relieved?"

She nodded, slowly. "Yes. He's done bad things, but I don't want him to be hurt."

He hesitated. "You don't?"

"No. You don't have enough family as it is. And he didn't have Lucas and Elijah like you. He—"

"He had your mother."

She ran on. "Yes, I know, but she . . ."

He put his fingers over her lips, stilling her words. "I think he got out."

She tugged his hand away. "Where is he?"

"I don't know for sure. A military transport left City Airport soon after you moved the stone back here." He looked down at her standing on it.

"So how do we find him?"

He pulled two red booklets from his pocket.

"Passports?" Lily grabbed them, seeing fake names, birthdays.

"Your dad gave me yours. Stedman did the rest. New identities."

"Dad?"

"Yes, your dad. I told him what you did at FutureMed. He's proud of you."

Lily looked down, swallowing back tears. "Did you tell him about Mum?"

"Yes. I didn't know how not to."

She bit her lip. "How did he take it?"

"He was upset. Then he was okay. Thanked me. Said it was finally closure." He took a breath, almost nervous. "He says you have to call him when we get there. Let him know you're okay."

"Get where?"

"I'll explain on the way, but time's short. And he said it was your choice. That you had to decide."

"Decide what?"

"To come with me. But you have to leave everything. Right now. In forty-eight hours Ed will list you as a missing person and you will, officially, become nothing more than a statistic."

"A statistic? Slow down, I don't understand."

"You don't have to come."

"I haven't said I'm not coming, but you have to explain!"

Carefully he touched her cheekbone with the back of his fingers. "We think you'll be safer this way."

Lily thought about it. "So, I disappear. And what then?"

"We find Ellis and convince him to join us."

"And if he doesn't see it our way?"

He took her face in his hands. "We'll *make* him see it our way. He's my brother. I won't give up on him. And we take the fight to them. The Agency is already back up and running. We need to know what data they managed to salvage from the power station." He grinned. "And for that, we need you."

She nodded, serious. "Oh. Right. Yes, of course. Data. That's me."

"Plus, I need help."

"You do?"

"Yes. I met a smart, funny, beautiful girl and then bad things happened. Terrible things. She almost died. I need you to talk to her for me. See if she's still interested."

Lily raised an eyebrow. "Sounds like I've got competition."

"Nothing *you* can't handle." He put his arm around her waist, hauling her up against him and kissing her. "And besides," he said, "all my friends tell me we're made for each other."

"Friends?"

He looked almost shy. "Yep. Turns out I have one or two."

Lily laughed. Her laugh echoed around the station like a church bell as she wrapped her arms around Regan's neck and hugged him tight, her knees curling as he swung her around.

He set her back on the stone and pushed her away, putting distance between them again, unsure. "But like Lucas said, there's always a choice. And I want you to be the one to make it."

The Dartford train arrived and hundreds of commuters rushed through the barriers past them. A young woman, luminous with happiness, was standing on the London Stone, looking up at a handsome, heavily tattooed young man.

The expressions on their faces were hard to judge. Most imagined they were saying good-bye. One woman paused in the middle of texting her daughter and looked at them for a second longer, deciding that it was more like hello. The other passengers went on their way to jobs, offices, and coffee shops. And no one noticed as the girl jumped down, taking the hand the boy held out, and together they disappeared into the City's lesser-seen streets.

ACKNOWLEDGMENTS

On a winter day outside St. Paul's, I saw a small, pale girl in skinny jeans and boys' boots, with the most beautiful hair. She was looking at her phone, head down. Then she shoved the phone into her back pocket and strode away toward Cannon Street, full of purpose. I watched her go, and I knew her name was Lily. Wherever you are now, thank you.

My Lily has lived many lives and Katie Sedler has been there for all of them, and believed in this story from the moment I could talk about it on a balcony on Hatton Garden, so many summers ago. Lily, Regan, and I couldn't have done it without you, baby.

Yet another hat tip to my husband, Richard, without whom none of this would be possible.

Thanks to my agent, Kirsty McLachlan, always, and to the team at David Godwin Associates.

Thank you to my editor, Imogen Cooper, for taking such good care of my girl.

To everyone at Chicken House for their boundless enthusiasm and love for what they do.

And thank you to Barry Cunningham, curator of stories. To be published by you is a dream. Mine came true.

ABOUT THE AUTHOR

Lucy Inglis is a historian of the eighteenth century and curator of the award-winning *Georgian London* blog. *City of Halves* is her first book for young adults. She lives in the shadow of St. Paul's Cathedral in London with her husband and their Border terrier. You can visit her online at www.lucyinglis.com.